MW01493272

The Chronicles of Tap

By Chet and Kim Brackett

Dedication

This book is dedicated to "The finding."

What an incredible journey this has been "finding" at first, only the names of those who had lived before us and forged a way for us to live a better way. Names like Tap Duncan and Ira Brackett, names that in previous days stirred up in us a curiosity then a longing as we mixed a few legends of family lore and precious photos, trying to conjure up reality of the lives that our people actually lived.

Then realizing that Chet had "found" some amazing papers written by his Uncle Chet, that had been hidden away from view for a period of years just waiting quietly amid the dust and spiders in an old attic, waiting until the time and circumstances were right for those stories to be told. Then "finding" that the stories that we had to tell struck a chord with other folks that shared our family tree.

We are so grateful for the folks and their stories that we have been lucky to find and those still out there waiting to be found. This work has truly turned our hearts to our fathers. The folks we share in common with all of you. We hope for you dear reader that these stories might inspire you also to join the "Find." Getting to know our ancestors through the stories and written histories left behind has brought sinew and flesh to an otherwise large valley of dry bones.

And as we see the animation, the life that these stories have given our ancestors, as we get to see them and feel them and breathe with them in their adventures in return they have given our lives a grounding and strength. We wish and hope for you too that you can find those of your blood who lived before and get to know them.

We hope that you enjoy this, our story of the "finding."

Acknowledgements

There have been many people who have helped us with the writing of this book and we would like to take a moment to thank them.

First of all we would like to thank Michael K. Youngman for the hand drawn pictures that this book contains. Mike's passion for art and for the Wild West makes his drawings something special as they seem to come alive before your eyes.

There are many precious family photos that have been included in this writing and we would like to thank you all for them.

Jerry Marshall

Amanda Weatherford

Michelle Drumheller

Skipper Duncan

Margaret Pehl.

Kristin Scholl

Dennie Anderson

Carol Hardin

Ronda McCaw.

Mackie Duncan

John Steele

Cowboy Dave

And for the help in getting the book ready for publication we wish to thank Michelle and Mike Drumheller. Their help and insight has truly been appreciated.

Contents

Pictures and Illustrations

Foreword

I, Chet Brackett II, found these notes written by my Uncle Chet when I purchased his old family home. In the course of remodeling the house, I came across journals. They were aged with time, and written in a disorganized manner.

They were the ramblings of an elderly bachelor, with nothing but time on his hands. So, with no electricity in his home, he picked up his pen and began reliving the stories of his younger years during long and lonely winter evenings in Three Creeks.

Uncle Chet wrote about the Duncan family because he had many experiences with them through the years and found a fascination with the lives they lived and wanted to live it again through writing about it.

This is a story about an amazing man Tap Duncan.

There seem to be several climacteric moments that shaped his life we have uncovered them and would like to share them with you.

- A trail drive when he was just 16.

- The hanging of his brother who he knew first hand was innocent of the crime for which he was accused,

- Even-ing the score for that hanging, then,

- Leaving his settled home in Texas and heading for the unknown territory of the newly settled state of Idaho because of it,

- Killing a man in self-defense there, and once again finding it necessary to find a friendlier place to live,

- Moving to Arizona and starting a ranching empire there

- Being invited to rob a bank,

- Even-ing the score for a very dear friend

- Being told by his wife to straighten up and fly right or she was gonna leave him, and because he chose his wife and family over his walk on the wild side of life,

- Living out his later years with family, good friends and surrounded by cows and a ranch that encompassed 1.4 million acres, the ranch that finally belonged to him.

How do you measure the effect of the events that happen in course of your life? That is a question I hope to one day ask my amazing great uncle, Tap Duncan.

We will begin to tell some of the tales of Tap by starting at the beginning with his parents Abijah and Martha.

Duncan Lineage

Abijah Elam Duncan 1828-1903, married December 15, 1855 to Martha Muscaga Blanchard 1824-1928*, in Freestone County, Texas

Abijah and Martha's children are:

- Abijah Elam Jr., (Bige) November 20,1856-1915

- Alex A.[1]

- Harriet, April 17,1858-1927

- Josephine Jane, March 3,1860-1870

- James P., (Jim), February 17, 1862-1943

- Richard H., (Dick), December 6, 1862-1891

- Osa Ola (Osia) June, 1864-1930

- Nancy Ann, (Nannie), February 1, 1865-1955

- Julia, 1866

- George Taplin (Tap), February 4, 1869-1944

- Frances Fanny, June 5,1873- 1967

Martha had been married previously to John Asbury Mullins and they had three children. They are:

- Mary, 1850

- John Wesley, 1851-1925

----

[1] Alex A. Duncan is included in an 1860 Texas Census as one of Abijah and Martha's children, but Abijah is not. Alex does not appear on other subsequent census, but Abijah does, so Alex may actually be Abijah. Also we have found various spellings for Martha's middle name as Machoga, Muscaga.

- Elizabeth, 1853-1917

Spouses of children born to Abijah and Martha:

- Abijah Elam Duncan (Bige) married Nancy Blake Ketchum, December 11, 1879. In Texas.

- Josephine married Edward Fairman in Texas.

- Harriet married Henry W. Harkey in 1878 in Texas.

- James P. Married Elizabeth Helsley in 1898 in Idaho.

- Richard H. (Dick) was hanged at Eagle Pass, Texas in 1891 at the age of 28, He never married but had planned to marry Annie.

- Osa married Thomas Cravey in 1880 Cravey died in Piedras Negras in 1890. She later remarried Tom Cox.

- Nannie married Sam McKee, a Methodist minister in 1880. He divorced her after Richard was hanged. She moved to Hackberry, Arizona and married Captain John Greele.

- Julia married Gomez Martinez and moved to Mexico.

- George Taplin (Tap) married Olga Ann (Ollie) Binnion in 1890, in Goldwaithe, Texas.

- Francis Fanny married Frank Comer in 1890, in Goldwaithe, Texas.

We are excited about the information we have found through our research into the Brackett and Duncan genealogy and welcome historical information and other family who may be on the same search as we are.

Chapter 1: Leaving Tennessee about 1863

Abijah was exhausted. He was tired of being held in the prisoner of war camp, and groveling at the feet of the Yankee guards. The North, with all her men and war factories ground the South to defeat, despite the valiant efforts of brave Southern warriors.

Abijah's term of enlistment was over. If he thought it would make a difference he would reenlist, if only he could get out of this camp. He wanted to go home and see his wife, and his children who were growing up without him.

He missed the open grasslands of Texas, and the wide open skies where he could see forever. He'd been in the camp ever since his commanding officers had surrendered, and the victors kept promising that any day now, all prisoners would be exchanged or released if they signed no combat papers.

Any day now. He was so sick of hearing those words. In the meantime he had to clean up after the Yankee soldiers, and take care of their horses and pretend to be happy to serve them.

Years before, Abijah had watched many a slave pretend to be in awe and servitude to their white masters, then turn around and defecate in the food that was served at big table in the big house.

Yes master, right away master, whatever you say master. A few of the rebel soldiers had talked back, gotten into fights with the Yankees, and ended up in the gallows or in a mass grave.

Abijah stood quietly, waiting outside the officer's club to take care of their horses. An officer galloped up, jumped of his sweaty and dehydrated horse, and tossed the reins to Abijah.

"Give my horse some grain, rub him down and have him back outside by the hitching rack in an hour," the officer shouted at Abijah.

He couldn't help but feel sorry for the poor horse. But as he was rubbing his lathered coat feeling his well-proportioned muscular frame, he took a second look, and his sentiment towards this horse went from pity to awe. This was truly a magnificent animal.

Abijah walked the horse around, cooling him off, and gave him and a bite of grain. Then he saddled up and rode the horse down to the front gate.

As he started to leave, the gate guard stopped him.

"This horse needs water or it will die. I need to go now," he told him.

In the shade of the trees near the coolness of the creek, the horse took a long and thirsty drink. Abijah had to pull his head out of the water so he wouldn't get water colic. Then he again admired the magnificent creature.

A smile began to grow across his face. I'm outside the Yankee prison camp, he thought. This was his chance to go home. He crawled on to the back of the horse, and rode through the willows down the creek.

No one followed and he put the horse in an easy ground covering lope and headed west for Texas.

As he rode, Abijah thought about how he had gotten to where he was. Before the war he'd lived in Georgia and had drifted into the job of slave overseer for his neighbor and old family friend John Mullins.

John was in poor health and needed help running the farm. The Negro field hands had slacked off and the plantation had gone from an orderly well run farm to one that could barely pay expenses.

Despite Abijah's abhorrence to slavery, he'd taken the job and he worked with the Negro field hands. He explained to them that if they didn't help grow good crops, the plantation and they, the slaves would have to be sold. It was highly probable that their new owners wouldn't treat them as well as Mullins had. So for the next few years Abijah worked the plantation and grew good crops.

John Mullin's health continued to deteriorate. He confided in Abijah that he was worried about what would happen to his wife Martha and their children.

Georgia was not a good place for a single white woman with children. Too many big slave holders with too much power would surely take advantage of a grieving widow. Martha and the children would have no future in Georgia.

If Abijah would help him, they could sell the plantation, take the slaves and move to Texas. It held promise for a better life.

The plantation was sold and in keeping with Abijah's belief that no man should be another man's property, the slaves were offered their freedom. However most of them asked to go to Texas with the family. Abijah and Mullins had been good to them. They were fearful if they stayed in Georgia most of them would soon be back in chains and sold to a new owner. The local slave holders didn't want a bunch of freed slaves around causing trouble.

Abijah arranged for the sale of the plantation. Then he bought provisions for the move to Texas, loaded John Mullin's and his family, and the freed slaves into wagons and headed west.

Arkansas, Texas, was their first stop. And even though it was better it was still not quite what they were looking for.

Mullins was still worried what might happen to Martha and the kids if he died. At first, he begged Abijah to stay and protect them and run the farm. But then, as he watched Abijah taking care of Martha and his children, he decided that no one would do a better job of caring for them after he was gone.

He made Abijah promise to marry Martha. While Abijah could plainly see that Martha was not only a beautiful and extraordinary woman, he didn't believe any man or woman should be told who they should marry.

But, little by little, after Mullins death, Abijah began courting Martha. At first she said it was like having her younger brother courting her. Four years was not really that much of a difference but soon to her pleasant surprise she realized she was falling in love with this young man.

They soon married and began a wonderful phase of their lives having children and raising them together.

This is a story about the lives of some of the children born to these hardy pioneers.

A representation of the Tennessee stud that Abijah used to escape the prisoner camp. Photo courtesy Chet Brackett.

Martha Muscaga as an old woman. She lived to be 105 years.

Abijah E. Duncan on his return to Texas after his service in the War Between the States.
Photo courtesy of Mackie Duncan.

Martha (old mother) Duncan bottle feeding a bum calf at Tap's Diamond Bar Ranch in Arizona.

So sturdy and strong pioneers were the stock from whence Tap and his siblings came. The next chapters tell of another a couple of other significant events that shaped Tap Duncan;s life: The hanging of his brother Dick and a trail drive to New Mexico when he was just 16.

Chapter 2: Richland Springs[2], Texas 1888

Dick Duncan was a true cowboy. He could rope and ride and outlast the best of them, and he took an enormous amount of pride in his skill.

In 1880 Texas, his kind of horse skills gave him lots of opportunity. But, for today he was tired of riding the horse beneath ~~him~~ his knees. He was hot and tired and real sure he smelled WORSE than a skunk. How sweet to his eyes was the sight of his family home at Richland Springs. He and his brothers had been gone from home for a long time now it seemed.

Pushing horns on this cattle drive north had lost the adventure for him. The trail seemed even longer now that he knew that his sweet Annie was waiting for him. As his thought drifted more to her, he gigged his steel gray gelding just a little faster when he ~~had begun~~ *began* seeing the landmarks that spoke, telling him he was near his home.

He and his brothers, Jim and Tap, had once again signed up to drive some longhorns to the rail head up north. Several times he had done this and every time, he had enjoyed the adventure. But this time, not so much. Perhaps, he actually was ready to settle down, because every day he just looked forward to signing for the paymaster and to the jingle that he put in his pocket.

Always before he had enjoyed that pay because of the promise of whiskey and women and, oh what a party that it paid for… but not this time.

This time, the promise before him was that this pay, from this cattle drive would add the last dollars needed to buy the little farm that belonged to old lady Williamson.[3]

---

[2] Richland springs was a small community located just outside of San Saba, Texas. Both Richland Springs and San Saba are used synonymously. In this text. San Saba being certainly the larger of the two communities, the Duncan's are listed as the first of the settlers in the area arriving in the late 1850's.

[3] 1880 United States Federal Census for Mary Ann Williamson: taken in Precinct 115, San Saba, Texas. Household members (with ages): Mike Williamson (53), Mary Ann Williamson (51), Ft. Been Williamson (13), Columbus Williamson (11), Bula Williamson (6), Levonia Homes (29), Maggie Homes (6), Jonnie Homes (1). The 1880 Texas census reflects that, at that time, Mary Ann had a husband named Mike and that they had another son Columbus and that Levonia had two small children. We have not

That farm that was just a short ride from his folks' place at Richland Springs. Probably Dick's excitement wasn't as much for the farm he was buying, it was that Annie was a part of the future he was planning.

"Oh Annie." He muttered aloud. She was a pretty one. He had his eye on her for a while now but she always seemed to be attached to someone else.

Last spring however, when his little sister Julia got married, at their family home, Annie was there. What an event that was. Julia had fallen in love, head over heels with a handsome young rancher from Chihuahua Mexico, by the name of Gomez Martinez.[4]

He had and his caballeros had travelled to San Saba in search of those "fabulous Duncan horses" as he called them. And that was so true, the blood lines that came from that Tennessee stud, the stud that his father Abijah had brought back with him after the War Between the States was now producing some of the finest horses in all of the south.

Gomez had liked the look of the horses for sale but he liked the looks of the pretty young Julia even better. So when he negotiated a price with Abijah Sr. for the remuda he wanted to take back to Mexico, he said he would take all the mares for sale but the little filly with the reddish hair and the green eyes had to be included, His eyes drifted over to her as she stood quietly near the table where the deal was being made. Abijah turned to glance her way to see just how it might be that she felt about such a proposition. And as he did he caught her blush and smile. He could tell that she was hoping that he would agree.

As Gomez held his hand out to Abijah he swallowed hard, "I will pay, sir, whatever the price."

---

found anything to point us to their whereabouts. If anyone reading this knows more information, please share! The family lived a short distance from the Duncan's ranch. Dick had paid them $400.00 for their farm and was planning on settling there and starting a life with his intended, Annie. The four family members that Dick accompanied to Eagle Pass are: Mary Ann the mother, Lavonia (sometimes spelled Levonia) Holmes. Ben and Bulah Williamson. Bulah is spelled differently in the court files and we have used that spelling (Beulah) for the rest of the story.

[4] This is the only information that we have on Julia. She married Gomez Martinez and moved to Chihuahua, Mexico. We know of one son named Jesus. This information came from Margaret Pehl. If anyone reading has any further or other information we would love to know about it.

Truth be known, Julia didn't mind his desire to take her home with his remuda. Of course Abijah was a little taken aback by the thought of "selling" his daughter. But he smiled back at Gomez,

"My wife and I will take it under deep consideration." He replied.

Julia and Gomez had a short courtship and the wedding party was in fact an event that perhaps most if not all of the San Saba River inhabitants attended. All of the family, close friends and relatives, such as the Binnions, the Ketchums and the Browns they were all there, and oh, what a night it was.

Dick and the boys were playing the dancing music. He could play his fiddle like no other. Annie was attending and she was wearing the most beautiful yellow dress he had ever seen. He and his brothers Jim and Tap and those single boys in the Ketchum clan (Tom and Sam) all decided right then and there to call for a beauty contest. The bride of course, couldn't be included. After all, she was already the star of this summer's evening.

The winner would have a special song played for her.

So, all through the night, those single ladies paraded around twirling and smiling and flirting with the boys in the band who were the judges. Dick played his fiddle especially well every time as Annie would dance his way. At the end of the night unanimously, Annie was chosen by the boys as the winner. Martha had gathered up a batch of yellow roses from out by the gate and as Dick presented them to her, their eyes met for a long moment. For Dick it seemed as time stood still. He wanted to kiss her tender lips, and he felt that she would have kissed him back if there hadn't been so many people

And well ... that Annie she was a proper girl.

All of these thoughts were playing in Dick's mind as he rode the last of the miles returning to his home near Richland Springs.

As much as he wanted to see his girl, he needed a shave and a bath to soak the trail dust off of him.

He passed by the Williamsons place as he rode home and old lady Williamson was outside setting on her porch. The shade of the roof made the day seem pleasant and as she saw Dick she yelled out to him. Even though he wasn't entirely ready to negotiate the farm purchase with her, she insisted on pulling Dick's ear to hear her terms.

It seems that she had been considering what might become of her and her family after the farm was sold. The tone of her voice sounded full of stress, maybe even a bit desperate, and Dick was afraid she was gonna change her mind about selling out. So he stopped and got down off his horse and set on the porch with her for just a little while. She yelled thru the window to her daughter Beulah to bring Dick some sweet tea. She smiled as he settled back in the chair across from her on the porch. She seemed content to have his company.

She began to ask him about Julia and her life in Mexico. She wondered if that Gomez might have some brothers that might be interested in Levonia or Beulah. Dick blew lemonade out his nose as she made that remark. He tried to brush it off that it was a cough from all that trail dust and she began to talk more about Julia and Gomez and this wonderful place called Chihuahua Mexico.

"Well," she said she looked at Dick very seriously, "If we're gonna sell we need someone to help us get there. You know, to that Mexico place."

Dick's heart began to sink. He shore wasn't looking forward to being gone from home for any length of time again. He had looked forward to the end of this last ride precisely so that he could spend some time with his Annie. However it seemed that old lady Williamson had her mind set.

Yes," she declared, she would in fact sell him the farm and at a good price but he would have to take them to Mexico. Dick felt his face flushing red. But he didn't want to blow this deal. He reluctantly agreed to take them but sure wasn't happy about it.

He bid her goodbye and headed for the ranch house. After a bath and a shave he set out to find his Annie. She greeted him warmly but was less than happy when he told her what he would now need to do for the Williamsons.

"Oh Dick, it seems like you'll never have time to just be with me," she cried.

"Is this the way it will always be?" Dick held her close and tried to reassure her that this would be the last of his travels.

"She won't sell the farm to us if I don't help her move. Annie".

Finally she conceded that Dick being gone for another extended period of time probably was the only way to their future. Dick rode back home late that night with a heavy, heavy heart.

Please see the forward for a list of the Duncan Family members.

Chapter 3: Late January 1889

A short time after that visit, Dick rode over to Joe Clark's smithy shop to pick up the brand new wagon that he had purchased to move the Williamson family to Mexico. It had been a wet winter and Dick made sure the wagon sheet was pulled tight over the top of the wagon. He had traded some of their belongings for a set of horses that could not only make the trip to Mexico but that were young enough to break ground for the new farm they hoped to acquire there.

To further dramatize the chaos of the events of this January of 1889, Dick's sister Osa had just arrived in San Saba with the news that her husband Tom had died in Piedras Negras, Mexico. She brought her young girls up to stay at the house with Martha but had left her 10 year old son, Ben in Mexico with their father Abijah. At ten years of age Ben wasn't all grown up but he sure was able to care for the stock and other chores at the little ranch. Dick's father Abijah had been down there with Osa and Tom and their family for the better part of the last year helping out during the time that Tom had been so sick.

So as Dick prepared to head down south with the Williamson's, Tap headed out with his sister on the train. The brothers had decided to meet in Mexico and bring their sister's household belongings and Abijah and Ben back to San Saba

It was late in the evening when he got the wagon outfitted and to the ready. The Williamson's insisted on loading for the trip south that very night.

He had said his goodbyes to Annie. She wasn't happy at all about this trip but she recognized that it was something he had to do for them. But, she told him she really didn't like the way this was turning out at all. Being alone and waiting for him all the time just wasn't the way she wanted to live her life. He got madder with every item he loaded in the wagon. The fact he had to be gone and everything else this trip couldn't have happened at a worse time in his life.

But, true to his word, Dick would accompany this family to Eagle Pass and help them after the crossing into Mexico. Old Lady Williamson and her family really weren't well suited for travelling alone especially on the Mexican side of the Rio Grande. In fact, it might be rather dangerous. Truly they would need Dick's protection to get them settled.

When they first started loading the wagon Dick had a pretty hot head, full of steam churning in his head. But by the time they got the last of the furnishings in the house to the wagon Dick had talked his blood pressure down a lot. He had even begun to feel a rekindled kindness toward this family who in all reality his friends.

However, the last straw came as the last of the household things were loaded and Beulah Williamson announced that they were ready to hit the road.

"Mexico, here we come!" She shouted.

It became apparent to Dick as they all loaded up in the wagon that they were leaving right then and there[5]. It was close to midnight and although a full moon was out he was not keen on guiding a wagon anywhere at this hour and he told them as much.

"Fine!" Beulah shouted, "Ben can drive: She thrust the reins into his hands.

"Best get to it Ben." She demanded.

Dick bid a farewell to them pointed out the easiest path to the hard road and headed for his family home. His conscience caused him to stay awake most of the night worrying for them even though his irritation had been rubbed raw. The next afternoon he caught up to them on the road south. He really was sort of fond of that family.

---

[5] Testimony in the Dick Duncan vs the Texas Austin Term 1891 Tom Hawkins: "About 11:00 that same night I heard the noise of a wagon start from Mrs. Williamson's house. Tom Hawkins was a neighbor to the Williamson's.)

Chapter 4: The Trip to Eagle Pass

Dick decided that he really didn't have to travel every moment with them and actually he could enjoy the trip a lot easier that way. There was even a day or two when he even had time to sit a spell at some town or another and sometimes he found time and a saloon where he sat to play a hand of cards.

He did become leery however; as the family got near people or towns. On several occasions, the girls, Levonia especially, liked to flash around and talk about all that money that Dick had paid them for the farm and that they had gotten for their other belongings. He became more than a little nervous thinking someone might sneak up on their camp in the dark of the night and take all that cash. He warned Levonia to keep her mouth shut but she just sneered at him and said he was jealous of all the attention she was getting.

"You had yer chance with me Dick Duncan," she tried to tease. He gigged up his little sorrel and decided he needed to get some distance from himself and this bunch for just a little while.

As they broke camp one morning not too far from the border, a single horse pulling a new buckboard headed in the direction of the town of Brackettville[6], pulled up near to them. Levonia's face lit up and she began to straighten her hair with her hand.

A handsome cowboy was driving the wagon that had a wagon sheet pulled over the wagon box. Levonia began to call out.

"Jed, Jed, why Jed, don't ya remember me?"

Jed pulled his wagon to a halt. His stomach, now had a sickening knot in it. He thought about ducking his head and just passing by. But the other wagon was awkwardly pulled to the middle of the road. With the wetness of the past wintry days he didn't want to pull off the roadway and get stuck. That would only make matters worse. So he pulled up his horses and decided to chat. Truth be told he wasn't in a real hurry anyway.

---

[6] The town of Brackettville, Texas is commonly referred to as Brackett as well, as Brackettville. This town in Kinney Co. was settled in 1852 by relative of the author, Oscar Bernadotte Brackett.

He did know in fact, know this ragged looking lady who hailed his name. Drunk and in need of "love", he had had a couple of encounters with her when he up north was in San Saba a few years back. Now, he was partners in a freight company in Eagle Pass and he was out on a delivery run.

Levonia began to tell him that they were on their way to buy a ranch in Mexico. Proudly, she said they had sold their farm in San Saba and it had been worth,

"Well more money than I've ever seen!" She said as she patted her breast protectively as if to indicate that there was where the money was hidden.

Now a smile grew across Jed's face. This conversation was getting more interesting by the minute. He decided that stopping for a chat had certainly been worth his while.

"Well, Imma thinking I might like to have a closer look at the money Levonia," his voice trailed off as if he was propositioning her. She smiled sweetly.

"Dick Duncan's taking us to Eagle Pass to cross the Grande there."

Jed wasn't sure how much money these folks might be sporting but he was thinking it might be worth his while to find out.

"Hell," he muttered to himself "I'm was delivering this load of smuggled whiskey for less than the price of a farm.

"Vonie darlin," he said "I'm headed to Brackett to deliver my goods...but I will be back to Eagle, shortly, why don't ya all wait for me there?" He winked at her and tipped his hat to one side.

"I can cross ya over and help ya settle south of the border...I've got a few connections there."

About this time Dick rode up on the wagon to see what the holdup was. Levonia introduced Dick to Jed stating that he was their guide to Mexico. After a few moments of chit chat Jed gigged his horses up but as he did, he looked at Levonia,

"Remember what I said Vonie," he looked her up and down as if he was admiring a fine piece of art.

She smiled sweetly looking at him, shyly and patting her breast again. He smiled, tipped his hat to her and drove on his way.

"What in the hell was that all about Levonia?" Dick demanded.

She looked at him and curtly replied, "Ain't, well … it ain't none of yer affair Dick."

A few days later the wagon and the Williamsons pulled in to Eagle Pass. Dick was anxious to get crossed toward Piedras Negras.

However, by the time they arrived in Eagle Pass, Levonia had convinced her family that Jed was gonna come to guide them to Mexico and she had even convinced herself these last few miles that he was planning to marry her.

"You all heared him," she said.

Dick had truly been tested to the brink by this trip. He wasn't in any mood to argue. If Jed was willing to take them to Mexico, then Dick was more than willing to concede this job and that would mean he could be on his way back home to San Saba and to the arms of his pretty Annie.

He took that family down to a grove of trees near the Rio Grande. He unloaded their things from his wagon and he left his wagon sheet for them for a tent. He didn't know how long they would stay there waiting for Jed to ride in like a white knight to save them, and honestly he didn't care. He wanted to get to Mexico and help his kin move his sister and get back home to his Annie.

Dick crossed on the ferry and travelled the short few miles to Fred Bernt's ranch. He was glad to see his father and brother. They had to wait a day or two to permission to put Cravey's body in the ground.

Chapter 5: She's Slipping Through My Fingers

Time, for Dick, seemed to drip slower than molasses on a cold winter's day on this trip.

The more anxious Dick was to get moving the slower it crawled. He tried hard to set Annie and his thoughts of her to the side and focus on the task at hand.

Osa and Tom Cravey had acquired some livestock and she had more than enough household goods to load down both of the wagons.

Finally, all the preparation had been made to leave and Osa[7] and her son Ben went to Piedras Negras to catch the train. Dick and Tap and their father would now herd her livestock to the crossing. It was just a few miles, and they left just before daylight hoping to avoid too many encounters with the locals.

All should have gone well until someone warned the Federales there was some Gringos. Two wagons with white men herding some cattle, horses and a burro north toward the Crossing. The Federales soon surrounded them near a grove of trees just south of the river. The Duncans knew just enough of the Spanish to sort of understand their chatter but when they pulled the guns out and indicated that several of the horses had to stay, Tap especially was glad that it was only a livestock tax they wished to extract, sort of a road tax they called it, for the pleasure of traveling to the crossing.

When they finally arrived at the ferry, Osa's livestock herd had been reduced to four horses and Ben's burro. About a year ago ,a Mexican

---

[7] Osa Duncan 1864 was born to Abijah and Martha M Duncan. On January 1, 1880 she at the age of 16 she married Thomas (Tom) Jefferson Cravey. On the 1 of April of 1881 their daughter Belle was born and then Benjamin J. came along on the 22nd of December 1882. A third child was born to them in 1885 they named her Fanny. We have read in the testimony of the Duncan vs Texas trial that Tom Cravey had some trouble in San Saba, being accused of cattle theft. From what we gather he had moved his family to Mexico in search of a better life. Abijah Duncan (Osa's Father) had been in with them south of Piedras Negras for the better part of a year when Tom passed away. See Tap Duncan's testimony: 30th court of Appeals report, Texas Dick Duncan vs. state of Texas court of appeals reports Austin Term 1891.

neighbor had taken a shine to young Ben and had given it to him because it was just his size. Ben was really proud of that burro. He could make him go by guiding him with a stick. Truth be told though that the burro just followed the horses like a dog. Wherever those horses went that burro followed.

When the group finally arrived at the ferry the horses were the first to load. Putting them on first meant that as they would be in place to pull the wagons off of the ferry on the American side. The little burro got left behind as the horses were being tethered at the front. That burro hawed and he hawed until he found a spot where he could get on and get up to be near the horses.

Then came time for the heavily loaded wagons to board. As the first wagon was loaded the planks of the flat shifted and the horses spooked. They, however were tied securely and couldn't go anywhere. When they loaded the second wagon the planks shifted again and the horses already agitated spooked again. The horses were shivering with fright the whole length of the crossing. They did however float to the American side without a real incident.

However, when they prepared to unload, Abijah jumped down from his wagon the planks shifted again and the horses, this time, began to jerk wildly against their tie ropes. Their jerking scared the little burro and he decided that he had had enough of this circus. He was getting off this ride. He headed straight for what he thought was solid ground, Dick however, was standing in the way. He was surprised when he looked up saw the little burro headed so fast his way and it took a second for him to realize that he was just about to be run over by that little rat. The only defense he had in his hand was his rifle and he swung it hard with both hands at the burro. He hit him squarely on the head knocking the burro sideways and Dick straight into the Grande[8]. The spooked little burro kept heading as far away from that raft as he could.

Dick was now fit to be tied. But it seemed that their father Abijah matched Dick's emotions. He walked over to the shore near where Dick

---

[8] One of the circumstantial facts that lead to Dick's conviction was that some of the state witnesses stated that the bodies of the Williamsons that were pulled from the rain swollen depths of the Rio Grande, appeared to have been hit in the head with a blunt object. Others, including Jacob Meyer who first found the bodies in the river, never spoke of trauma to the head. Because Dick Duncan's rifle had a bent magazine the state sought to draw a conclusion that Duncan had used the gun as the murder weapon.

sat in the water. He pulled him out of the river by the nap of his neck. He was threatening to use that gun on Dick just as like he had used it on Ben's burro. Dick was embarrassed and angered and ready to fight. First, because of being knocked in the water and secondly because of his Father's anger at him. He was shouting right back in his father's face. Tap smiled. He was glad that wasn't him. He went ahead and got the ferry unloaded and just let them fight it out.

By the time that Tap had gotten the ferry emptied, Dick had walked off in a huff and Abijah was sitting on the grass and his face was grim. Tap walked over and sat on the ground beside him and asked permission to make a small suggestion.

"Pa, "he began, "why not send Dick on up north towards home. He's really just wanting to get back to see Annie. We can load our wagon heaviest and let him make a faster trip."

Abijah agreed. Somehow his youngest son seemed to have a gift for making things make sense. Tap helped Dick lighten his wagonload, and Dick hit the trail for San Saba.

Chapter 6: The Rangers

Dick couldn't believe his luck. He travelled the 35 miles to Spofford and planning to head steadily north on the road to Brackettville. He knew that if he would keep travelling at a walking pace, his horses could take him about forty miles in a day and it would be possible to see his girl soon. But to make that speed he would need corn for these horses to fuel them for the trip. So he stopped at Spofford to trade some of the household goods in his wagon for corn. He hated to take the time for the stop but he knew the little pulling geldings would need that corn.

He grained the horses and bid farewell to that town. Even though it was nearing dusk he was anxious to keep putting the miles behind him. Just a short ways out of Brackettville though, his harness broke, luckily he had his sorrel tethered to the wagon so he saddled him up and rode on into town.

He arrived there late. He couldn't find a suitable leather and didn't have much money **and** he had left his trading goods at the wagon. He used what he had to buy some rope to splice the harness together until he got home to San Saba and he could fix it right. By the time he got back to the wagon it was plum dark. And there was not much for light in the sky. He would have to spend the night there by the roadside.

The next morning as he prepared to fix the harness he discovered that his knife was gone. It must have fallen in the river when the burro dumped him overboard. He muttered a few more choice words about that critter. He honestly hoped that his pa would never find that animal. But deep in his heart he knew that his father wouldn't give up until he found him. Dick could just imagine his father saying,

"You know it is more than enough that little Bennie lost his pa. I will not go back and tell him he lost his burro too."

Dick found himself smiling at that thought. He found a sharp rock that he used to cut the rope. He hobbled the team and snuggled in the box of the wagon under Osie's quilts and slept.

Finally after the sun shone straight up in the sky Dick got started north again. Sure not a lot of time saved on this go around! He thought.

As Dick drove his wagon along the warm sunshine made him relax even in the early spring weather. He had decided that he need to just slow down and take each day …. One day at a time. It seemed that the faster he tried to go the further behind he got. His little ponies were getting tired but he wasn't that far from home.

He wondered how Tap and his Pa were getting on. Not too long after he was thinking on them, he heard the sounds of a wagon approaching from behind him. He looked back and saw a wagon with two men. He smiled thinking, hoping it might be his kin. He slowed his pace just enough to let them easily catch up with him.

Sure enough it was his Pa and Tap. They whoaed their horses and stopped to visit for a few moments. Dick noticed they had found the Burro. It seems that he had been so spooked and knocked little bit loco from the Winchester being bent over his skull, he kept travelling all the way to Spofford. But now back again with his horses, he again just followed the along like a dog.

While they were parked along the road, a group of men approached on horseback. Tap was first to see the Ranger tin stars glistening in the mid-morning sun. He got an eerie feeling as they rode past. They eyed the Duncans as if they suspected them of some sort of nefarious behavior. Tap tipped his hat to them. He and his kin had no reason to be wary of them, however the looking over they gave them and their wagons caused the little hairs on the back of his neck to stand up straight. He gigged his horses and headed on toward home. Abijah had gotten in Dick's wagon. He wanted to ride with Dick a ways just sort of mend the harsh words they had spoken to each other in Eagle Pass, at the Crossing.

The Rangers rode on past but a couple of miles down the road they stopped and had a chat. They circled back and caught up with the wagon. When one Ranger pulled his horse up short in front of their team, Abijah and Dick began to look questioningly at one another. Dick was the first to speak. He was very polite.

"Can we help y'all out?" he asked

"We see y'all got some weapons in this here wagon *boys*. And you got some goods y'all brought up from south?" One of the Rangers stated.

Abijah especially hated being called "boy." It reminded him of those arrogant Northerners back at that prison camp. Dick grabbed his Pa's arm to hold him back as he began to respond to what he had obviously been meant as an insult.

"Ah... Yes?" Dick replied courteously. The Rangers with their guns out informed the Duncans that they were going to have to run them in on "weapons charges,"

Tap, who had been a mile or so ahead of Dick and his Pa had slowed his pace down when he realized they weren't behind him. Soon the Rangers soon overtook him.

All the Duncans were escorted to Barksdale and held for further investigation on smuggling charges[9]. Abijah and Tap were released[10] but Dick was held for further investigation. The Rangers remembered seeing him earlier in February, the 7th in fact, at their camp when he stopped to have dinner with them as he travelled south to Mexico with the Williamsons.

---

[9] Texas Court of appeals ,Austin term 1891 Dick Duncan vs the state No. 6694 testimony of John Hughes pg. 7 "on the first day of March this year sergeant Aten and myself arrested the defendant....Also Tap Duncan was with them. We arrested them on the west fork of the Nueces River...We arrested them on the suspicion of smuggling. After we arrested Tap we carried them all three back to Barksdale and placed a complaint against them for carrying pistols. The reason we did this is we suspected them of smuggling and wanted to investigate the matter."

[10] Texas Court of appeals, Austin term 1891 Dick Duncan vs the state No. 6694 testimony of John Hughes pg. 7. Tap was released on lack of evidence.

Chapter 7: Dick Loses Annie

Here it was the First day of March. The bluebonnets were blooming and oh, the spring was turning out nice. It had been a cold and wet winter in west Texas and Dick had planned to be home in Annie's arms by now. Hoped to have even proposed marriage to her.

Yet here he was. Sitting inside a jail cell listening to his Pa and brother being interrogated by the Rangers.

He still wasn't sure exactly what it was they brought them in for. One moment he heard them asking about the guns they carried then asking interrogating them about Osa's household goods.

Now finally it was his turn. He was so irritated by this unreasonable delay that he told them to either arrest him, if they had cause or let him be on his way. He had to swallow hard to try to not sound as irritated as he was about this whole ordeal. He promised the Rangers that if he had done something to break the law it was innocently done.

They did let Abijah and Tap go, but the Rangers kept Dick for further investigation, until they were satisfied that he hadn't smuggled Osa's household goods from Mexico. When they finally released him later, Dick was even more anxious to head for San Saba. What a tale he would have to tell when he finally reached his Annie. That is if she still would talk to him.

As he drew near to Richland Creek, Dick stopped to pick a batch of the pretty flowers growing on the side of the road her. He headed for her house. He was so excited to see her that he didn't even stop at home and do the Gentlemanly thing and clean himself up before he went to see her. He licked his hand and tried to straighten his hair. He planned to just drop by and ask if he could come to call later that evening.

When he pulled the wagon up in front of her house she was sitting out on her porch with a man that he hadn't seen before. Dick had a wary feeling about the oddness of this situation but hoped that he was just be a business acquaintance of her family. Under his breath however, he muttered,

"But why the hell you sitting on the porch with my Annie?"

Dick face started to turn red. He just never was good at hiding his emotions. The lightness of his somewhat freckled skin which was a Duncan characteristic, against his reddish blonde hair showed vividly the rise or fall of blood pressure as his mood changed. He stopped at the wagon and gathered the flowers he had picked for her. He took a deep breath.

"Miss Annie," he called out, as he took his hat off and bowed to her, "permission to come to call on you?"

Dick, in his dramatic ways always did make her smile and truth be told those ways warmed her heart.

She looked at her visitor with a sideways glance and told him she needed to speak with Dick. The visitor reached out and grabbed her hand as he said his goodbye.

Now Dick's blood was boiling. He reached the porch as the visitor departed. Forcing a smile he tipped his hat to him. Then he focused back to the prettiest girl he had ever seen.

"Oh Annie," he whispered. "You are a sight for my sore eyes!"

She smiled at his kind words. He did make her feel pretty.

"I ... I was beginning to think you wasn't coming back, Dick." She smiled a crooked little smile.

Dick asked if he could sit with her for just a minute and she offered him a seat on the porch swing. As a sort of afterthought offered her the flowers. She was slow to take them and Dick felt a huge pit forming in his gut.

"Can I ... Could I call on you tonight, Annie ... after I've had a proper bathing and all?" She smiled at him again.

"Dick, yes, she looked squarely at him, "you should come to call. We have much to speak of."

With that Dick touched her hand lightly and promised to see her later. Then he hurried to get to his wagon. He didn't want to let her see the tears forming in his eyes. She hadn't said it but when she pulled her hand back as he touched it, he knew that in his being gone for all this time, her heart had in fact slipped away from him.

He gigged the horses up and headed for the Duncan Home. But he really needed a stiff drink. He stopped at the saloon. Didn't have any money in his pocket but he did have a couple of cartridges in his pocket. He took one out and slammed it hard on the bar. "A shot of whiskey" he called out. This was not turning out how he had planned at all.

The Duncan family home near Richland Creek. About 1885 photo compliments of Skipper Duncan and Margaret Pehl.

Photos courtesy Margaret Pehl also Skipper Duncan. The home in San Saba burned
sometime in the 1890s

Chapter 8: Dick Tries to Clear His Name

When Dick heard the rumor that he might be accused or wanted for questioning for the murder of the Williamsons he went voluntarily to the sheriff's office in San Saba.[11]

Sheriff Howard put Dick in his jail shaking his head. He told Sherriff Howard that he had consulted a lawyer who told him he should be following the setting sun. "You ought to be listening to that advice, son." Dick looked at Howard and shrugged his shoulders,

"But I have nothing to run from," he replied.

"It might not matter whether you are guilty or innocent Dick. This case is taking a life of its own. Everybody in Eagle Pass, the Rangers, all the way to the governor's office want someone to pay for this crime. Someone will hang, guilty or innocent, it doesn't matter," said Sheriff Howard.[12]

Shortly thereafter, the Rangers soon came to visit. They asked Sheriff Howard where they might find a man named Dick Duncan the sheriff told them that Dick was there waiting for them.

It wasn't but five minutes after they began to interrogate him and Dick knew this was trouble.

Yes it was true, the Rangers had seen him on the road to Eagle Pass and he had seen him with the Williamsons. He had stopped on night and

---

[11] Newspapers.com San Saba News and Star (San Sab, Texas) Fri. march 29, 1889.

[12] Quote from article "From no Account to Just Plain Mean by Chris Weatherby. "The murders had come at a time when Texas was desperately trying to curb outlawry in the state. Officials were anxious to have the murders solved quickly. Word of the crime spread fast. Most of the newspapers in the state carried the story. Rumors had preceded Aten to San Saba. People there already had heard that Dick Duncan was suspected of committing the crimes. Duncan also had heard the rumors and had asked a lawyer to meet him outside of the town to discuss his chances in a court of law. Duncan was told that the possibility of an acquittal was slim because of public sentiment regarding the murders, because of the circumstantial evidence, against him and because of the bad reputation that Duncan had. The lawyer told Duncan that, in his opinion, the only chance that he had to save himself was "To follow the setting sun and never look back." In spite of this advice, however Duncan turned himself in to the Sheriff at San Saba and was put in jail."

they took supper with them at their camp. So had many other people. It was a matter of fact that he had helped that family go to Mexico.

Dick tried to assure them that he had nothing to do with the murders. He had held a fondness for the otherwise strange family. He had just bought their place and had big plans.

I am innocent he said, saying it louder and louder every time as he was becoming more and more fearful of the outcome this interrogation might hold for him.

The interrogating Ranger became rather arrogant and stated that they now had their man.

"Dick," Ranger Aten began … "We have two men in Eagle Pass who tell us they saw you murder that family." He wiped his hands together as if he had finished a dirty job. Dick could feel the blood rising to his face and a gaping hole growing in the pit of his stomach. Dick swallowed hard. His head was spinning He looked at Aten with pleading in his eyes.

"Who could that be?" He mouthed.

He stood with his arms open palms out looking, at the ground as if he was searching for a lost answer.

Ranger Aten walked over near Dick. He put his hand on his shoulder. He sat on the desk near him.

"Dick," he began, "I can't tell you who these men are. They are a part of an ongoing investigation. We use them to help us to curb some of the smuggling activity that is going on at the border."

Aten straightened up to walk toward the other men. Dick started to grab at his shirt as he left the desk and the Ranger near him took that as a threat. He got right in Dick's face as if to emphasize his control in this situation was total and complete.

"Go ahead and do it boy." He invited with a threatening tone.

"Touch him, and I betcha one of us will get trigger happy if ya know what I mean."

All of West Texas was in a fury. Call it hue and cry or fear and outrage, the public, from Eagle Pass all the way to Austin, didn't feel safe and demanded that someone needed to pay for these horrendous murders. And these Rangers were gonna solve this case come hell or high-water.

Mexican bodies floated in the Rio Grande all the time[13] and mostly they were merely pulled out and buried in an unmarked grave unless, for some reason or another, the Mexican government came to claim them.

But for today, four white bodies had been found in the swollen river and the whole of Texas seemed to be unnerved. So the cry went up all the way to the governor and he sent the declaration to the Rangers that someone needed to hang for this crime.[14]

Dick Duncan, in his innocence naively wandered into the Sheriff's office thinking that justice would be served and truth would be known. He had no fear of the law because he had left those folks, his friends and neighbors, alive and well down at the river.

The Ranger now shoved Dick to the floor.

"'Let's be on our way boys...I think we are finished here."

The sheriff escorted Dick back to his jail cell. The sound of the steel lock engaging made his heart sink. Dick sat on the floor and the thick adobe walls of the jails seemed to close in on him. He needed some air. He walked over to small barred window.

"What is happening to me?" he moaned. Fear filled his heart and tears fell. He wondered if he could somehow get out in fact run. But his family could never live in peace if he did. Vigilante justice was not unknown in this part of Texas in the 1880s In fact, San Saba seemed to be the heart of it, but Dick sure didn't expect the Rangers to ever be using it and most of all not on him. Taking a deep breath he hoped that his innocence would be proven ... he was innocent.

---

[13] Also a quote from it is in article: <u>The hanging of Dick Duncan</u> by John C Myers for the Maverick Co. Centennial Edition of the Eagle Pass News and Guide September 16, 1971.

[14] ibid.

Chapter 9: The Indictment

The Rangers stayed in San Saba for a short time investigating and interviewing folks about the Williamson family and about Dick Duncan. Sheriff Howard had warned them that they needed to have their facts right about Dick Duncan or he said,

"Someone from these parts that hear you all accusing him, why they might take those fancy pistols ya all have and shove them down yer throats. Just a warning mind ya." He smiled.

"These folks are all just a little salty. Watch yerselves!"

Shortly afterwards Dick was transported to Maverick County to the Jail. Sheriff Howard told those Rangers that if Dick Duncan didn't for some reason make the trip SAFELY to Maverick Co. that he would personally hold them responsible.

On May 23, 1889 Dick Duncan was indicted for murder 1 for the murder of Ben Williamson, Beulah Williamson, Levonia Holmes and Mary Ann Williamson.

Dick and his lawyer met and they made busy sending out notices to appear and testify in court.

Court was set and Dick's witnesses were lined up and ready to testify, however the prosecution decided they needed more time and sued for postponement. They appealed to Judge Kelso saying that the depth and importance of this case required that all the facts be brought to light. The Judge agreed.[15]

So a set new date was set and this time around the Sheriff's office did not notify all of Dick's witnesses or simply couldn't find some of them. In fact one of the State's witness had died in the meantime. The new case was set for December 2, 1889. Before this date in late November, the Defense asked for continuance because not all of Dick's witnesses had been served for the second appearance.[16] The most important of his

---

[15] Duncan v The State Texas Court of Appeals Reports Austin term 1891. Pgs. 27-28

[16] Actual court transcripts obtained and copied at maverick County courthouse. "By the witness Joe Bryan, Jim Miller and Nat Johnson Defendant's application states that he

witnesses Jo Grimes, Jim Miller and Nat Johnson all of whom had seen Dick on his way home to San Saba were slated to testify they had later seen the Williamsons alive and well near Eagle Pass. These men were either not served or were for other reasons unable to attend. 2 As the Judge Kelso reviewed Dick's Appeal for continuance he wrote there was little chance that men from San Saba actually had seen the Williamsons down by Eagle Pass so he concluded that they were probably be lying[17]. At this point Dick wanted to call San Saba Sheriff Howard to wit but he was off on another case in Brady as well and was and unavailable. He had applied that Sheriff Howard would testify that as soon as Dick heard rumors that he might be charged in the murder of that family he voluntarily went to the sheriff's office and turned himself in.

Judge Kelso decided that the sheriff would only be a character witness and Dick's character was not on trial. In the ordinary course of a trial the jury would have been instructed that Duncan's testimony would be accepted as the fact unless refuted by other witnesses.

But the judge refused to instruct the jury as to that fact.

So on a sad and dark day the trial at Eagle Pass, Texas began without the witnesses and the support that Dick needed to prove his innocence. The Rangers and prosecution spent the bulk of the trial proving that the Williamsons were in fact the people that were murdered. Because it took a while for the bodies to be identified a large portion of the testimony was dedicated to identifying the bodies. Several people testified that their

---

could prove that on or about the 21 day of Feb. 1889, they saw the defendant in the western portion of Edward co. on the road to Junction City. And they had all been well acquainted with defendant for many years. And that the next day they saw Mrs. Williamson her daughter Levonia Holmes Ben Williamson and Beulah Williamson at camp some 6 or 7 miles west of Spofford Junction in Kinney County that they were well acquainted with the Williamson family. That she was looking for a man who lived across the river some 20 miles from Eagle Pass. She showed the witnesses what seemed to be a lot of money that she said she had got for her place." These witnesses were available to testify at the trial but when the state had sued for a postponement appealing to Judge Kelso that due to the gravity of the crimes the prosecution needed time to insure they had all their witnesses. When the December 2nd court date arrived some of the defendants witness weren't there. Duncan Made his first application for a continuance which was by the court overruled, the Defendant excepting. Pg. 25 Defendant was then placed on trial which resulted in his being convicted of murder in the first degree and accessing the death penalty.

[17] Duncan v The State Texas Court of Appeals Reports Austin term 1891. Pg. 36.

clothing on the deceased bodies matched those worn when by the Williamsons as they left San Saba.

Several people living in the towns on the road to Eagle Pass testified that they had seen the family traveling south in the company of Dick Duncan.

Some folks had testified that the bodies in the river appeared to have been struck in the head with a blunt object.

Some other testified that there was no mark on the heads.

However no one testified that they had seen Dick and the Williamsons within 25 miles of the Rio Grande together.

But this was a very foul and hellacious crime and someone had to pay for such a deed. Dick was the last person to see the Williamson family alive the court had concluded and because his witnesses weren't there to testify he couldn't refute the evidence other than by his own and his family's testimonies.

Dick's Lawyer began to instruct the jury that his testimony unless otherwise refuted was to be taken as truth but the judge wouldn't allow that instruction.

So the jury weighed Dicks life in the balance on the circumstantial evidence brought forth.

Yes Dick had accompanied the Williamson Family to Eagle Pass Texas.

Yes, the magazine of Dick's rifle was bent.

Dick had hit Ben's burro with it.

The State claimed he used the gun to bash the heads and murder the Williamson family.

Yes Dick had purchased some rope in Brackettville, Texas.

Dick didn't have the money to buy the leather that he needed to fix his harness so he bought rope in Brackettville to patch it until he returned home.

The State claimed that the rope he had bought in Brackett was the same type used to tie the bodies to the heavy rocks used to weight them down in the river.

Not a single witness for the prosecution proved anything other than those circumstantial events. Not a single witness had seen Dick and that family together within 25 miles of the place they were found floating in the river.

Yet, with only one side of the story told, the Maverick Co. court in Eagle Pass, Texas found Dick Duncan guilty of murder. Guilty of the murders of Beulah, Levonia and Ben and Mary Ann Williamson. Dick was shocked, stunned, and mortified. All the feeling had gone from him.

When Judge Kelso pronounced the verdict he asked Dick if he had anything to say as to why death sentence should not be pronounced upon him, Dick looked at him as if he thought the judge must have been living on another planet during all these proceedings.

"I suppose I have lots to say but I don't suppose it will do me any good now."

As he descended the staircase from the upper floor of the Maverick Co. Courthouse on through misty eyes he saw his family waiting for him at the bottom of the staircase. His sister Nannie reached out and grabbed his hand. "What do you think they will do with ye now Dick?" Dick looked at her with tears dripping down his otherwise stoic face. Squeezing her hand he replied, "I reckon they'll hang me."[18]

Appeals were launched and delays requested. As Dick's lawyers and the prosecution got together in closed sessions to discuss the motions put forth, the Rangers said they had specific witnesses that saw Dick murder that family. When Dicks lawyers asked them to bring the men forward. The Rangers said that bringing them forth would compromise an ongoing investigation they had launched to curb stolen property and smuggling of goods into the States. Dick and his lawyers said that Dick had right to face these men in open court and to hear the ACCUSATIONS THEY LAUNCHED AGAINST HIM so that Dick, his lawyer, and the jury could decide for themselves if they were credible witnesses. The Rangers

---

[18] The Galveston Daily News, 19 Sep 1891, Sat, Page 2. Also UNIVERSITY MICHIGAN PROSE: DUNCAN VS. TEXAS 1891.

invoked protection for them stating that they had helped them solve previous criminal cases and if their names were brought forth they could lose the value they served to the state as undercover investigators. It might ruin further criminal investigation. But the Rangers vouched for their credibility.

It was clear to the court that Dick could not have committed these murders by himself. As of right now it was accepted by insinuation that Picnic Jones (Walter Landers) as they called him was who they suspected was his accomplice but since they couldn't find him, they decided that perhaps Dick may have killed him also. The Rangers could also use the fact that the Duncans were all arrested together as another piece of ambiguous evidence and suggested there could be room on the gallows for three. They made that clear. So Dick knew that if he raised too much of a dust up, well the evidence might start to point to Tap, and his dad Abijah, after all they were was also arrested in Barksdale along with Dick. His lawyer told him with a very somber look on his face that if any of this got out to the media there would most likely be three hangings.

During these ongoing negotiations between Dick, his Attorney, the Prosecution, and the Rangers, Abijah was fed up with all the secret hearings. He had heard enough to know that all was not being told. A jailhouse source had told him about the secret witnesses that the Rangers were supposed to have. He went down to the Prosecutor's Office and threatened to blow it all sky high with revelations to the press about the Rangers secret witnesses. The prosecutor told him straight out, if he did that, then the prosecutor office would have no choice but to charge him and Tap with the murder as well. Both he and Tap had testified they had been with Dick at all times. "Ya best let well enough alone and only Dick would hang, raise a stink and all three would hang."

Abijah was beat, he would risk his life in a heartbeat, and he had always stood up and done what was right. His life he would risk but he could not bear the thought of risking Tap's life too. It was bad enough losing one son, he could not bear the thought of losing two. Abijah was a beaten broken man. It would be many years before he would reveal what the Rangers had told him.

Finally the actual day for the hanging was set for September 18, 1891. An appeal had gone to the Governor for a stay of Dicks hanging but finally at midnight Bige brought the news from Austin, Dicks hanging was to take place.[19] Several reporters wished to record Dick's last conversations and action. He did grant to one reporter the access to the very last days of his life.

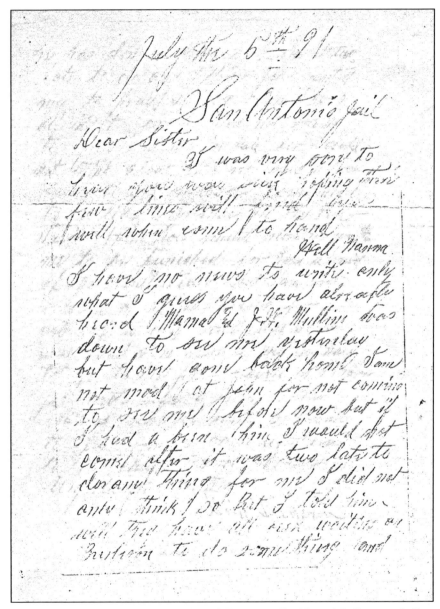

Page 1 of Dick Duncan's 1891 letter from jail. Transcribed by Michelle Drumheller on the next page.

[19] The Galveston Daily News (Galveston Texas) 12 Sep 1891 Sat • Page 3

Page 1 of the letter as transcribed:

July the 5th '91[20]

San Antonio Jail

Dear Sister,

I was very sory to

hear you was sick hoping these

few lines will find you

well when come to hand

Well Nanna[21]

I have no news to write only

what I guess you have already

heard Mama[22] and John Mullins[23] was

down to see me yesterday

but have gone back home I am

not mad at John for not coming

to see me before now but if

I had a been him I would not

come after it was two late to

do anything for me I did not

only think so But I told him

well they have been waiting on

Burleson[24] to do something and …

---

[20] The year 1891.
[21] Nancy Ann B. (Nannie/Nanna) Duncan, a sister
[22] Martha Duncan, Dick Duncan's mother
[23] Half-brother of Dick Duncan; son of Martha Muscaga (Blanchard Mulins) Duncan and her first husband John Mullins (Senior)
[24] Leigh Burleson, a San Saba lawyer appointed to represent Duncan.

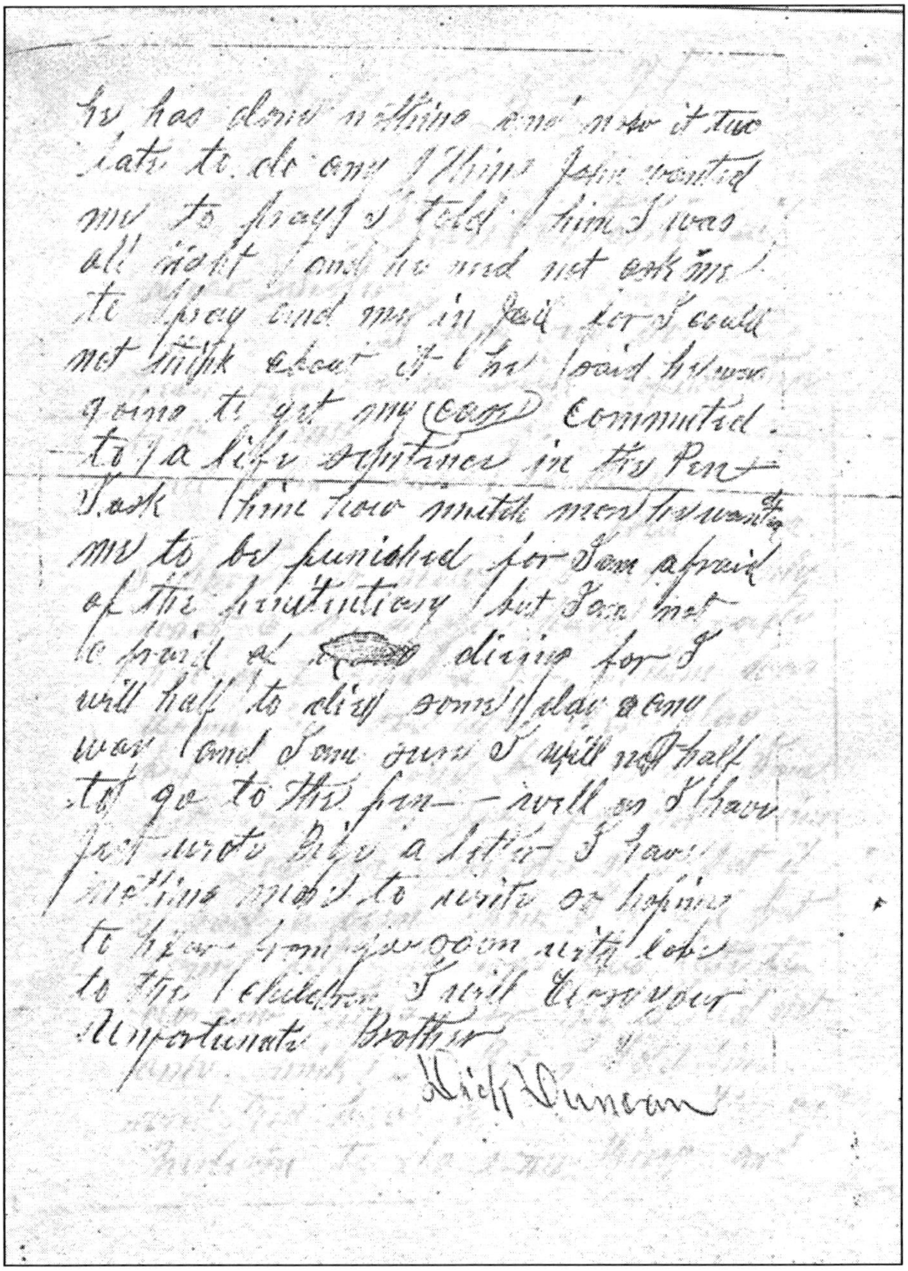

he has done nothing and now it too
late to do any thing John wanted
me to pray I told him I was
all right and he need not ask me
to pray and me in jail for I could
not think about it he said he was
going to get my (case) committed
to a life sentence in the Pen
I ask him how mutch more he wanted
me to be punished for I am afraid
of the penitentiary but I am not
to fraid of dieing for I
will half to die some day some
way and I am sure I will not half
to go to the Pen — well as I have
just wrote Bige a letter I have
nothing much to write so hoping
to hear from you soon with love
to the children I will close your
Unfortunate Brother

Dick Duncan

Page 2 of Dick Duncan's 1891 letter from jail. Transcribed by Michelle Drumheller on the next page.

Page 2 of the letter as transcribed:

he has done nothing and now it two

late to do anything John[25] wanted

me to pray I told him I was

all right and he need not ask me

to pray and me in jail for I could

not think about it he said he was

going to get my case commuted

to a life sentence in the Pen

I ask him how mutch more he wanted

me to be punished for I am afraid

of the penitentiary but I am not

 afraid of [mark out] dieing for I

will half to die someday [mark out] any

way and I am sure I will not half

to go to the pen --- well as I have

just wrote Bige[26] a letter I have

nothing more to write so hoping

to hear from you soon with love

to the children I will close your

Unfortunate Brother

Dick Duncan

Dick Duncan was hanged on September 18, 1891 at Eagle Pass, Texas, at age 28. Take note of the distinctive difference in the slant of the text of the body of the letter and the slant of Dick's signature. The script in the body of the letter slants to the right, like a right-handing writer. And

---

[25] John Mullins, half-brother of Dick Duncan.

[26] Abijah Elam Duncan was Dick Duncan's brother

Duncan's signature slants to the left like a left-handed writer. This indicates that this letter was written for Dick by someone else, probably a public official (the letter is formatted somewhat like a warrant) but signed by Dick himself.

Chapter 10: Will They Hang Him?

It was a hot and muggy day in Eagle Pass on September 18, 1891. The whole town had been eagerly anticipating this day. The original Appeals and delays had put the whole town on edge. In fact even until about midnight Dick wasn't positively sure that the proceedings scheduled for the 18th would carry forth. Then the call came from Bige. He had been in Austin awaiting the decision about the stay of execution from the Governor[27]. In reality they all knew how this would turn out but Dick's lawyer, Burleson conceded when Martha Duncan had insisted that they try.

"You can never deny a mother the right to exhaust every means possible," he said.

During the appeals that the defense had filed Hogg, who was now governor. had ridiculed their efforts to get a fair and equitable trial for Dick[28] and Bige in fact brought the news that Hogg in fact ordered that the execution continue as schedule.

There were rumors that the Duncan /Ketchum gang was going to ride into town. Shoot things up and break Dick Duncan out of jail. The Rangers and sheriff's office were prepared. Anyone attending the hanging had to check their guns before they could enter the town square. Most of the residents were more than ready to see the this whole murder ordeal put to rest and the final finishing touch was that Dick Duncan would hang.

A reporter from the Galveston Daily news was granted access to Dick and all the proceedings of the day. Dick woke early. Truth be told he didn't sleep at all but he closed his eyes and tried to imagine the peaceful place the minister kept describing to him. At times he felt like telling him that if it was so great why didn't he go there himself and let him alone but by this day, Dick's fight had gone plum out of him. He just accepted. The

---

[27] Bige read the letter from Governor Hogg to Sheriff Cooke: "After careful investigation, I decline to commute Dick Duncan's sentence. Let the law take its course. Inform him of his fate so that he may prepare to make peace with God." James Stephen Hogg Gov. This telegram is still located in the archives of the District Court in Maverick Co. Also a quote from it is in article: The hanging of Dick Duncan by John C Myers for the Maverick Co. Centennial Edition of the Eagle Pass News and Guide September 16, 1971.

[28] Ibid

Sheriff did grant him a bath and even a shave. The suit that his father brought down from San Saba didn't fit him really well anymore. He had lost some weight these 18 months that he had fought to prove his innocence.

The last time he wore this suit was when Julia married Gomez. He had a photograph taken of him and choked up as he thought back too Julia's big fuss on her big day,

"At a wedding, Dick, you should always have a picture taken of you." She straightened his tie and kissed him on the cheek.

"So you get dressed real nice Dick Duncan, and you will have your picture taken today." She had smiled very sweetly at him but he knew if he messed this up for her there would be hell to pay.

Dick, for, just a moment thought about what it might have been like if things had worked out with his Annie. By this time he would have got a photo picture taken of him but for a much happier reason. He would have smiled so proudly. Those thoughts broke his stoic facade and after he recovered from the pain he composed himself.[29]

His reverend baptized him and he took the sacraments of his new church. They spent some time reading some words from the Good Book together and Dick thought about how his mother had taught him and his siblings to read from this book. At 10:00am the Sheriff Cooke began to read the death warrant. Then Dick had called upon those against whom he held the greatest bitterness and told him that he forgave them. He also asked for their forgiveness.

At 11:00 am the final preparations for the execution began. When the guards came to his cell to shackle him, he called out to Sheriff Cooke pleading for them not to tie him. "Please grant me this as a dying favor?" He called out. Cooke granted this to him and Dick and the priest linked arms and firmly ascended the scaffold.[30]

Dick looked out on the crowd. The large room was packed. "Wow," he said to himself thinking how popular he was on this day. He searched

---

[29] Photo taken of Dick before hanging.
[30] The Galveston Daily News (Galveston, Texas) 19 Sep 1891, Sat, Page 2.

the faces through misty eyes and saw his friends and family. Not many of them there other than those Ketchum boys and Tap.

He asked for permission to talk with them and Cooke granted it. He knelt down on the scaffold and talked briefly with them. Then he stood up and took a deep breath.

He looked at Sheriff Cooke and said, "I want you to forgive me ... God has forgiven me and I have asked him to forgive me as I forgive my enemies."

He breathed in deeply again then continued, "I feel he has heard my prayer." He smiled a crooked smile then he looked at all the folks gathered to watch him die. "Goodbye," he said. Then he added, "I hope we meet in Heaven." His voice sort of drifted off. "I feel that I am going there. I feel that I have committed no crime and feel that I have been pardoned and washed whiter than snow." He spoke a few more words to the crowd and invited anyone who wanted to come shake hands with him to come to the gallows. Finally he looked at the sheriff, and said

"I am ready any time you are Sheriff Cooke." The sheriff tied his feet and they placed the black hood over his head. As steely as his resolve was he was more than a little frightened by the hood being placed over him. He asked for it to be removed for just a moment. Cooke granted that also. He told the Sheriff and the guard that he was grateful that he had not resisted them at all for these years he had been in their charge. He asked the father to say a prayer for him. He asked Cook to tell him when they were going to drop him.

"Please have mercy," he pleaded.

The hood was placed back over his head. His nervousness was showing, "Don't choke me with the rope please?" he asked.

The Sheriff now asked if he was ready. His reply was, "I am ready." Instantly the trigger was pulled and Dick's body shot through the trap. His body gave only one or two convulsions. And it was over.[31]

---

[31] The Galveston Daily News (Galveston, Texas) 19 Sep 1891, Sat, Page 2.

Dick Duncan

Historical Marker about the Dick Duncan murder trial.

Dick Duncan, Ola Shields (cousin) and Fannie Duncan.

Chapter 11: The Murder

Tap had stood in the crowd and he tried to calm his shaking nerves. The September sun seemed hotter than usual even for the mid-morning hours. Anger just kept filling up his mind and agitating his soul, but he vowed,

"No matter how sick nor how scared looking at that hanging rope made him feel, he would stay and watch."

But despite his rock solid resolve, when that hang man put that black hood over his favorite brother's head and they stood on the gallows near the noose ... Tap's guts, Oh how they twisted up. He had to get out of the crowd ... the Eagle Pass heat made him feel like he couldn't breathe. He stepped outside quickly then behind a big nut tree. There he vomited. He tried to pull himself together quickly but he vomited again and again. He knew he was missin' the hanging for sure but his insides just wouldn't quit. It was like he was trying to purge himself of all the happenings of this day.

Finally he bent down on his knees and just held his head in his hands. It seemed like hours that he just sat there looking at the watery bile he had just expelled. When the stench of it finally brought his thoughts back to the events at hand, he stood up. He took a deep breath and stepped back inside to the crowd. And it was done. He saw Dick's lifeless body attached to the hangman's noose.

Tap felt dizzy, like all the blood from his head suddenly drained to his feet. Maybe, he thought, grasping for some sort of reality check that really isn't Dick with that black hood and all. For a fleeting moment he was sure he was experiencing a bad nightmare in living color, and when he woke, he and Dick and their father would simply get in the wagon and head for home.

As they lowered Dick's body to the floor of the platform, Tap walked over to the Hangman. He had been invited to escort the body to the undertaker. Tap went along just to make sure that Dick was treated respectfully. It made Tap sick to think that Dick's body would be put on display in front of the courthouse for the rest of this day. But, as quickly as the sun rose tomorrow, Tap would put Dick to rest put to rest in his state issued pine box. Tap could take him home to San Saba.

Obviously, not everyone in here in Eagle Pass knew that he wasn't guilty of those murders and not only had the hanging been a major commerce draw but the viewing of Dick's body as he lay in the coffin outside the courthouse would make the locals feel that justice had been served.

As courthouse tower cast its shadow from the mid afternoon sun on Dick's now lifeless corpse it would symbolically say to the passer-by

"Pay attention you all, this is what the long arm of the law does to those who commit heinous crimes."

Dick had known well what the sentiments of the people in Eagle Pass were. He told the newspaper reporter that his dying wish was that he didn't want his name in the papers

"I have been more persecuted than prosecuted. My friends know me (and know that i am innocent) and no one else here will believe me. I have forgiven my enemies. I just want the matter to be forgotten out of regard for my relatives," he said.[32]

So putting his corpse on display for all these folks here in Eagle Pass who knew nothing more than the outcome of this mockery of justice, would have been as disgraceful to Dick as the accusations were. So for this and many other reasons, the Maverick County sheriff had required that Tap not wear his pistols in fact, they all had to leave their arms, weapons of any kind at home as a condition of being in town on Hanging Day.

---

[32] The Galveston Daily News (Galveston, Texas) September 19, 1891, Saturday, page 2.

Dick Duncan at the gallows.

Tap helped the doctor carry Dick's body to the wagon outside. Later he headed back to the House to meet his Father and his brother Bige. Martha, his mother was simply too distraught and angry to make the trip to Eagle Pass. She was so sure that Dick was innocent just like he said, that she spent considerable funds on a gravestone that stated that Dick had been murdered in Eagle Pass.[33]

His other brother Jim stayed behind in San Saba to look after their Ma and the ranch.

But for now Bige, Tap and their father, they would have to spend yet another night here in the boarding house in Eagle Pass. So far away from the soothing embrace of family. Tap needed that so much right now and so did his father.

When they had awakened this morning, before the hanging, his father told him that he just couldn't go to watch. So Tap had left him at the Boarding House. Bige stayed behind to look out for him.

---

[33] The Galveston Daily News (Galveston, Texas) September 19, 1891, Saturday, page 2

"Dick's always looked out for me Pa." Tap told his father that morning, "I gotta go to get his body."

When Tap arrived back at the House, he found his father just sitting in the street looking at the ground. It scared him to see how old and weathered his father looked. Tap reflected on how strong he had always thought his father was. How he loved the story his mother used to tell him about being the only man on her plantation in Georgia who could keep the slaves in line without the cruelty of a whip. He could coax work out of the boys almost like drawing bees to their honey she would say with a warm smile. Tap felt so proud especially when she later told him how he held her plantation together after her husband Mullins died of consumption. Shortly afterward she married that strong man.

As Tap reflected on this story he just couldn't see the man his father was, who was now sitting there in the dirt in the streets of Eagle Pass, even sitting on the back of a horse.

His brother Bige who had arrived late last night from Austin with the edict from the Governor, was on the boarding house porch just watching their old man. At sixty-three years Abijah wasn't all that old wasn't that old but somehow today, he just looked hollow.

Tap stepped inside to the bar and ordered himself a glass of whiskey. Mostly though he just fingered the rim of the glass. Since the beating that he had taken in a bar in New Mexico a few years ago, his drinking was much disciplined. He might have a drink to wet his dry throat or even calm his nerves but there was no way on God's green earth he would ever allow himself to drink and be off his guard the way he was in that bar in New Mexico after the trail drive. As his mind settled back on the events of this day, he stepped outside to sit with Bige on the porch.

Chapter 12: Life Ain't Fair

How things got to this deadly point he just couldn't figure. Tap knew for a fact that Dick was innocent of the crimes that he had been hanged for. He had been with him during the time the family was murdered[34]. The Republic had cried for a man to hang for those awful murders and it was too easy to pin it on Dick Duncan. Dick had in fact been tainted by the petty crimes and his associations with cousins Sam and Tom Ketchum but these brutal murders, they weren't his doing.

Tap couldn't sleep that night. Every time he closed his eyes. The scenes of the day mixed with the past few years kept playing over and over in his head. He had a special bond with all his brothers but especially Dick.

Dick had always been there for him. He thought back to the cattle drive when he was just 16.[35]

What a time to be alive! Times were tough in their part of Texas. Money was hard to come by. Tap and his brothers were ambitious and they were all excellent horsemen. They would catch wild horses, make trades for others and they could ride anything with four legs and hair. But now in this part of Texas, new homesteads were settled, it seemed every day. There wasn't much room for expansion and less for young men to do. So when a trail drive started up to take cattle to New Mexico, the Duncan brothers were among the first to sign up.

And in the mid-1880s, Trail driving was hot and dirty work. Water, some days, even a sip to drink was scarce. Other herds that had passed this way had grazed nearly all the grass.

After nearly three long, dusty weeks on the trail with not much more than mud holes to wash in, sleeping on the ground, ground that grew harder each night and eating food that camp cooky bragged would make you sick, they finally reached the trail's end. They had in fact earned every

---

[34] Texas Court of appeals, Austin term 1891 Dick Duncan vs the state No. 6694 testimony of Tap Duncan.

[35] Story written by Chet Brackett 1 and rewritten and published in Chet's Reflections by Chet Brackett ll. A collection of stories written by Chet bracket from actual accounts of the Duncan family life as told to him by his father Ira Brackett, Jim Duncan, Tap Duncan and other actual events.

cent that paymaster issued them. What an adventure this was for a boy thinking he was turning into a man. Tap was sure he had found his calling in life.

So, in high spirits, and with a pocket full of jingle, Tap's brothers took him to the saloon for his first real taste of whiskey, even before they found a bath, some clean clothes and a bed for the night.

His brothers, Dick, Jim and Bige taking him to the saloon for his first taste of whiskey should have been a simple rite of passage. But some ornery New Mexican raunchies took exception to the brothers and began making fun of them for dressing and smelling like Texans. One big bully in particular, who didn't smell so good himself took particular offense to them. Full of firewater and foiling for a fight this man singled young Tap out.

While Tap was good sized and thickly muscled, he was about four inches shorter and at least fifty pounds lighter than the bully. Tap had turned his back to him and tried to ignore his foolishness. But when he accusingly called Tap a "momma's boy",

"Why," Tap thought, "that was about the stupidest thing I've had ever heard!"

Being young, untempered and, full of the whiskey himself, he dared to say so …out loud. The bully saw that as the opening to start the fight he was already set for. His huge fist slammed hard to the side of his head, knocking Tap off of his barstool before he could've said he was sorry, even though he wasn't planning to.

Already light headed from his first few drinks of whiskey, Tap tried to scramble to his feet but stumbled badly in the attempt. As quickly as his brothers moved off their stools to help him, the drunk bully's friends drew their pistols warning them to stay back. The man who knocked Tap down kicked him first in the stomach with the sharp point of his boot. That stung like nothing Tap had ever felt before. Tap kept wondering why this was happening to him, he hadn't done anything to this man. The bully then kicked him in the nose then in the throat and chin. Tap's thoughts now were total panic. Blood was gushing everywhere and he just couldn't breathe. Next came a series of kicks to his chest and stomach.

The brothers now had seen enough. This bully would kill Tap if it went on any longer. Dick quickly grabbed the gunman closest to him by the arm and slammed his wrist hard on the bar, when the gun fell to the floor Dick quickly kicked it toward Jim. Bige took cue from Dick's movement and body slammed the other gunman to the floor. Even though he was thin and wiry, the unexpected force of Bige's body knocked him easily to the ground.

With the gun packing friends contained, Dick now turned to Tap's attacker. His red hot temper matched his fiery hair. He quickly grabbed the pistol from Jim. Then he shoved the bully hard forcing him to back away from Tap. Again and again he shoved. Until the Bully tripped over a chair. He hit the ground hard as he fell. As Dick stood above the man with his foot on his throat, time in that New Mexico saloon seemed to slow to a crawl, a killing it seemed hung thickly in the smoke filled air. Bige sensing the tension, loudly cleared his throat, walked over to Dick and put his hands on both sides of his brother's face and whispered to him.

"Dick whatever we do, to this pile of donkey dung, he has friends who will tell the story different than we do." He swallowed really hard.

"Dick … look at me. Look at me now." Bige pleaded yet half commanded in such a voice that only brothers can use with each other.

"We ain't' in Texas." Dick's gaze was still on the bully but Bige had pulled his face upward so that he did have to look him in the eye. He tousled Dick's reddish hair "its best ya leave it be Dick," he warned.

As Dick's stance on the man's throat loosened, Bige tried to take the gun but Dick, well, his grip was like steel, he wouldn't let go."

"Just give me a minute Bige." He choked the words out.

After what seemed like eternity, Dick finally took his stare off the bully lying under his boot. He was listening to his brother. He turned the gun in his hand, took a deep breath. In a sort of afterthought, he leaned over and struck the man in the face hard across the nose with the butt of that pistol. He seemed to be speaking to the downed man but the intent of his voice filled the room as if everyone in that room might feel he was speaking directly to them.

"My righteous brother here told me I caint kill ye now … He hit him a second time hard, with the metal butt of the colt pistol.

"butifinya ever, ever mess with me or mine again," Dick continued, "My righteous brother might not be here and I just might kill ya."

With that, the brother's kept those pistols, picked up Tap's badly beaten body and vacated that saloon.

Tap had become unconscious but later woke up in the street hurting like he had never hurt. His head was in Dick's lap. They were outside laying in the shade of the water trough. Dick was dipping his scarf in the cool water and wiping Tap's swollen and bloody face. Bige was standing nearby with his scatter gun threatening to shoot anyone who dared to come their way. Dick was talking to him in a soothing, quiet voice that reminded Tap when as a young boy his mom would talk to him and rock him to sleep when he had bad dreams.

Even as strong as he was, it took weeks for Tap to recover. Dick sat with him day after day. Encouraged him and changed his bandages, calming his hurt. He did have his rite of passage to manhood however on that trip. Before they left New Mexico, with some of the money he had earned on that cattle drive, Tap bought him a pistol that seldom, if ever wasn't carried at his side.

And now sleepless, in this boarding house in Eagle Pass, as he thought about how Dick had been there to nurse him back to the living he opened the window to the outside. The fresher air seemed to help him breathe better but he still felt as if he would leave the contents of his guts on the hard Texas ground.

Dick had saved his life. Tears stung his eyes.

Yes, Dick had saved his life … and yet today as that hangman led Dick to the noose and put that black hood on him, Tap was helpless to do anything. It was truly a good thing he had to turn his pistols in to the sheriff. He would have most likely used them today. Not so much on the hangman. He was only carrying out instructions. He surely would have used them to pull his brother out of this mob that was lynching him.

After all, Tap knew that Dick had left that family to camp outside of Eagle Pass when he had left for Mexico when he came to Bernt's ranch just out of Piedras Negras to help them move Osa after ben had died. They had been alive and well the last Dick had seen them as he headed for Mexico.

In the wee dark hours of the warm Texas night Tap's anger seemed to be growing out of control. He forced himself to breathe deeply and steadily. That seemed to calm him down. He couldn't let his father see his anger. It might only add to his grief.

When the first light of dawn began to announce the day, Tap realized that he hadn't slept a wink. He went to his father's room. Bige had already filled the water basin and got him a fresh cloth to wash with. They made sure their father ate a bit for breakfast, then they took the wagon to gather up Dick's body. The state had provided a pine box and Tap was surprised how relieved he was not to have to handle Dick's lifeless body any more.

It had ripped his heart out yesterday as they carried Dick's body like a bale of cotton. The box was opened long enough for Tap to acknowledge that Dick was in there. Then was loaded into the wagon. Tap thought back on what he thought was a dream yesterday. Yes, he and Dick and their father were in the wagon leaving Eagle Pass but it wasn't like Tap had hoped.

Even on this warm September morning, he saw his father shiver. Tap reached for the blanket that lay tucked behind the wagon seat and he pulled it over his father's thin and bent shoulders. As they drove by the livery stable on the edge of town, Tap spat his tobacco on the ground.

"I Will be back." he muttered under his breath.

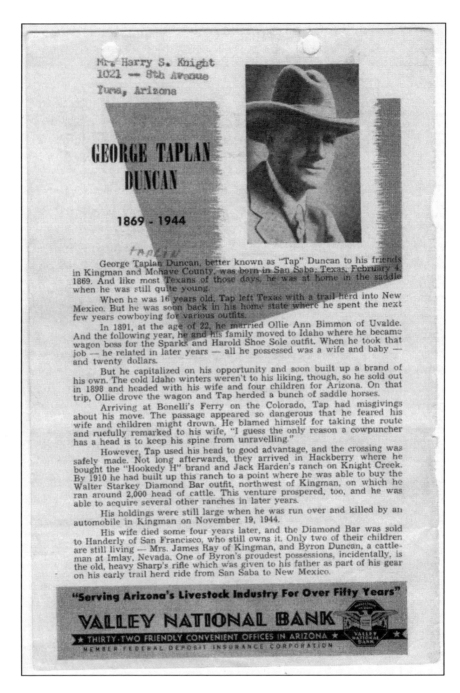

Mr. Harry S. Knight
1021 — 8th Avenue
Yuma, Arizona

GEORGE TAPLAN DUNCAN

1869 - 1944

taplin

George Taplan Duncan, better known as "Tap" Duncan to his friends in Kingman and Mohave County, was born in San Saba, Texas, February 4, 1869. And like most Texans of those days, he was at home in the saddle when he was still quite young.

When he was 16 years old, Tap left Texas with a trail herd into New Mexico. But he was soon back in his home state where he spent the next few years cowboying for various outfits.

In 1891, at the age of 22, he married Ollie Ann Bimmon of Uvalde. And the following year, he and his family moved to Idaho where he became wagon boss for the Sparks and Harold Shoe Sole outfit. When he took that job — he related in later years — all he possessed was a wife and baby — and twenty dollars.

But he capitalized on his opportunity and soon built up a brand of his own. The cold Idaho winters weren't to his liking, though, so he sold out in 1898 and headed with his wife and four children for Arizona. On that trip, Ollie drove the wagon and Tap herded a bunch of saddle horses.

Arriving at Bonelli's Ferry on the Colorado, Tap had misgivings about his move. The passage appeared so dangerous that he feared his wife and children might drown. He blamed himself for taking the route and ruefully remarked to his wife, "I guess the only reason a cowpuncher has a head is to keep his spine from unravelling."

However, Tap used his head to good advantage, and the crossing was safely made. Not long afterwards, they arrived in Hackberry where he bought the "Hookedy H" brand and Jack Harden's ranch on Knight Creek. By 1910 he had built up this ranch to a point where he was able to buy the Walter Starkey Diamond Bar outfit, northwest of Kingman, on which he ran around 2,000 head of cattle. This venture prospered, too, and he was able to acquire several other ranches in later years.

His holdings were still large when he was run over and killed by an automobile in Kingman on November 19, 1944.

His wife died some four years later, and the Diamond Bar was sold to Handerly of San Francisco, who still owns it. Only two of their children are still living — Mrs. James Ray of Kingman, and Byron Duncan, a cattleman at Imlay, Nevada. One of Byron's proudest possessions, incidentally, is the old, heavy Sharp's rifle which was given to his father as part of his gear on his early trail herd ride from San Saba to New Mexico.

Photo courtesy of the Myrtle Stowe Duncan estate.

It was interesting to learn from another source other than Uncle Chet's writings that the trail drive was an important moment in Tap's life.

Chapter 13: Jim and Tap Devise a Plan

Leaving Eagle Pass, Tap headed the wagon north to the Binnion Ranch outside of Uvalde. Tap was so relieved to see his wife Ollie[36]. Their baby son Charlie had been born last spring[37] and Ollie had come here to stay with her kin. Tap had been spending so much time in Eagle Pass and this way she was somewhat closer by.

All this time that Tap had been gone trying to help clear Dick's name he hadn't realized how much he had missed out on. He couldn't believe how his little Charlie had grown. Even though he had vowed not to, he nearly forgot how pretty his wife was. What a sight she was to his weary, weary eyes. All he wanted to do was hold her. He buried his face in her soft brown hair and as he breathed in her light flowery scent his head became light. Oh how he loved this strong woman. Tap packed up her belongings and made a nice seat for his father in the wagon bed. Bige saddled Ollie's horse and would ride it alongside the wagon as they journeyed to back to San Saba.

When Ollie set Charlie in the wagon near his grandfather, Abijah turned his back to him. As Tap thought about what having his own son meant he finally realized why his father was now so despondent. He gathered up Charlie and held him tight. Ollie, who could handle the wagon nearly as well as he could took the reins and let Tap get to know his boy.

Back in San Saba, Martha, their mother had gotten a tombstone made for Dick's grave. It said that Dick had been murdered at Eagle Pass on the 18th of September. A funeral was held and friends came to call. Tap began to feel a little better but he still couldn't sleep. He tried to get back to breaking horses and working whatever jobs he could find. But mostly he was making plans to start out new somewhere that life and people would treat him fair. Everyone was trying real hard to adjust.

Jim came to visit him a short time later. He said he had sold a couple of fancy colts to a ranch south in Brackettville and needed Tap to help

---

[36] Tap Duncan married beautiful Olga Ann Binnion. (Ollie) in 1890. Goldwaithe, Texas.

[37] Charles Duncan was born 21 February 1891 in San Saba Texas. Three other children would be born to this happy couple Byron Tellis, February 7, 1893, Tappie Lou, November 24, 1894 and Lora Clare June 26, 1896. All three of these children were born in Three Creeks, Idaho.

deliver them. Truth be told both men were ready to get away from San Saba. The once prosperous and happy Duncan Estate at Richland Springs was now a very sad place to be.

Traveling along the very road that held a lot of bad memories, Tap began to open up to Jim about all that had happened and his feelings about Dick's predicament. He said he couldn't remember the last time he had really slept.

"Yeah, I get a nap here and there but I can't ever really rest." He blinked hard and looked away quickly from Jim.

"Dick's last words keep haunting me, do you know what they were Jim?" Tap wrung his hands slow and hard almost as if he wished he could rub the skin off. Jim shook his head no. Tap looked squarely at his brother,

To his dying breathe he said "You're hanging an innocent man. Someday it will come to light who really did this." Those were his words.

"Every time I close my eyes Jim and try to relax … I see Dick looking thru that black hood for me. Like he knows for sure he can depend on me, like he knows that I am gonna help him."

"I see it every time." Tap choked back the heavy emotion that hung in his voice.

Tap held a clenched fist his to his face. "And I, I was helpless to do it Jim."

Finally Tap and Jim both swallowed hard. Tap straightened up his back cleared his throat and gigged his horse to move a little faster. Jim spurred his colt up to catch up.

"He helped me Jim, you know … in New Mexico when I was so close to dying I was wishing to. But every day Dick made me hang on he made me want to live." Jim was nodding and holding back his own tears.

Soon afterwards they arrived at the ranch where they delivered the colts. Money always burned a hole in Jim's pocket and he was itching to go to the nearest saloon for a drink. Tap decided that he too might enjoy a drink, but mostly thought he needed to unwind.

Inside the dimly lit saloon the brothers headed toward the bar. Tap began to share with Jim how he kept remembering that the Rangers had said there were two men in Eagle Pass. Those TWO said had they had seen Dick commit those murders. Tap wondered if they might have been the ones who killed that family and were happy enough to let Dick swing for them.

"I have some gut feelings but Jim I don't know for sure. I wish I could go there and just look around and listen."

He paused took a small draw from his whiskey glass, "But with spending the time at the trial and all ... It seems like I am recognized wherever I go."

Jim looked at his brother "Why, Tap maybe I should go. Let me do it. I ain't never been seen in Eagle, 'sides you got a woman and kin to attend to," he smiled and winked at Tap. He moved his chair in closer to Tap.

"So tell me some more of whatcher thinking," he said.

Photo of Tap Duncan from family photos however the original photo is in possession of Jerry Marshall and is a hand drawn piece of art.

Photo Ollie Binnion courtesy of Dennie Anderson and Carol Hardin.

A couple of run-away matches caused a little breeze Wednesday. Tap Duncan and Miss Ollie Binion and Frank Cromer, commonly known as Frank Parker, and Miss Fannie Duncan were the contracting parties. They stole away in the silent watches of the night and went to Goldthwaite where the ceremony was performed.

Clipped from the San Saba News and Star 23 May 1890

Amid the awful tragedy that was occurring in the lives of the Duncan family with Dick's trial life still went on. They lived life. Tap and his sister Fanny took their intended's and eloped.

Chapter 14: A Stranger in Eagle Pass, Winter-Spring of 1891-92

Two weeks later, a scruffy looking stranger drifted into Eagle Pass. He rode a broncee brown gelding. The handle on that horse was green at best, but he was stout and could carry his man across the desert and back. The stranger was dirty and his clothing was worn and torn. The only clean thing about him were his weapons, a repeating Winchester rifle tied down to his saddle, and the gun that hung on his left hip facing forward. Another pistol hung in a grungy holster under his left arm and a large bowie knife hung along his right hip. He walked with a limp, his left foot was pronounced at an awkward angle. Despite his deformity, he carried himself as a mysteriously, dangerous man.

Town people whispered among themselves wondering who he was. None among them could remember having seen him before, and no one seemed to have the courage to approach him to ask. He had money, gold coins in fact. The rumors began that he must have been involved in a payroll robbery to have that much money. He kept pretty much to himself riding out of town early each morning and returning late afternoon. He always took his supper in Eagle Pass settled in at a corner table in one of the bars, drank some whiskey and played some cards.

He would retire to his room at the boarding house at a respectable hour. Pretty soon he had settled into the saloon run by an ex-Texas ranger who seemed to be connected to the local smuggling organization.

Looking dangerous and like he was surely hiding from the law, one night the saloon keeper ask what his name was? Jim stammered and stuttered a bit and then mumbled: Alonzo[38]. The Saloon Keeper ask, "Alonzo who?" Jim shot a very serious look in his direction and said roughly, "just Alonzo, don't need any other name."

After that he was known as just Alonzo to anyone he met in Eagle Pass. Jim began to complain to the Saloon Keeper about the crookedness of the Texas rangers and how arrogant they all were.

---

[38] Alonzo was Jim's alias as he spent time in Eagle Pass according to writings of Chet Brackett 1.

"They want the law to apply to everone but theyselves." Alonzo hissed.

The Barkeep liked this mysterious stranger. He started giving him work. Hauling freight to different towns all over west Texas. The Barkeep had a warehouse where he stored incoming freight. Most of the freight was legal, goods that needed to be transported from the crossing. The legal freight gave a good cover for any questionable goods. The Saloon Keeper had a thriving business, it seemed.

Late one night a group of Mexicans from across the river came into the bar. They started out the evening friendly enough. They ordered lots of whiskey, played a few games of cards and even joked with some of the other drinkers.

But about five empty bottles of low grade, rotgut whiskey later, things started to get interesting. One of the fellows playing poker decided he had not understood the rules of the poker game that he was now losing.

He accused the Yankees of cheating him. "Yankees" as an expletive seemed to be the worst insult these Texans in 1891 could hear. The losing Mexican pulled out his pistol and said he was taking back his money the filthy Yankees were trying to steal from him. The rest of the Mexicans stepped back and pulled their pistols backing the angry card player.

"Teees is our loot, he waved his pistol around in a circular motion as if indicating the card table. It's ours and we're taking it."

The Mexicans scooped up the money from the table and started to leave. The Saloon Keeper pulled his shot gun from under the bar and told them to put the money back and get out of there. Another Mexican sitting quietly at the bar pulled out his pistol, holding it against the Saloon Keeper's head and told him to drop the gun.

As this scene unfolded Alonzo, stepped forward, he reached for the pistol that hung on his left hip with his right hand. He drew it quickly and shot the Mexican that held the pistol in the arm wounding him. That gave the Saloon Keeper just enough of an edge to grab the pistol from his hand.

As the wounded man was looking at his arm, the Saloon Keeper grabbed the shotgun that he had just surrendered. He ordered the wounded

Mexican to take the rest of the vermin he came in with and get outta his bar.

The Mexican's friends must have been surprised to have encountered these tough and armed Texans. They dropped their loot and held their hands up in the air in an effort to distance themselves from their drunk friend's offense. Mumbling in words that no one really understood, they helped their friend to his their feet and funneled toward the swinging doors.

Alonzo gave the last man a good shove with the end of his boot out on to the dusty street.

The Saloon keeper yelled, "Don't you ever come back here!" He shot the shotgun in the air for effect and then yelled,

"Or this one will be for you!"

Those boys headed off for the cover of the river glad to be alive.

"We work together almost as well as my pulling team!" The Saloon Keeper said looking at Alonzo.

After that night the Saloon Keeper considered Alonzo a friend. Late one night when the Saloon Keeper was drinking heavily Alonzo finally began to hear the very information that he had been waiting for. He began confiding in Alonzo how he used the bar as a front for his real money making business: Smuggling goods across the river and the border.

Mostly, he and his partner would fence those stolen goods but generally, they did whatever it took to make a dollar. They got a lot of stolen whiskey that they distributed to other establishments in these parts.

"People in this hot Texas desert are thirsty," he smiled.

"My men go all over west Texas with different stolen and smuggled goods as well as my legal freight all the way to Brackett and any other parts of West Texas. We distribute a wagon load of whiskey once every couple of weeks."

He was drawing big circles in the air as if to indicate the enormity of his business.

The Saloon Keeper said that he had been burned badly by trying to be a law abiding citizen. Said he had once been a Ranger and got drummed out because his captain said some accused him of stealing.

"Never could prove anything."

He smiled then slyly added, "I am just too smart for that!"

Even though he was no longer with the Rangers he had friends who still were.

"They keep me informed of what is happening," He took another deep draw from his whiskey bottle,

"And in exchange I do my civic duty," he chuckled at his own cleverness.

"I *inform* them about smugglers."

He smiled even bigger, "and other undercover actions that are happening in the neighborhood. I have even helped them solve some of their crimes." He was having a hard time containing his pride as he continued:

"Let me tell you Alonzo, if a Ranger comes here, I always have a meal and even cut rate drinks you know, just for my friends the Rangers."

His smile kept growing bigger with every sentence. He clearly was proud of what he considered his excellent cunningness.

"As they tell me where they are investigating crimes, I fill them in on what is happening, who did what and where to find different people they are looking for. Then, I make sure my illegal shipments are where those Rangers aren't."

He stopped in the middle of his story and looked Alonzo squarely in the eye.

"You know I could use another good partner. I ship my goods all over west Texas."

Leaning in closer to Alonzo he lowered his voice then added,

"My partner, he's sloppy, and what an idiot. Nearly got us all hung."

Even though this seemed to be the very conversation Alonzo had worked for nearly two months to hear, he showed no surprise. He arched his eyebrows in a look of curiosity, then he fingered the rim of his whiskey glass grunting affirmation as the conversation required.

"How's That?" Alonzo inquired coolly

"Psst." he scoffed. "Them Mexicans turn up dead in this grand river all the time. Never causes a ruffle with the locals let alone a Ranger. But cha get an Anglo floating in that river and well it will cause quite a stir."

He looked around as if to make sure no other ears were listening. Even though the saloon had been empty for hours.

His voice lowered to a whisper. "My partner, Jed, you know him, in his two bit thievery and desire to hump anything that'll stand still for him nearly got us hung."

Jim drank some whiskey in an effort to act like this conversation was just like any other he had shared with this man.

The Saloon keeper continued, "There was this white family camped outside of town a year or so back. Headed to Mexico. They had sold out up north and headed to Mexico for a fresh start. An old lady and her grown children. Her daughter was not only ugly but a bit touched in the head. They had a wagon full of all their earthly goods and a nice wad of cash. Jed convinced them to ditch the cowboy that was taking them across the border. Promised that he would take care of them and even hinted to that ugly girl that he'd like to take her hand in marriage." He paused as he looked up at the ceiling.

"Now Jed, while he is a little guy, he is good looker and actually quite the lady's man, He had that family eating outta his hand."

Alonzo was fighting hard to contain his astonishment. It was all just as Tap had claimed. Alonzo's mind was racing as the Saloon Keeper rattled on.

"Jed had convinced me that their money was like a ripe pecan just ready for the taking."

He sucked on his bottle of whiskey. Alonzo turned his head and let out a heavy breath.

Dick was innocent.

Now His heart was racing fast. He had to hear this story out though trying not to show a bit of emotion. He hoped another shot of whiskey would help him calm down. So he sucked on his bottle.

The Saloon Keeper put his own bottle down and smiled wryly.

"When that cowboy left them here, he took the wagon that hauled them down here … so Jed and I took a wagon over to their camp. After everything was loaded we drove them down by the river, we was taking them up to cross by the old mines you know, instead of paying for the ferry … we told them. He put his hand to his mouth as if he were whispering a secret to Alonzo.

When we got to the ford we told them we'd have to take our wagon and their stuff across first then we would swim them across on the horses. As they climbed out, we clubbed them one at a time. Not one of them knew what happened to the other. I had my horse tethered to the wagon. After we had got the money and what was any good for selling, and let me tell you there wasn't much ... I mounted up and headed back to Eagle Pass leaving Jed to get the wagon out of sight and bury those bodies before someone came along. He promised to bury those bodies so deep that not even God could find them.

He paused then said thoughtfully, "That was a nice wad of cash and we got them goods, what they had, distributed nicely." He smiled again.

"I was actually proud of my partner for the first time. But then a few days later, a washerwoman outside of town found a body, and it was a white body floating in the Rio Grande.

More investigation and more bodies were found. No one locally could identify them and the sheriff put them out on display there by the street, outside his office." He pointed as if he was indicating the direction of the sheriff's office.

"It was gruesome, and oh, that stench, it would bring you to your knees. Finally they wrote down descriptions of them and just buried em."[39]

"Women and kiddies avoided that part of town for weeks!" He shook his head as if trying to get rid of the imaginary smell he had conjured up.

"Well, when Jed got back from his whiskey deliveries up north, I nearly wrung his scrawny neck. He whined that the ground had been too hard for diggin' so he got himself a great idea. He had taken in some rope in trade in Brackett for some of the last shipment of whiskey. He got him some big rocks and used that rope to tie those rocks to those bodies."

'When I threw them in they sunk clean to the bottom." He told me.

Then added that he was plum glad to bid them goodbye.

Then the Saloon Keeper said "You know I heard tell that as them bodies decomposed the gasses they make, brought them up to the top of the water[40]. Now believe you me, Jed just ain't the smartest, but who would have thought of that?" Alonzo nodded in feigned a look of amazement.

Saloon keeper's voice drifted off in thought and it seemed as if he were about to fall asleep. Alonzo got worried because he really needed to hear the rest of this story. He slammed his glass on the table and said he needed more whiskey. Moving to get the bottle seemed to wake the man up.

He continued as his head hung low and he wobbled.

"You know if I hadn't remembered that the Rangers arrested that dumb cowboy with the red hair for carrying his guns and accusing him of smuggling, no telling what might have happened. Turns out, he was last person to see them alive.

The pause here was a long one. Alonzo cleared his throat and it seemed to help the man regain attention to this conversation.

---

[39] The hanging of Dick Duncan by John C Myers for the Maverick Co. Centennial Edition of the Eagle Pass News and Guide September 16, 1971
[40] Testimony of A.H Evans MD Texas court of appeals reports Austin term 1891

Saloon keeper let his hand fall heavily on the table as he tried to illustrate his point.

"Just a hint here, a rumor there, and soon my Ranger friends were looking for him. Turns out that a lot people knew he was gonna guide them; you know that family, to Mexico. And after all that Dick Duncan," the Saloon Keeper leaned nearer to Alonzo, then continued,

"I heerd say he had a real, well, reputation as a bad boy."

With those words, Alonzo felt the anger rising in his body. He so was glad for darkness in that saloon. Every fiber in his being wanted to grab his knife and cut that slimy man's throat right then and there. He coughed slightly in an attempt to hide the emotions rising in his throat

But that wasn't part of the plan. The Saloon Keeper continued. "Everyone wanted those murders solved and the killed consigned to the ground, and..." The Saloon keeper smiled.

"I found a way to steer them from us."

He paused and yawned heavily. Jim could tell this conversation was winding to a close.

"So I need me a new partner, Alonzo what would you say?" Alonzo stood up, he smirked as he held back the words he truly wished to say to this bucket of pig slop. He was ready to make his leave.

"Let's talk it over when we both have had a bit less whiskey to drink ok?"

Alonzo walked slowly to the door careful to remember to keep his foot sticking out to its deformity.

Back at his room, he kept thinking about going back to that saloon and shooting that man in the head right then and there. But he knew he would need to stick to Tap's plan. He wasn't sure what Tap's plan was exactly but he did know that he had to let Tap know what he had found out.

Two days later, on his next delivery out of town for the Saloon keeper he sent a telegraph to Bige in Knickerbocker, telling him to send him telegram in care of the saloon in Eagle Pass. He instructed Bige to relay a message to a man named Alonzo saying that his mother was dying and if he wanted to see her had to come home.

When the Saloon keeper gave Alonzo the telegram he asked what this would mean. Alonzo told his Saloon keeper that he needed to attend to some family affairs, but as soon as he could ... he would be back.

Alonzo looked the Saloon keeper squarely in the eye, "You have really helped me out my friend! This is a good deal." He said

The next morning he mounted his brocee brown gelding and rode out of town.

Chapter 15: The Duncan Boys Split Up

Jim was surprised how quickly that gelding covered the 250 miles to San Saba. He did stop one night but travelled the rest of the way with unrelenting focus. He could not wait to share this whole nasty tale with Tap. Jim stopped at Tap's place first. Bige had come from Knickerbocker to be filled in on Jim's findings.

Tap's wife, Ollie fixed dinner for them. They didn't leave the house to talk this over, Tap told both Jim and Bige that Ollie was certainly aware of all that Jim had been doing.

So Jim began to unfold the story. At first Tap felt heart sick then his anger began wash all other emotion out of his body.

"I knew it," he kept muttering over and over to himself.

Their brother had in fact been framed. Bige stood up so fast he knocked his chair to the floor. He grabbed the shotgun he had leaned against the wall by the door.

"Who are they Jim, I'm going to shoot those son of bitches right now." Tap stepped in front of his path as he headed toward the door. "Bige. Bige," he said gentling pushing him back towards his chair.

"Sit down please! We have got to think this through."

Jim was ready to go tell the sheriff right then.

Tap stopped Jim by grabbing his arm. He looked him squarely in the eye.

"You know we can't do that Jim," He said. "Think about it! They promised to hang pa and me if Dick didn't stay quiet about being innocent. You remember that?"

There was a long pause. Then Tap continued, and more than that, do ya think the Rangers would let it stand, an accusation from **us**, that they had been misled?"

"Even a hint that they'd hung an innocent man?"

"Dick was convicted in a court of law period. No matter how unjust and wrong it was and all most folks know is that the Rangers rode in and made their everyday lives safer. He nearly choked on his next words...

"And now Hogg that great prosecutor, is the great governor of this state he had a chance to give Dick a break but just couldn't do it[41] ... you think he's gonna eat crow in front of all this state?"

Jim looked puzzled at his brother. "So you saying I have wasted the past couple of months of my life for nothing, Tap?"

Tap ran his fingers through his hair scratching his head thoughtfully.

"Slow down Jim," he said. Tap was quiet for a few minutes as if he was trying to frame his thoughts into words. Then he said, "Imma, no we are fixing to leave Texas, he drew his finger around in a circle in the air as if to indicate Ollie and his son Charlie also, then he asked, "Jim, you wanna come with me?"

Jim gave him a funny look wondering why Tap would be changing the course of the conversation just when Jim had told him this disgusting news.

"Leave Texas? Where to Tap?" came a tired reply from Jim. Tap smiled a crooked smile.

"Remember that little horse wrangler from Cherry Creek, Ira Brackett? We met him when we got those horses from New Mexico and took them to Denver?"

Tap lifted his eyebrows at the cleverness of the way he framed this sentence. Jim smiled and nodded too. They had acquired some horses in New Mexico and some New Mexican loot sort of all by accident or guilt by association.

---

[41] Letter from Governor Hogg to Sheriff Cooke: "After careful investigation, I decline to commute Dick Duncan's sentence. Let the law take its course. Inform him of his fate so that he may prepare to make peace with God." James Stephen Hogg Gov. This telegram is still located in the archives of the District Court in Maverick Co. September 15, 1891.

"I got a letter from him a while back. He's made it there and Jim, it is all that we had heard and even more. Big sky and green grass and horses that run in great herds like the prairie buffalo.

"The picture that he now paints of the Idaho now that he is there is even better."

"Yes, it is where the grass is stirrup high on a horse and free for the taking but the biggest deal of all, why there ain't enough people to have folks messing in your business." Jim was smiling. This picture that Tap was painting was paradise.

Tap continued, "But first y'all we need to finish some business in Eagle Pass for Dick." Bige and Jim looked at Tap. Bige asked point blank "We aimin' to kill those guys? Tap just smiled.

"Let's saddle up and go for a ride."

He took them to the cemetery that evening to one more time see Dick's tombstone

Barnett- Davidson Cemetery

Dick Duncan, San Saba Co. badman.

His last words:
I know that God has forgiven me and feel that I have heard from Him.
Goodbye, I hope we will meet in Heaven. I feel that I am going right
there and feel that I will be pardoned of my sins and washed whiter
than snow

Dick Duncan's grave marker.

"Read it, boys[42]..." Tap said, "Read what Ma had inscribed on it." Tap Bige and Jim stood silent for a moment then, Jim let out a deep breath. "It's true, he muttered.

Dick had been murdered by the Republic's desire to distribute a façade of justice at whatever the cost even if the man they hanged for the crime didn't commit. Jim just stared at the headstone a long, long time. The brothers, both …right then and there, knew they were in fact, ready to leave this place, for practically anywhere.

The brothers visited some more. It was decided that while it was important that Bige knew the whereabouts and whyfores of his brothers but just couldn't be involved in this endeavor. He had a rather large and growing family in Knickerbocker that depended on him. Tap and Jim would go south and take care of business and Bige would go back to Knickerbocker. They would keep him informed as to where they were and what went on.

As we talk about the influences that shaped Tap's life one that we must introduce to the reader is Ira Brackett. In this chapter is the story of how Tap and his brother Jim while in the company of their cousins met Ira in Colorado. And why Tap leaving Texas decided to settle in The Idaho.

---

[42] Grave marker. Dick's mother Martha felt so strongly, and the family knew for a fact that Dick had not murdered that Williamson family that she had a gravestone made for his grave that said he was murdered in Eagle Pass.

Chapter 16: The Ketchum's and Duncan's Come to Colorado 1884

This story is a part of the book we put together called *Chet's Reflections* that was written in part from stories we found from our great Uncle Chet Brackett. He was the youngest son Of Ira Brackett. This tells of when Ira Brackett met Jim and Tap Duncan and their cousins Tom and Sam Ketchum from San Saba Texas.

A hot whizzing bullet cut through the leather of Tom Ketchum's coat. His shoulder burned.

Tom Ketchum gets shot.

"I'm shot, so do I die now?" He wondered. He was breathing hard and the tears he was fighting were stinging his eyes. "If I cry Sam will stick the point of his boot in my back end." He was trying really hard to hold back the tears. He was really scared.

He could see the others in a plume of dust ahead of him. He spurred his horse to keep up with the others. New Mexico, he decided isn't a very friendly place[43]. The men were moving fast, afraid for their lives that a posse might be catching up. Tom just didn't get why they were so mad over just a little bank robbery. Especially when all they stole was about $2000. In gold. That sure was not the big haul that he had heard of from that sort of acquisition.

Tom and Sam Ketchum and their new cousins, Jim and Tap Duncan (from the marriage of their sister Nancy Blake to Bige Duncan) had all come to New Mexico in search of work. They had heard there was plenty, but when they arrived, it seemed that the work was mostly just day to day jobs and it sure was hard. Even harder than when their brother Green Berry Ketchum expected them to work for him.

Since Tom's dad had died when he was just five and then his mother just a few years later, Green Berry had to step in and try to raise his siblings while building a life of his own. Tom and Sam it seemed had a hard time fitting into his perception of life.

So now they had drifted into Folsom, New Mexico, hot, tired, hungry and broke. Jim ran into an acquaintance he called Lazy? Or maybe it was Elzy? Tom couldn't rightly remember. That man was there checking out a bank. Tom's grasp of the details from there on out became a blur. Next thing he knew they were in the bank using their guns and asking for money. It didn't really hit Tom until later that they had just robbed a bank. He had no clue at this point what he was really doing but he did know now, that if he lost the riders ahead of him in that plume of dust he was in big trouble. He spurred the horse to go faster, more out of his own life's preservation than loyalty he followed. They had ridden for a couple of hours and their horses were fully lathered and completely exhausted.

---

[43] Tom (Black Jack) Ketchum and his brother Sam formed one of the Wests deadliest outlaw gangs. Sam was shot during one of their robberies and died in the penitentiary in Santa Fe New Mexico in 1899. Tom was injured in a solo train robbery later and eventually caught. His arm was amputated and he was later hanged in Clayton Co., New Mexico. April of 1901.

Tom wondered what was next. "Boy if we had a plan it would sure help, he muttered to himself. The group slowed their horses and let them catch their wind. Before long they rode up to a corral full of horses.

Fresh horses.

Elzy or Lazy and the Duncan's quickly pulled their saddles off their spent horses and pulled the log gate that served to keep the horses in. They quickly caught themselves a new mount. Sam saw Tom just sitting on his horse and told him to get down his backside down and catch a new ride. Tom didn't move. He looked like the scared little brother that Sam remembered after their mom died. Tom was young and Sam too but somehow helping Tom be brave made Sam feel braver too.

"I … I think I got shot Sam!" Tom blurted out. Then he added that he sure wished that he had one of Nancy Blake's cinnamon rolls. "They were the best I ever tasted." Tom was just about to cry. Sam was getting worried that Tom had really been hurt. Because he was the youngest of the family he had been doted on by his siblings especially his older sister. Eating her sweet bread and cakes made him happy. Sam quickly looked at Tom's shoulder. He saw that the bullet had only cut through his coat. Then he was drawn immediately back to the situation at hand.

"Tom," Sam said in a very stern voice, "You are ok. You get your ass in gear and catch you a horse."

"You **just robbed a bank**. You need to catch a horse and get outta here.

"NOW!" Sam kicked at the back of Tom's pants with his boot.

"These men, Tom," Sam said pointing to the corral, "will shoot you iff en you slow them up." Sam looked sternly at Tom. Leave ya for the coyotes or worse yet the posse!

"Do you know what they do to men who rob banks and steal horses?" Do ya Tom? Emphasizing his words with his hands as if they were a rope around his neck he continued,

"They dangle him by the neck at the end of a rope until he's dead." Tom grimaced a bit and rubbed his own neck.

"Get along and catch ya a horse. You can't just quit halfway through this mess and say you're sorry they'd just hang ya anyway!" In disgust, Sam grabbed his own rope and headed for the corral. Tom followed. Somehow Sam could always make Tom understand what he needed to do. His stern words gave Tom the courage to go on.

In the corral, Tap, Elzy, and Jim had already caught their new horses. Tom took a deep breath. A sleek black stud walked near him and he reached out his head and sniffed Tom's hand. Somewhat surprised, he said "I think he likes me Sam." Tom caught that black stud. Sam caught one for himself and both the Ketchum boys took their new mounts out and threw their saddles on them.

Elzy then announced that the group was slowing him down too much and he was heading east He was splitting the gold 60/40. That left $800.00 for Tom Sam, Tap and Jim to split. More money honestly than Tom had ever seen really seen. And other than the scare from the bullet, the nerve wracking run from the posse Tom decided this was not a bad way to get money. He sure liked it better than driving herd that was for sure.

The boys watched Elzy ride off. Jim muttered something like good riddance to ya under his breath. They finished tightening cinches on horses and stashed the money in the saddle bags. Sam opened the corral gates. They headed the all those horses north. The corrals held about 20 head of horses besides the mounts they rode.

The sun had begun to set low in the sky and Jim said they would ride until it was too dark to see. But much to the delight of the four travelers, a full Comanche moon began to rise in the quickly darkening nighttime sky. As they kept moving it was as bright as a reading light. Sam reached into his saddle pack and pulled out a chunk of beef jerky and handed it to Tom. These new horses were fresh and kept making good time until well after dark. But the riders did slow their pace to more carefully pick their trail.

Finally about four in the morning, sleepiness began to overtake them all. There was a small box type canyon up ahead where they could corral the horses and get just a wink of sleep. Even though it was chilly, they chose not to have a campfire just in case a posse might be following. They hadn't seen hide nor hair of the posse since the horse thief corrals where Elzy took his own trail. But just to be sure they stayed cautious.

They headed steadily north for the next couple of days. Early one morning they began following a creek down to a valley. Jim and Tap stayed behind near a grove of trees. Near the end of the meadow there were two substantial log houses and several barns and out buildings. Near what appeared to be the barn there was a large corral. In that corral they saw a man with a large cowboy hat working a rather wild horse. A couple of kids sat on the log fence. About the time that the riders reached the corrals, the man in the hat sent the smaller of the children to the house. He had tied the lariat attached to the wild steed to the snubbing post in one of the smaller pens. Then he walked over to the gate and nonchalantly strapped his gun and holster to his hips. The horsemen stepped off their horses and cautiously walked over to where the man in the cowboy hat stood.

Sam reached out his hand to shake, "Sam Ketchum's my name." He said. "My brother Tom." He added leaning his head in Tom's direction. Ira took off his big hat and wiped his forehead with his shirt sleeve. He sensed a friendliness from Sam.

"Ira's mine." He replied.

Sam explained to Ira that they had come up from the south looking to sell some horses at the railhead in Denver.

Ira kept eyeing that beautiful black horse that Tom sat on. Oh it reminded him so much of the gelding that Ozro had used to gather the maple back in Vermont. The same horse that had pulled the wagon that he and his brother Levi just six and eight years old at the time had driven from Wisconsin to settle in this the great American West.

Ira nearly teared up as he thought of that old horse. As he was growing up, next to his brother, Levi, that horse was his best friend. Sam and Tom both took notice of Ira's interest in the horse. When Ira's asked if he had a name Tom looked at the horse thoughtfully then replied, "Jack. Black Jack that is."

It now occurred to Sam that they could use this horse to cut a deal with this man. The Duncan's and the Ketchum's needed a place to stay and get the stolen horses ready for Denver stock sale and Ira, well, he really wanted Tom's horse. They chatted on a bit then Sam proposed an offer to Ira. For room and board in his barn for say the next few weeks…while they touched up their herd for Denver, the beautiful black stud would become Ira's horse.

Ira truly wanted that horse and he quickly agreed. The men shook hands on the deal and Tom and Sam went to the grove on the creek to fetch Tap and Jim and the rest of the horses. When they returned Ira invited the men to join him at the house for dinner, to which the men eagerly agreed. A good hot meal was something they had all missed for the last few months.

Ira took them to the smaller of the two log houses. He pointed to a water trough near the fenced yard where they could wash up.

"My wife's kinda big on having clean hands to eat with." He smiled and began washing his own hands.

He walked into the house and was warmly greeted by his lovely wife Sarah. Standing there in the late afternoon sun, holding their little Mary Inez, Ira couldn't have imagined a more beautiful sight. That black stud that Tom had ridden in on hit a real close second, but it was second. Seeing her smile so brightly holding that baby was a real boost to his heart, After their first born, Earl Clark died, it was a long time before her saw her really smile.

Ira told her that they would be having guests for supper that night and then he added with a more with a question than a statement, And for the next few weeks?

That wasn't a problem for her. Sarah never really knew how many mouths to feed there would be at her table for whatever meal so she fixed. So she always cooked plenty. Even though her mother in law Lucy did well by her children, with fourteen of them, time and plenty for a kid to eat was scarce at her house. So they often set their boots under her table.

After dinner, Ira and his guests visited well into the night. The Duncan's spoke of the tales they had heard of the Idaho territory from the Texas drovers who took herds up to that country. Con Shea had been the first to reach that country. He and his drovers had brought back tales of a land where the range was open and a cowboy could go for weeks seeing nothing but himself, his pony's ears, and whatever home they made of their cow camp.

Sure sounded great to these boys from Texas, ever since the Comanche had been reigned in fences started sprouting up like Texas bluebells, just everywhere. That was when the cattle drives north started up. Cattlemen had heard stories of lush grasslands. Tap and Jim thought they might sell their horses and head west. The word pictures they painted intrigued Ira.

At some point in the night they excused themselves and headed out to unsaddle horses and put their bedrolls in the barn. The rest of the horse herd, they had already put in the small pasture near the corrals. At the rising of the morning sun, Lucy's big cast iron bell began to toll. Breakfast would soon be served. The outlaw crew reluctantly rose with the bell toll.

True to the deal they had made earlier last evening, Tom led the black stud now called Black Jack, to the larger pasture that held the mares. The men stayed with Ira for nearly two weeks working their horses and getting them ready for sale in Denver. Along with working their horses they also helped with chores around the hay ranch.

Ira and Tap seemed to share the same love of horses and for the idea of the wild open spaces of the west. Ira carefully watched all the men's techniques with their horses as he tried to glean from them tips that he could use on his own horse workings. He especially liked matching his own skills with those of young Tap. Sharing their skills challenged them both. This friendship would prove to run deep.

When at last they decided that the horses were ready to for Denver, Ira was truly sad to see them go. He had so much enjoyed having other accomplished horsemen in his midst. And, it seemed that since they had arrived, every night he dreamed of the wide open spaces with less people, where cows grazed without boundaries. He liked his new friends and he liked the tales they told of the Idaho Territory.

Tap had immediately developed a deep friendship near to a kindred spirit with this little horse wrangler named Ira Brackett, even though he was several years older than Tap. They shared a love of wild horses and of taming them, a love of the Wild West and they both hoped someday to tame just a little piece of it for themselves.

As Tap reminded his brothers about Ira, he began: "I got a letter from him a while back. He's made it there and Jim, The Idaho, it is all that we had heard and even more. Big sky and green grass and horses that run in great herds like the prairie buffalo. And the biggest deal of all … ain't enough people to have folks messing in your business."

Jim was smiling. This picture that Tap was painting was paradise.

Tap continued, "But first Jim we need to finish some business in Eagle Pass for Dick."

Bige and Jim looked at Tap. Bige asked point blank "we aimin' to kill those guys? Tap just smiled.

"Let's saddle up for a ride." He took them to the cemetery that evening to one more time see Dick's tombstone[44]. 2

"Read it, boys." Tap said,

"Read what Ma had inscribed on it."

Tap Bige and Jim stood silent for a moment then, Jim let out a deep breath.

"It's true, he muttered.

Dick had been murdered by the Republic's desire to distribute a façade of justice at whatever the cost even if the man they hanged for the crime didn't commit. Jim stared at the headstone a long, long time. It was here, the brothers both … right then and there, decided they were in fact, ready to leave this place, for practically anywhere.

The brothers visited some more. It was decided that while it was important that Bige knew the whereabouts and whyfores of Tap and Jim he just couldn't be involved in this endeavor. He had a rather large family

---

[44] Grave marker. Martha felt so strongly and they knew for a fact that dick had not murdered that Williamson family that she had a gravestone made for his grave that said he was murdered in Eagle Pass. As we have gone through the stories that the Duncan's left us as family legends and reading carefully through the trial transcripts Dick Duncan was innocent. One especially poignant comparison being the difference in how he and one of his best friends Tom Ketchum approached their impending hangings. Dick sought to forgive and be forgiven and even to his last moments, proclaimed his innocence. On the other hand, Tom (Black Jack) Ketchum proclaimed his guilt and seemed to fully embrace it. Told the boys hanging him to hurry up so he could have breakfast in hell. These men were not only cousins but they were friends. They had grown up together and it is Author's theory that the hanging of Dick, in his innocence created, in part, the Ketchum gang's disregard for the laws of life and the land.

in Knickerbocker that depended on him. Tap and Jim would go south and take care of business and Bige would go back to Knickerbocker. They would keep him informed as to where they were and what went on.

Ketchum's Lineage

Green Berry Ketchum 1818-1868, married 27 January 1842 to Temperance Katherine Wydick 1820-1873

Their children:

- James Laurence 1843

- Joseph-1845

- Elizabeth 1848-1933

- Green Berry 1850-1914

- Samuel (Sam) 1854-1899 died in penitentiary in New Mexico

- Nancy Blake* 1860-1937 Married Abijah Elam Duncan Jr December 11, 1879

- Thomas Edward 1863-1901 Tom was hanged for robbing a train in Clayton Co. New Mexico in April 1901

* Nancy Blake is Great Grandmother of Author. And her husband Abijah Jr (Bige) is great grandfather.

The marriage of Nancy Blake and Bige Duncan was one of the unions intermingling Ketchum and Duncan Blood. For the purpose of this book this union is the focus. Also the information listed is to the best of our knowledge as of today. If the reader has other knowledge and would like to share we would love to hear it!

Tom and Sam Ketchum both became notorious outlaws after the hanging of their friend and cousin Dick Duncan. It is the theory of the author that a contributing factor to the total disregard for the law that these men held was due in a large measure to the injustice perpetrated on their innocent friend and Cousin Dick Duncan. During the latter part of the 1890s they made up on of the Deadliest outlaw gangs in the west.

Chapter 17: Return to Eagle Pass

The next morning Tap loaded Ollie and baby Charlie in the wagon with food and their most necessary possessions. Jim arrived a while later. A satchel carried all that was important to him. Otherwise it was mostly clothes. Money and food; his guns, he wore. His steer lap robe was already in the wagon.

Ollie had piled quilts up and made a soft bed in the box for Charlie. Tap and Jim would leave Ollie and Charlie in Uvalde for a few days while they headed south and finished Dick's business.

As their horses plodded toward Eagle Pass, Jim asked several times for Tap to tell him his plan. Finally Tap pulled up his horse.

"Jim it ain't real solid yet. I keep building it as I ride along. But... I promise you I will tell you when I settle on it ok?"

The wagon pulled up to stop at the Binnion ranch and Tap left the wagon for Ollie and Charlie as they visited her kin. Tap carried their things inside and Ollie followed him back to where his horse was tied. Ollie kissed Tap and whispered that she would be ready to leave as soon as he and Jim returned.

She squeezed his hand tightly,

"I Love you Tap! And I know that you have to do this!" She paused, her eyes sparkling with just a bit of a tear, "but, Charlie and I, we need you." She smiled so sweetly,

"So be careful."

She turned quickly away from him and he and Jim headed their horses south.

A short while later,they arrived at a grove of trees outside of Eagle Pass.

"Jim, let's camp here tonight." Tap said.

They unsaddled the horses and even cooked a small meal that Ollie had sent with them. Tap finally poured himself a cup of coffee and came over to sit nearby the fire.

"Ok Jim," he said, "Here's the plan." He cleared his throat then continued.

"Early in the morning before dawn, we will ride on in to Eagle Pass. The Saloon Keeper rooms above his bar right?"

"Yeah," Jim replied. "He is the only one up there."

"Good," Tap replied.

"Jim, you will stay in the alley out back with the horses. Keep them quiet and calm. I will climb up on the roof and get in his room by the window, when I return we will get outta town fast ok."

Then he added, swallowing hard,

"But Jim, if I don't come back you … you go get Ollie and Charlie and take them home you hear me?"

Jim had a puzzled look on his face but nodded in agreement.

Tap smiled. "Jim, you are my back up, really you always have been. So if for some reason I don't return it's up to you to care for my wife and my son."

Jim felt a twinge of panic at what Tap said. He had known this was a dangerous thing they we doing but it had never occurred to him that Tap might not return. But he could tell that his brother had thought this out very carefully, and he didn't know enough details of Tap's plan to argue.

"Ok. Tappie," he replied.

They sat for a long time and just stared at the glowing red embers of the dying fire. At some point Jim just drifted off to sleep but Tap's mind was busily going over and over in his mind plans for the early morning events. As the fire burned low, Tap just would gather more wood and keep it going.

There was a pleasant silence in Eagle Pass just before dawn. Especially this close to the river. Tap and Jim rode quietly down to the saloon. Leaving his horse with Jim in the alley, Tap climbed the pylons to the roof. He quickly crawled near the Saloon Keeper's bedroom window. Opening the window further and being as quiet as he could, he slipped into the dark room. The Saloon Keeper lay snoring loudly in his bed.

Tap began unfolding his plan;

Tap. Tap. Tap. As he stood behind the long drapery, he knocked on the window pane with a lone bullet in his hand.

"What is that sound?" the Saloon keeper, wondered.

He was still locked in his dream state but some irritating noise was loosening sleeps grip on him.

A powerful, recurring dream kept him captive: Things hadn't gone so well for him since he got kicked out of the Rangers. While he was with them he had pretty free rein. He did really, as he pleased. That badge had given him power and frankly he liked it. Investigate, cover up. It worked well for him especially where there were injustices he needed to "fix." Then along came those allegations that he himself might be corrupt. They hadn't been able to prove a thing. Still that Holier than Thou captain had kicked him out. He had half a mind to take care of that self-righteous bastard. Given half a chance he'd take him down a notch or two.

But that captain, he was a dangerous man not to be taken lightly.

Tap.Tap.Tap.

There was that damn sound again. Now he was beginning to wake more fully from that dream about the state of his life. His mind was still groggy from last night's inebriation. More often than not he really hated how he felt in the morning but how could one tend bar and not have a drink or two and more often than not, five or six.

Tap. Tap. Tap.

What was that irritating tapping noise? He was now fully awake headache and all. If he heard that tap on more time he thought his head might explode. As his mind got clearer he realized his window was fully open and a cool early spring breeze off the Grande was blowing in. He shivered.

"When did I open that?" He shivered again.

He tried to think back on last night's events.

As he sat up in bed feeling like he really needed to find his chamber pot to answer morning nature's call, there came a cold voice … no a bone chilling voice from the shadows.

"Rise and Shine!" The voice said then added, "There is so much to be done today."

Now the Saloon Keeper was fully awake. Somehow he felt he had heard that voice before. He grabbed for the pistol that hung at his bedstead. He pointed his gun in the direction of the voice. In the faint light of the early, early dawn he could make out slightly, the figure of the man the voice belonged to. With his gun pointed in that direction, the stranger kept talking,

"Saloon Keep you have a lot to account for."

The Saloon Keeper cocked his pistol and warned the stranger,

"You stand still or I will shoot you."

Tap smiled and continued: He tossed the bullet he was using to make the tapping noise on to floor by the bed.

"I know the world seems a bit unfair at times but my friend," he continued, "I am here to fix some of that.

"Hearing the "friend" part and still thinking of the dream he had just had, the Saloon Keeper thought somehow the stranger was there to help him. Tap walked closer to the man. He picked up the kerosene lamp by the bed, struck a match and lit the lamp. He wanted the Saloon Keeper to be totally and completely aware who he was talking to. As the Saloon Keeper recognized Tap his grip tightened on his gun.

"Don't you come any closer!" he warned.

Tap smiled and drew near the bed. The man frantically pulled the trigger on his pistol.

Misfire. He pulled again,

Misfire again.

Tap smiled as he reached in his own pocket and showed him the bullets he had taken from that man's pistol just minutes before as he lay sleeping.

"You do know me don't you?" Tap asked.

Nodding the Saloon Keeper said, "You are that kid from San Saba, you're … your brother hung here last fall."

Tap wasn't sure if that was a question or if the inflection in his voice was from fear or just from an urgent need to answer nature's call. Tap smiled. He was starting to enjoy this just a bit too much. Then he realized he might be spending too much time here. He sat down matter of factly next to the man on the bed.

Tap looked the man squarely in the eye.

"all ya all," Tap emphasized this part knowing this man hadn't worked alone on the murders,

"You all framed my brother Dick, for those awful murders that you committed;" he paused, looking the Saloon keeper squarely in the eye.

"Didn't you?"

The man slightly nodded his head. Tap stood up and turned his back as if he was starting to leave. But he paused slowly turned back to the man squirming in his bed.

"My brother told everyone that he was innocent", he peered curtly at the man,

"And you knew it first hand, didn't you."

The Saloon Keeper smiled slightly.

"Yeah," Tap said out loud to himself.

"But ya' all framed him anyway."

Tap whirled the barrel of his own gun, emphasizing his emotion, and then he pointed his pistol toward the man's head.

"BUT you framed him. Anyway."

Tap was surprised. Instead of cowering or indicating any type of repentance the man on the bed just got arrogant.

"The case is closed and your brother is hung." The Saloon Keeper sneered. Tap swallowed hard and thanked that man under his breath for saying that. "You just made my job easier." Tap said out loud.

He thoughtfully spat his tobacco on the floor. He realized the dawn was quickly coming and decided he needed to hurry and finish this business.

But he allowed himself for just a brief moment to picture in his mind Dick with that black hood standing near the hangman's noose. To Tap's surprise, this time, he didn't feel the urge to throw up time just as he had before every other time he thought on his brother's hanging.

"Well, maybe that's a good sign," he muttered to himself.

Tap stood up like he was getting ready to leave, but turning back toward the bed the pointed the pistol to the man's head.

"I need to know where you partner is." Tap said. The Saloon Keeper seemed to think this was a ray of hope for his own life and he began to spill all he knew.

"He took some whiskey up to Brackett two days ago. He is due home today." "I can hook ye up to him. Gladly." he added.

What a slime this guy is Tap thought. Tap walked near the bed stead and pulled the pillow from behind the man.

"Thank you for your help. I got what I came for."

Relief washed vividly over the man's face. He was somehow thinking that Tap would now just leave.

Tap really was new at this sort of thing and sort of making it up as he went. He truly wasn't quite sure what to do, but somehow that vision of Dick standing there in the black hood flashed into his mind again. Smiling resolutely to himself and straightening his back to his full height, he wrapped the pillow around the pistol in his hand held it to the man's forehead. His gun spit muffled fire and thunder. When Tap felt the man's body go limp, he placed the pillow back on the bed. As Tap looked more closely at the man, he saw that a third eye had appeared in his forehead.

"There you go Dick. I love ya!" Tap whispered as tears filled his eyes.

Tap straightened his again, took a deep breath and slipped quietly through the open window. He slid off the roof and mounted his horse that Jim was holding for him in the alley. He could always rely on his brothers to have his back. Duncan blood runs deep.

Against the ever so slight pink sky of the morning sky, they rode quietly but quickly out of town. Jim kept alongside him as they headed off North West toward Brackettville. Although he was very curious about what had gone on upstairs from that saloon Jim knew better than to ask point blank. He decided just to ride, confident that Tap would share in his own time.

They rode quickly for about five miles. Their powerful colts were starting to lather and they slowed them so as to let them catch their wind. Jim wanted to be sure he understood the next part of Tap's plan. So he finally asked what they would do now. Tap kept his horse walking at a steady gait he began to share his plan with Jim.

"That Saloon Keeper said that his partner was due home today from a whiskey delivery to Brackettville. I am hoping we will meet him on this very road sometime later this morning." Tap smiled.

The brothers rode steadily but not fast enough to tire their young horses. They were both on colts that had the heart to go all day. The rest they took as they slowed to a walk after the five mile trot out of Eagle Pass only served to bring out their running edge. As the brothers walked along the road to Brackettville, the colts under them were firing up and building for energy for another run.

About midmorning a horse and rider appeared a ways off on the horizon. The brothers thought perhaps they would be looking for a man driving a wagon but Jim had learned that sometimes the smugglers would take a stolen wagon to deliver their goods and they would sell the wagon as well just to get it out of the territory. As the rider drew nearer, Jim in fact began to recognize him.

The rider was plodding along barely staying in the saddle. Last night's drunken party left him with a pounding headache. Barely aware of Tap and Jim, he pulled over and started to ride on past. As he drew even with him, Jim rode closer and reached over and grabbed the horse's bridle and drew him up to a halt. As he was focused on Jim Tap reached over and un-holstered the man's 45.

Tap looked the man squarely in the eye.

"You remember me?" Tap asked the man.

The man barely nodded and pulled his hat down more securely on his head.

"You remember a little lady, name of Levonia Williamson, Jed?"

"You got some answering to do for her, but mostly," Tap had grabbed the man's rope and untied it from his saddle, "for my brother."

"No, I don't. And she weren't no lady," Jed sneered.

"That trials all done, justice has been served."

He gigged his horse and attempted to get away from the brothers.

"Let him go Jim," Tap said. A huge smile grew on his face.

"You remember how we run horses Jim." A grin grew instantly on Jim's face.

"Well, I'll take the first go Tappie."

Jim's colt was young and the walking pace they had set for the last bit had given him rest enough to gain his second wind. Jed was riding an older gelding and had travelled the bigger portion of the miles from Brackettville to Eagle Pass. Jim turned loose of the reins of Jed's horse.

Tap slapped the horse on the rear spooking him. He jumped and nearly threw Jed off before he broke into a frightened run.

Jim headed them in circles for a while. Jed's older horse just didn't like the way the Jims colt kept pushing him in. He pinned his ears back and tried to bite a chunk out of Jim's colt's neck. Tap kept a short distance off in case Jed would break of in a run, he would haze him back. When Jim finally decided the fun was up and headed them towards a high plateau that towered over the old dry river bed.

Tap had meandered his colt across the dry bed and began picking his way up the southern edge of it. Jim kept edging the rider and his horse toward Tap and the hill. Finally in the mid-morning heat Jim delivered a much lathered horse and a rather angry rider to Tap when they reached the top of the plateau.

Tap was fingering his roping and began building his loop. By now both man and horse were completely exhausted and Tap knew it was time to end it. "Get on one side of him Jim and I will take the other. Send him down the hill."

Tap looked at Jed. "This game we are playing here Jed… Well, ya see, it's for my brother Dick."

This time Jim whipped the lathered horse on the back end with his loop. The little horse squealed and bolted down the hill. Tap quickly swung his rope and threw it, with the exactness that comes from only from hours and hours in the saddle.

The loop landed on the ground just in front of the horse's next front foot step. At the instant that both front feet hovered just at the opening of the lasso and Tap quickly pulled up and jerked his rope tight. He dallied hard and fast to his saddle horn. Tap sat back hard on his colt as the rope pulled tight but still the weight of the thousand pound horse dallied to his saddle pulled him forward as it stumbled.

As Jed's horse tumbled, and quick as lightening, Tap loosed his dally and let his rope follow the wreck. It was a tumble, heels over head again and again down that old river bank. Jed flipped with the saddle for the first two tumbles but then was thrown loose as the horse finished its last rolls.

Jim rode quickly over to Jed's limp body. He pulled out his pistol ready to finish the job. Tap held his hand up as he rode over. With one look at Jed, Tap knew that the job was already done.

"Holster your pistol, Jim." Tap dismounted his colt. He shook Jed's body with his foot.

"I'm sure his neck is broke."

"This way no one will ever know other than his horse stumbled with him, Jim. Let's leave 'er that way."

Jim agreed, Tap always made so much sense.

Tap smiled a wry sort of smile, "Ain't it ironic that he met death at the end of a rope, Jim…. just like Dick did."

Tap gathered his rope, got on his horse and the brothers headed at a fast clip toward Uvalde. "Let's just skip Brackettville Tap." Jim winked and Tap agreed.

They kept those little colts moving at a fast clip the rest of the day. They arrived at the Binnion ranch the next morning. When they rode up to the ranch. Ollie was outside hanging laundry on the line. She smiled at Tap.

Oh, that smile just melted his heart.

As he rode near her. "Darlin'," Tap called out, "You hear that?"

Ollie smiled, "Hear what?" she called out curiously.

"The Idaho," he said, "it's calling your name!"

Tap stepped off his horse as she neared him. He gathered her up in his arms as tenderly as a rich man touches his gold.

"Ollie," he whispered in her ear, "it's time for us to go."

She knew how hard this whole ordeal with Dick had been on him and the whole family. The great Duncan clan had just fallen apart.

Tap's pa just wasn't the same. He just stared into the sky.

Tap's ma was stricken in her grief. Last she had seen of Jim he had quit shaving and bathing and had become a grungy mess.

Nannie's husband, a Methodist minister was threatening to leave her because her brother was a hung as a murderer,

And the house on Richland Creek, the beautiful house that had once been full of laughter and Dick's music, had been reduced to ashes. No one was sure if unfriendly folks who thought Dick had really murdered the Williamsons did it or it was just an accident. None the less their lives resembled those ashes.

They had believed in the justice of the Republic. They knew for a fact that Dick didn't murder the Williamsons family, Tap had been with him. The deputy even believed that Dick was innocent. He told Dick's mother that the jail door would be left open and Dick could run. When she told him what the jailer said though, Dick told his mother that he did not do this and if he ran now he would be running for the rest of his life.

How funny it seemed, that now, it would be Tap doing the running.

But, Ollie thought, as she straightened her slender and tall frame, a new and grand adventure lay before them in a new place called the Idaho. She really was however, quite glad that her kin had gone into town. If they packed quickly she would be gone long before they returned. She would simply write a note telling them she had gone back to San Saba for a family emergency and would write soon. Tap tethered his saddle horse to the wagon already packed with clothes and food, hopefully enough to reach that place where was grass stirrup high to a horse and … for now a good hiding place … in Idaho.

Author's note Intro Ira Authors note here we change course so we can introduce to the reader one more of the more significant relationships in Tap Duncan's life, Ira Brackett. This story was a part of a hand written stories that we found in the attic of the house where my great uncle Chet lived. He was the son of Ira Brackett. We introduced Ira briefly in a previous chapter but now we would like to tell you the story of Ira and of his because Ira and Tap were drawn together not only by their love of horses a desire to conquer the west but also that they both had a brother that was murdered. Which is a major component of the whole of the story.

So we will begin the story of the Bracketts: as Ira's father leaves Wisconsin with his family in a covered wagon, to conquer his piece of the Great American West.

Brackett Lineage

Ozro Brackett 1813-1889, married 20 May 1849 to Harriett Blackstone 1828-1853

Their children:

- Levi: December 28, 1850- 8 October 1888 killed in Arvada a suburb of Denver Colorado.

- **Ira:** February 26, 1852- 28 march 1920 died of tick fever.

Harriet passed away and Ira remarried to Lucy Philena Stone.

Their Children:

- Alonzo Haines, 1856

- Ellen May, 1857 captured by Indians never seen again

- Samuel, 1859-1966

- Anson, 1861-1947

- Addie, 1863

- Edmond Hilton, 1866

- Charles, 1867

- Minnie Etta, 1868

- Alice P., 1870

- Luther, 1873

- Ozro Jr., 1874-1877

- Amos, 1876

- Effie Amy, 1878

- Dora Belle, 1880

Ira Brackett: born February 26, 1852 and died March 28, 1920 of Tick fever. Buried in Twin Falls, Idaho. Ira married February 1, 1880 to Sarah Elizabeth Mauldin: January 10, 1862 and died 1934, is buried in Twin Falls, Idaho.

Their children:

- Earl Clark Brackett: 21 may 1881 died 15 February 1882, buried in Franktown, Colorado.

- Mary Inez: January 9, 1884 died in 1963. Buried in Twin Falls, Idaho.

- Noy Elbert l: August 19, 1886. He was born shortly after the family settled in Three Creeks, Idaho. He is buried in Twin Falls, Idaho.

- Chester Earl I: October 10, 1888 -1972. Buried in Twin Falls, Idaho. The author of this book is named after him. He wrote many of the stories that we put together for this book and the Chet's Reflections Book.

Ira is author's great grandfather, his son Noy Elbert I is author's grandfather.

While Tap Duncan and Ira Brackett were not related by blood, their friendship extended into the next generation. Tap's niece and Ira's son were introduced because of their deep friendship.

Noy Elbert (Bert) Brackett: August 19, 1886 - October 18, 1934, married February 3, 1912, to Ora Lee Duncan: March 1, 1891 - 11 October 1966. Ora Lee was the daughter of Bige Duncan and Nancy Blake Ketchum, grandmother of author.

Their children:

- Noy Elbert Brackett ll: September 11, 1913 - August 27, 2002

- Mildred Elizabeth: September 30, 1915 - 30 June 2000

Chapter 18: Bracketts to Colorado about 1860

The creaking old wagon came to a halt. Ozro pulled his team of horses up so that he could stop to read the rough map that he had carried with him since he left Wisconsin. This looked like good land he thought. There weren't as many trees but here, you could see the sky, lots of sky.

The wagon train the Bracketts had joined on this journey west had dwindled down to just a few. Most of the travelers had left the train farther north, closer to the actual town site of Denver. But with its nearly 100,000 new residents, it was just too crowded for Ozro's comfort so they just kept rolling on. They had traveled now two days south and found some land that looked to be excellent farm ground.

Ozro asked his father to come look at the land with him. Samuel, who was now 68, climbed out of his wagon and joined his son. Here lay the promise, the makings of their good new life. Trees were plentiful to the west and the foothills looked to have promising quarry loads. Father and son looked at each other and smiled in agreement. Here will be our new life, our new home.

Life in Wisconsin had been good. The Portland Quarry that they had owned was a flourishing business and the land they had invested in at Sugar Island had trees that yielded lots of maple syrup. But since Ozro's wife Harriette had died, he just didn't seem to have the passion to keep it all going. The winters were cold and seemed so lonely without her.

For the past few years, mostly to fight off his loneliness, he had taken his sons, even as young as they were, with him to gather the trees on Sugar Island. One fall and winter when Levi was four and Ira was yet two, he taught the boys to sit on the big black gelding that he used to travel between the maples to gather the syrup. Little Ira would sit, it seemed, so tall on that horse and move in rhythm with each step as the giant horse plodded along, tree to tree.

Levi and Ira ride the big black gelding.

It made Ozro feel whole to see his son smile. All that fall he let the boys accompany him on the syrup trips. It even seemed as if little Ira would guide that horse with his tiny legs as they went along. Levi enjoyed the rides too, but didn't seem to relish them as much as his younger brother.

Shortly after that in the spring of 1855, Ozro met and married a beautiful young woman, Lucy Stone. She would make a good mother for the boys and a great companion for him. Ozro now had found a new lease on life and was busy managing the quarry and the trees.

On a supply trip to Waterford, Wisconsin however, they found some news that would change the course of the Brackett lives once again. While he was waiting for his supply order to be filled at the general store, Ozro's father Samuel picked up the local newspaper. It was late summer of 1858. The headlines read:

Gold Discovered!!

Gold Fever to stone masons and builders meant something different than it might mean to a wildcat miner looking for a lucky strike. The Denver area of the Kansas Territory was full of gold.

For the entire ride home after getting the supplies, Ozro and Samuel spoke of what discovering gold would mean:

The influx of people,

The growth of the cities,

The need for builders to build the buildings.

Their skills, they decided, could prove to be of great value.

So their families spent the winter preparing to leave. The quarry sold quickly and the land and maple trees at Sugar Island brought a handsome sum.

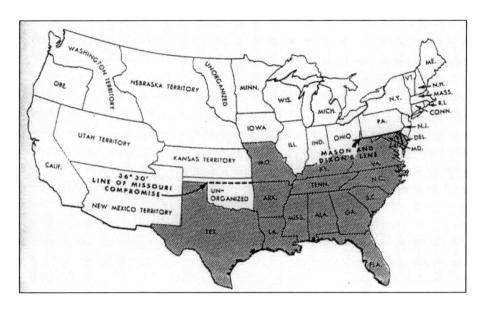

The United States in 1860.[45]

With Levi and Ira, now six and eight, Ozro bought an additional wagon to travel west. In this wagon would travel his masonry tools, extra food and a few of the household treasures that Lucy couldn't bear to leave behind.

Harnessed to this wagon was the black gelding that had carried Ira on the maple runs. Confident that the boys could manage this wagon, he loaded in his own, his pregnant wife Lucy and placed three year old Alonzo Haines and two year old Ellen May in a fortress of bedding and quilts behind the wagon box. Ozro's parents, Samuel and Amy in the third wagon were already loaded. Their own journey here to settle in Wisconsin from Vermont years earlier classified them already as trail hardy pioneers. Lucy's family came from Sauk County to bid them a tearful farewell.

When they began planning this new conquest, they had been heading west to what was known as the Kansas Territory. But with the gold rush and the influx of settlers it had now become the Colorado Territory. The land looked productive and Ozro was thrilled about the new life they were beginning.

---

[45] http://columbinegenealogy.com/records/civil-war/history/

Everyone needed to pitch in to make this Colorado grassland a home. Logs were cut from nearby timbers and corrals were built for the horses and cattle that they kept.

Ira's gentle and commanding way with horses gave Ozro an idea for buying horses and taking them to sell them at the various liveries around and eventually lead them to a very lucrative opportunity: that of selling horses at the Denver stockyards. His son, it seemed, possessed a natural ability to put a handle on any horse and simply convince him to do what he wanted. Maybe it was from his bonding with the black gelding at such an early age.

So as the family was busy building the barns and houses to live in, Ira was given the charge of the stock ... the horses especially. He still had to help with the everyday chores, but the breaking of the colts fell to him. As well as the taming of the wild ones.

The ranch that the Bracketts were building on Cherry Creek, (which would soon become known as Franktown), was on a major route south from Denver. Many travelers discovered after two days journey, that they had a horse not quite fit to the trail. Travelers' often stopped to trade a rather rank horse for one that Ira had gentled. That meant there was always some nasty bronc that needed some schooling.

A while later, after they had gotten established, Ozro took the boys on a trip to Denver to sell a horse that Ira had broke to ride. As it came his turn to show his horse in the ring, the horse bucked and then he bucked some more. He made a circle twice and didn't slow a lick. Eventually Ira gathered him up and got a hold of his head. He kindly but firmly convinced him that trying to lose his rider just wasn't worth it. Ira held his own, but it ended in a bust. No one wanted to buy that rotten piece of hide. That horse didn't bring a single bid. However, there was something else really interesting to come out of this attempt at a horse trade.

A man who had been in the audience of buyers walked over and introduced himself to Ozro and young Ira. He was as a representative of the newly founded U.S. Mail delivery system called the Pony Express. He was looking for small, skinny boys under the age of 18, he said who could set a horse and ride him fast. He added that most generally they were looking for orphans but it wasn't a requirement. They would be interested in visiting with Ira further.

Ira's route would be about 75 miles and he would receive $25.00 per week for his pay. Ozro couldn't believe his ears. Twenty-five dollars, why that was lots of money even for grown men in these parts. Many a man could work hard all day and make only about $2.00 a day.

Ira taught his horses to do tricks that most ordinary men couldn't. One day on his mail route when he was in a stretch of known Kiowa country, he had an eerie feeling that he was being followed. Looking behind him without slowing his gait, sure enough he spotted a small band of Indians trailing him.

Just up ahead of him lay a few rolling hills and a grove of trees. He angled his path to reach those trees about the time the band caught up to him. He ducked into the forested area. When he was in far enough to feel sure they couldn't see him, he headed his horse back to the south. Here, in a grassy gully he gently asked his horse to lay down.

He reached up and covered the horse's eye in an effort to keep him calm as he lay quietly in the tall grass. He spoke to the beast in a soothing tone assuring him that he was alright. He could hear the Indians jabbering and yelling as they seemed to be looking for him. Finally after what seemed to be a whole day, the voices were gone. When he felt sure that he could get up and on his way he gigged his pony up and they resumed their route.

The Pony Express job only lasted a few months as the mail system adapted to new travel. However, the money that Ira earned helped to get the ranch in Colorado up and going. Ozro and Samuel with the help of the boys were building a ranch, making a water system and helping to establish Franktown.

Chapter 19: Ira – Master Horse Trainer

As Ira grew, he developed an even greater talent with horses. He and his father both recognized the potential that lay ahead of him in the horse trade.

At Cherry Creek they had a small band of broodmares and a very fine stud. As the colts were born in the spring of the year, Ira would be there with them. He would play with them practically from the second that they were born. He would hold their heads in his hands and look them in the eye as if he were communicating with them telepathically. They bonded with him. But the colts weren't his only strength.

Travelers trading horses at Franktown had slowed, so Ozro would often take the boys , now men, to Denver with him and at times they would stop at the stockyards where the horse trade was being conducted.

They would wait through the entire auction until the especially broncy horses were left. Ozro with Ira's advice would buy a couple of them, at a substantially reduced price. After all no man had successfully shown them or ridden them that day. Then they would head their acquisitions back to the ranch.

Ira would spend most of his days working with these purchased horses and by the time the next auction came along he would have a fine mount to show in the arena. It made him smile to know that he could work so well with the animal. It made him smile even more when an ornery piece of horsehide that he had purchased or $20.00 sold as a well-trained and mannered pleasure horse for about $65.00. They had been trading horses for several years and he won more often than busted.

One of these horse trading trips in particular would shape Ira's future in a remarkable way. Ira had bought a horse with an especially hot disposition. He worked many hours trying to calm him. On this particular morning, Ira was having a devil of a time trying to keep him traveling in the direction of Denver. Usually that 25-mile trip to the stockyards would cool most horses' blood, but not this roan that he was riding today.

Truthfully, Ira was glad when they arrived and he could get off that bad cayuse. He would never let on to anyone, especially not to his father, but he was a just a little afraid of that horse. Somehow he felt that his ability to handle a horse was tied to his father's pride in him. As Ozro got the horses consigned it seemed that there was a lot of confusion coming from the gate near the street. A big husky man was bragging about his superior race horse and that no horse west of the Mississippi could beat him. He was even going as far as betting the flesh. The winner he said would take all. Money bet, horses ran and of course the fame.

As Ira looked longingly at the man's beautiful Tennessee sorrel stud, he thought back to the little Roan mare that he had ridden in from Franktown. Even after 20 miles his heart was still burning, blood pumping, he wanted to go. The sorrel certainly looked built to be fast. But through his chest he was thicker and his muscles seemed looser than the Roan he had just ridden in on.

Ira listened to the big man squawk awhile then he suddenly blurted out, "Why I could go to these corrals out here and get that nag of a roan in rode in here on and I could beat you!"

Ira was almost as shocked as Ozro at the challenge that had come out of his mouth. The man strutted over to Ira and looked down at him. Then he spit his tobacco, the wind caught it and blew it in Ira's face. That act in itself washed from Ozro any feeling that perhaps his son should apologize. This big man was obviously a bully and Ira had called him out. Ira however was grown now and old enough to make his own choices.

"You are on Sonny!!" The man half screamed, half laughed. "I'm gonna take that horse of yours," he growled at Ira. Looking at the crowd he had gathered he declared, "Today at the strike of two, we race our horses."

The crowd began to buzz. The news of a horse race seemed to attract people like flies. This rough Denver crowd loved a chance to gamble.

Ira was now really on edge. He was glad the race was later in the day so his Roan would have time to catch her wind. He was damn sure she could run fast but wasn't entirely sure about keeping himself in the middle of her. And all this time, out in the yards, money was being wagered. The horse betting was on.

Close to the hour of two, Ozro nodded to Ira. He made his way back to the stock pens and it seemed that all eyes were on him. Levi came to help him get his little Roan out of the corral. Ira knew that the horse would be fairly simple to catch but wanted to make a bit of a show out of it. Horse-trading depends a lot on the show, his father had told him years ago and he had adopted that as a motto for himself. He let his Roan pass by twice. The horse racing gambler started to chuckle.

"This might be even easier than I had previously thought," he remarked.

Ira grinned to himself. He now felt that he had made his statement. So, at the next circle the horses made he announced that he would choose the Roan. Ira fingered his lariat and started building his loop. As the rope nestled snug on the horse's neck, the Roan reared up. Holding the rope firmly and pulling the animal gently towards him, Ira talked soothingly to the horse.

Finally somewhat in show but somewhat actually struggling, he saddled that horse and led her down the alley and out into the street.

Maybe it was Ira's imagination but this crowd seemed to be on fire. The excitement seemed to make the Roan harder for Ira to keep still. Levi came over and told him that the odds were now 100 to 1.

"You can do this right?" he asked his brother with a grin on his face. Then he added, "That seems like one mean s.o.b. to me. After you beat him we better get out of town."

Ira nervously smiled. "Hold this little sweetheart while I get on, ok. I think we may have just found her niche."

Then he added, "Levi, give her an extra little tug on the back cinch as I pass through the gate, it'll make for a great show."

He winked at his brother.

Ira swung his left leg up to the stirrup and the other over the horse in liquid motion. Then he centered his backside ever so lightly in the saddle. It seemed as if the horse didn't even know her rider had gotten on.

The gambler's horse had a gangly youth on his back that looked to be a much younger than Ira, old age always will outwit youth every time, he had heard his father say. The horses lined up at the starting line.

The starter said, "On the count of three."

"One."

At the count of "Two" Ira's horse whirled and ducked his head.

Ira starts the race.

The starter smiled and not waiting for Ira to get his horse squared, he quickly yelled, "Three!"

He fired the gun into the air and started the race. The Roan bolted out in a huge hop and bucked about three times as Ira spurred and firmly coaxed her head in the direction they needed to go. As the horse saw an open direction and got Ira's cue which way to head she opened up the burner.

The gambler's horse however had taken full advantage of Ira's near spill and now had a significant lead. Ira again raked the steel of his spurs to the Roan's sides. That was like pouring fuel on the fire. Roanie jolted forward and Ira could feel the blood boiling in the veins of the horse beneath him. He knew his only job now was to cue this little race machine in the right direction.

Now Ira loosened his already soft touch on the horse's reins. He gave her full head and just let her run. He patted the side of her neck as she deepened each stride. He was rewarding her for her efforts and she knew it. He was delighted to see how the Roan was gaining.

By the time the horses reached the station where they would turn around and head back the roan was stretching her neck and sucking air even faster. Ira now was confident in how this horse would handle. He was only two lengths behind the Tennessee stud at the turn.

However as they came out of the turn the Roan swapped ends much faster than her opponent. By the time the horses were halfway to the finish line the Roan was pulling even.

At this point Ira leaned forward on his colt's neck and began encouraging her, "Come on Roanie, you can do this, come on!"

With that, Ira, one last time, raked his spurs to the Roan's sides. The Roan jumped forward and now was a half-length ahead as they crossed the finish line.

Ira smiled to himself as he thought that might have been an exciting race to watch. Trying to catch his breath he didn't really even hear the cheers and even louder moans of the crowd. Ira was feeling so happy inside. This was a rush he had never felt before.

"Roanie, now instead of making horseflesh cash, you'll be the star of this day's auction." He exclaimed.

Not even thinking about the race winnings, Ira was instead dreaming about what this little gold mine he was now riding was worth.

Levi was waiting for him and he grabbed the Roan's reins and pulled his brother down off the winner. He was dancing around and screaming, "We won! We Won!"

In the middle of one of his jumps of expression, he landed hard on the foot of the already humiliated and angry gambler who had come up behind them to speak to Ira. It was obvious that he didn't take kindly to losing.

The gambler's words were stern and in fact more of a warning than congratulations. Even though they were seemingly disguised as such. The message was delivered ..."you had better watch your backs, the both of you."

A chill ran down Ira's back. "That is one mean son of a ****," he whispered.

Levi protective as always of his younger brother shrugged it off.

"Leave this go." He said.

He grabbed Ira around the neck said, "Let's go see what we won."

Ozro was already with the man who had been the purse keeper for the crowd. He looked at Ira with a huge grin on his face. "$300 son ... THREE HUNDRED DOLLARS." He shook his head in disbelief. "I wasn't sure you were gonna make it here on that hide, let alone make a dime on her."

He held the money out toward Ira with a look of amazement on his face. He put his hand on Ira's shoulder, "Guess providence is smiling greatly on us today." He looked up toward heaven and Ira thought he heard him whisper a "Thank You."

Looking back at his boys he then added, "It just keeps getting better, let's go get your new horse, son!"

Ira saw his father do sort of a jig expressing pure excitement. He smiled himself thinking about his father's excitement and just the goodness of this day.

The auction got underway and the horse-trading kicked into high gear. The Roan brought $125. In the flush of money, they had forgotten the harsh and chilling words of the gambler. But when the beautiful stud horse that Ira had won came into the ring, the boys were reminded that the gambler felt that he had been skinned badly.

As he pranced majestically in front of the prospective buyers there was an audible gasp of awe from the crowd. Who would have ever thought that such a grand beast would be available at a common stock sale?

The man calling for the bids stopped and discussed the fineness of this horse and why he was here. Then he asked for $1000.00. Ira's jaw nearly dropped to the floor. Would they really get that kind of money for that horse? The bid caller did have to back down on his price but when he got to $800 the bids started flying. That fancy stud that Ira won did in fact bring the $1000.

He looked at his brother Levi "You know that horse brought nearly twice for we got for building the jail at Franktown ... and it was sure a lot less work!"

That gambler and a few of his pack dog friends were standing on the other side of the auction ring. His closely set eyes seemed darker than Ira had remembered. They seemed to pierce him to the core with a look of pure hate.

Ira shivered. "If that guy had a gun he'd shoot us," Ira whispered to Levi.

Ozro decided that for this night, instead of rolling their bed rolls out in the livery barn the boys would be treated to a night at the Broadwell house. After all, Ira had certainly earned it. The young men had never seen such luxury. They even purchased a hot bath and a shave. Then slept on sheets that smelled of summer sunshine. The next day they purchased supplies for the ranch and then headed the wagon and the new horses they had bought south to their hay ranch on Cherry Creek.

Chapter 20: Courting Miss Sarah

News spread fast in the now bustling town. Franktown's own Ira Brackett was a horse race master. The story was told over and over by everyone. He was fast becoming the town's newest celebrity. When he rode in to Franktown to deliver a horse to the livery he was surprised by the greetings that he received from all he met. He was really liking this attention, but especially so when as he was leaving the livery he came face to face with the beautiful young Sarah Mauldin.

Sarah's father Miles owned a ranch not too far from their own on Cherry Creek. Ozro and Miles had been friends for several years. They had even served together in the Third Colorado Cavalry[46].

Back in 1864 there had been some Indian raids, even in their own Franktown by the Arapaho and Cheyenne Indians. The government had retained a large company of black servicemen from the Civil War and stationed them all around Denver. The outer towns however were left to look out for themselves.

Ozro's own family had been the victim of one such raid. Lucy and a few of the children were traveling to Elizabeth Town one day to help a friend who was about to deliver a child. Ozro had sent Ira and Levi to ride along beside the wagon. Knowing that this trip was only a short distance the boys took to amusing themselves along the trail.

They headed their horses after a rabbit that had hopped across the wagon's trail. With both of them chasing, the rabbit ran off farther than it might have otherwise. As he circled and darted the boys soon found themselves headed in the opposite direction of Elizabeth, and out of sight of Lucy, the kids and the wagon.

They were just headed back in the direction of the wagon when they heard some blood curdling screams. They spurred their mounts. Up ahead, near a thicket of trees, a band of Indians had ambushed the wagon.

Providently, as the boys rode up, it spooked the attackers. Frightened as if they thought the cavalry was coming, the Indians left at a high rate of speed. But, as time would soon tell, not without having exacted their toll

---

[46] www.kclonewolf.com/History/SandCreek/sc-documents/ sc-colorado-third-regiment.html

from the travelers. Lucy began to gather the kids and count heads and panic struck. Where was little Ellie? In the confusion some of the kids had bailed out of the wagon and run to the trees for protection.

They searched under the wagon in the trees and in the draw. They hadn't heard her scream. The Indians must have had her mouth covered as they rode away. By the time they had searched for the missing girl and realized that she had been kidnapped, there was no sight of the band and no one really knew which way they had gone. Levi and Ira felt so bad. Lucy did realize however, that the boys riding up as they did probably saved all of their lives.

Heartbroken as she was to lose her little girl it was not Levi or Ira's fault. Finally, a few years later, she actually gave up and decided she would never see her little girl again in this life anyway.

So when the state of Colorado called for volunteers to serve in the cavalry to control the Indian raids on the settlers, Ozro didn't think twice about signing up. He hoped that somehow he might find his little girl among those Indians[47].

Their regiment was only together for a short time and they did get a bad name when their colonel led them to southeastern Colorado. There they engaged in a bloody slaughter of a large band of Cheyenne and Arapahoe prisoners camped under the protection of the 1st cavalry soldiers. As their regiment came upon the Indians camp and began to attack, it became clear that these were not the warriors that they believed they had come to fight. It was a camp of mostly women and children.

Ozro's heart raced. Hoping to find his daughter, he ran through the camp yelling at the soldiers to stop. His voice however was not heard and the slaughter continued. Ozro was sickened by the carnage. He went through the camp searching among the living and the dead for his precious little girl.

Ozro's anger at the Indians, who had caused so much sorrow in his community and more personally in his own home, disappeared as he saw the inhuman treatment of the captives by his fellow soldiers.

---

[47] http://www.historynet.com/sand-creek-massacre

Even after serving in the Cavalry, Ozro and Miles Mauldin remained friends. Later when Miles had lost his wife, his kids would sometimes come to stay with Lucy. Among them was a thin gangly girl by the name of Sarah who used to come out to the corrals and watch Ira as he worked the horses. She would offer to hold the reins or just to pet them. He usually told her to get lost. As Sarah grew, Miles was shot*[48] and later died. Ira began to treat her with a little more tolerance. Her uncle was now raising her and the rest of the family.

Even though Ira was little when his mother died, he still felt like a hole was ripped in his heart where her memory was. Sometimes Levi would tell him of a very sketchy memory he had of their mother. Ira sort of knew the pain of losing your mom but how much worse would it be to lose your father also, he thought. So he tried to be even kinder to her.

Time had gone on and the Mauldin children had pretty much quit coming to the Brackett ranch. Now as a full grown woman, that Sarah…why … she was beautiful. There were more than a few times that Ira regretted telling her to get lost. And now, she hardly even looked his way. She had all the attention of the young men in the area. At twenty-seven years, and ten years her elder, she probably thought of him more like an uncle than as a beau.

But now here they were, face to face, outside the livery stable and to his disbelief, she was smiling … Smiling at him. His heart thumped in his chest, He fumbled to take his hat from his head. Holding it to his chest he slightly bowed.

"Morning to ya, Miss Sarah," he said.

She looked him up and down. She said she had been in Denver and seen his horse race show. Then she added thoughtfully,

"I'm glad you beat that ole gambler."

---

[48] New York Times publication July 25, 1871 Attempt of a Woman to Shoot Neighbor: Tells the story of Miles Mauldin, Sarah's father, being shot by his sister in law in July of 1871. He was seriously wounded but didn't pass away until several months later, in December of 1871. So Sarah, at the age of nine years became mother to her siblings. An Uncle took them in but it was not the best of family situations.

She smiled sweetly and continued on her way. Ira stood as if frozen as she walked by. He could smell the sweetest scent of lavender and rose. Oh, she smelled pretty.

A couple of years ago his brother Levi had married the beautiful and sophisticated Clara Crowfoot. Since that time Ira had taken to thinking more and more about taking a wife of his own. As he thought about the obvious prospects with whom he was acquainted in the area, it was Sarah who seemed to occupy his mind the most.

Ira now found himself riding his colts more often in the direction of the Mauldin's ranch. Some unseen force just seemed to pull him in that direction.

One particularly chilly fall day as he was out riding, Sarah was out hanging laundry on the clothesline. When he saw her he tried to turn the colt quickly enough so that she wouldn't think he was coming by to see her. He turned but couldn't keep his eyes off of her long and curly hair.

He certainly wasn't focused on the young colt beneath him. Sensing a loosening of Ira's grip on his reins, the horse began to crow hop at first, then full out buck. Ira was grabbing leather and trying to steady his center, but it was too late. One more thrust and the colt had won. Ira landed hard on his backside on the cold, hard ground. What a fine mess this is, he thought. I haven't been thrown in years and now it has happened right here in front of Sarah. His pride was wounded certainly.

Ira gets bucked.

But the events of the next few moments seemed to unfold in Ira's favor. Sarah, hearing the commotion looked over her shoulder from her laundry just in time to see the colt's spectacular dance. When she saw Ira hit the ground she ran over to see if he was all right. He had wanted to jump up and act as if the whole embarrassing incident had not happened. Yet, as she knelt close to him, Ira decided he might like to sit there just a little bit longer. He did allow her to help him up and he leaned on her as he hobbled over to catch the colt that sullenly stood nearby.

Sarah invited him to the house. She poured him a cup of coffee.

"Never thought I'd see a horse get the better of you Ira Brackett." She smiled.

That day began a courtship that lasted through the winter and in February they were married. Ira took on more than just a wife though, when he took Miss Sarah's hand. She had become mother to her siblings after both of her parents had died. Ira knew that he had taken on a family[49].

---

[49] When Sarah and Ira married, several of her siblings came to live with them. Sarah's mother had passed away and her father had been shot shortly before the marriage by his sister in law Mrs. Gibson. Siblings Joel, Mary and William lived with Ira and Sarah (Lizzie) according to the 1880 Colorado census. All three of those siblings accompanied them to Idaho. When Ira married Sarah it was with the understanding that he was taking on her siblings as family. Later, when Ira's brother Levi was murdered in Colorado son Edward and daughter Cora Inez came to live with the Brackett's. There may have been others but we are certain of those two. Several documents that we have found, including inscription on the gravestone of Sarah Elizabeth Mauldin, include (Lizzie) in parenthesis. The stories that we put together from the writings of Uncle Chet had Ira calling his wife Sarah and consequently Chet called her Sarah when he referred to her that very well may have been Ira's special name for his wife.

Chapter 21: We Need to Get Out of Town 1886

Ira hadn't been to Denver to buy or trade horses in several years. In fact, the last time he came up here was when the Roan had run the now famous race. Ira smiled at the thought. But for today, had eight fine geldings for sale and they were ready to go. On this trip he brought with him his brothers Levi and Alonzo. He would need their help in showing the horses.

It was nearly evening by the time they got the horses consigned and fed for the night. The horse trading would start early the next morning.

As they drove the wagon to the livery to park it for the night, Levi looked skeptically at his bedroll. The spring weather was chilly and he commented that sleeping in his wife's warm, soft bed had made him into softer man.

"Boys," he smiled, "I am headed to the Broadwell House for dinner and a room."

Alonzo eagerly joined with him. He had only been to Denver on rare occasions. As the oldest of Lucy and Ozro's children, a lot of the responsibility of the hay ranch fell to him. So a night out on Denver's boardwalk he said, would suit him just fine. Ira, feigning reluctance, did in fact follow his brothers. But in all truthfulness, he too, liked a soft bed to sleep in.

They checked into their rooms and Alonzo insisted that he needed a bath. After all he didn't have a wife yet to make him clean up as much as the other two. He even had a shave.

As they wandered downstairs to eat dinner, they could hear a tinny piano playing one of their favorite songs. The music just seemed to call their names. So they skipped the dinner table and wandered out on the boardwalk. Alonzo found the swinging doors of a saloon and before Ira could object, they had walked into the hall where the piano played.

As they stood just inside the bar, Ira's blood ran chill. There at the poker table, staring at him was the gambler...the one who the Roan had beaten in the horse race. They hadn't exactly parted with words of friendship the last time that Ira saw him. Ira tried not to look at him and was silently praying that maybe, just maybe, he would not remember him.

The brothers walked to the bar and ordered a bottle of whiskey. Each poured himself a glass and stared at the mirrored wall that made the backdrop behind the bar. The gambler cleared his throat and folded his hand.

"Weren't good cards anyways." He muttered.

"Barkeep!" He growled.

"What do you mean serving such a little feller, why he gotta still be a boy as short as he is."

A few people in the saloon laughed. But some scurried for the door knowing that a brawl was brewing. Ira started to turn and look at the gambler but Levi grabbed the back of his neck hard and whispered sternly.

"Keep your eyes up here," he nodded toward the mirror.as the gambler walked over and stood close behind Ira.

"Didn't ya hear me Shorty?" he asked.

At this point Levi slid off his stool and stood between Ira's back and the big man. Levi saw in his eyes the same look of hate he had seen at the horse sale a few years ago.

"Why don't you just go back to your business, mister and we'll just mind ours," Levi suggested, trying to sound mean.

Even though Levi was taller than Ira, he was somewhat thin and only about half the width of the gambler. The Gambler looked at Levi and smiled. Then spat his tobacco on Levi's boot. Those were the nicest pair of boots Levi had ever owned and he was really proud of them.

"We had better get outta here." Ira whispered to Alonzo who was seated next to him at the bar.

As Alonzo shifted on his stool and the gambler must have thought he was making his move. A heavy left fist from that big man sent Levi scrambling to the floor. Now with Levi out of the way he grabbed Ira from behind. As he pulled Ira backwards, Ira grabbed at the half full whiskey bottle, he gripped it and slammed it hard to the gambler's head. As the gambler fell to his knees several more men joined in the fight. The blood and the brew began to flow. Ira heard the gambler cussing:

"You filthy Bracketts, stay outta my territory!'"' he yelled.

He was struggling to get up and began detailing all the things he was gonna do to them and their families if he ever caught them in his territory again. And even though Alonzo got a few good licks in he took more than his share. The saloon keeper, finally fed up with this behavior, pulled out his buck shot gun and fired it twice into the smoky air.

"The sheriff's on his way," he yelled in a very commanding voice, "and I suggest you all should be too!" He lowered the gun and aimed it toward the fighting crowd just for emphasis.

The brothers were, escorted out of the saloon. They felt a bit uneasy as they passed the dark alleyways on the way back to the boarding house. They weren't sure where the gambler and his compadres were. And they were relieved when they arrived safely back at the big house.

No one however slept well that night. Ira thought maybe he had a broken rib and both of Alonzo's eyes would probably be swollen shut.

"Would anyone buy a horse ridden by a man who obviously was beaten up in a barroom brawl?" Ira muttered to himself.

At the crack of dawn, Ira went out to the livery to get extra halters for the horses in the yards from the wagon.

Opening the livery doors, he was both stunned and sickened by what he saw. His sorrel gelding that he had used to pull his light wagon here to Denver, lay on the floor in a pool of blood. Somewhere in the night, someone had shot him and then slit his throat.

As Ira knelt down on the ground by this.one of his favorite ponies, he remembered the things that the gambler had said he would do to him, to his wife, to his family, if he ever caught him in "his territory" again. Ira was now sure they weren't idle threats. That gambler knew Sarah. He was friends with her uncle. He was always trying to hit on Sarah. One time when they were here in Denver a street dance was going on. That man asked her to dance. Because she was young and because she wanted to dance she said yes. He tried to kiss her and Sarah slapped him hard. Then her uncle beat her for that.

"That gambler helps put food on our table," He said. "I promised him he could have you."

So not only had Ira wounded this man's pride at the horse race, won his fancy horse, engaged in a nasty bar fight, but Ira's wife had turned him down too. Nearly comical Ira thought, but then as he stood sat pulling at the mane of his dead horse, lying there in that pool of blood...it didn't seem funny at all.

Ira pulled his hat off and rubbed his head as if to force some thoughts straight into his brain. He wondered if they should even stay long enough to finish their horse business. Leaving the halters he went back to find his brothers. He was getting more apprehensive as time wore on. Visiting with Levi and Alonzo, they decided to stay until they sold the horses and then hightail it out of town. They had to keep back one of the geldings to pull the wagon home.

On the way home Ira began to visit with Levi about the Idaho Territory. He told him of all the tales the Ketchum's and Duncan's had told about the Texas drovers and their herding stock to the Bruneau[50]. They had told of the open sky and endless fields where the grass grew stirrup high to a horse, and it was free for the taking.

Levi wasn't couldn't share Ira's desire for the beauty of it all.

"What could be more beautiful than my Clara and the ranch my father-in-law needs me to help him run?" He looked at Ira and said, "We are just beginning to grow a family and prosper."

As for Alonzo, well he was busy trying to keep his swollen eyes shut and his head from hurting. So Ira quit trying to recruit Levi. He could clearly see how good Levi felt his life here was. Truthfully, it was with Ira that the gambler had a problem. Even though Levi had been with him nearly every time they had problems with that man but if it wasn't for Ira's

---

[50] We have an additional story from the writings of uncle Chet that Ira may have purchased train tickets to another destination so that anyone looking for them would have a harder time tracing their whereabouts.

horse trading bringing them to Denver maybe the rest of them could stay out of that gamblers way.

Ira began to quietly add up in his mind what money he had and what he and what he and Sarah had to sell. He felt surer with each clop of the horses hooves that he needed to get out of town, and fast. He started to share the profit he made on the geldings with Levi when they stopped to drop him off at the Crowfoot ranch. Levi looked at the dollars that Ira had placed in his hand. He handed them back to his brother.

"I can tell that you've got it determined in your mind to leave for the Idaho, Ira.I wish you'd change your mind," He paused. "But if you are leaving you are surely gonna need this and some more."

He paused again, "If I can help you Ira, let me know."

Alonzo was worried about what he would face when he returned home. Ira told him that he would help explain it to their father. When Ira finally pulled the wagon to a halt by the barn, in his mind, he had already sold all of their liquid assets, booked a train west and started a new life.

Sarah came to the barn as he was unhitching the horse. She was such a soothing sight to Ira's heavy heart. He pulled her close. They walked hand in hand to the house. Ira sat her down on the porch.

"We have a lot to talk about," he said.

Sarah swallowed hard not sure what he was going to tell her. She listened intently. Her blood too, ran chill when he talked about the gambler. Even more so when he talked about the sorrel gelding. Sarah knew first-hand what a wretch that gambler was. She was so glad when she and her siblings were not at her uncle's any longer. But he knew where she was.

Then at the end of the conversation, Ira with tears in his eyes added, "and I didn't get you that blue dress at the dry goods store. I sure wanted to," he said.

Sarah's heart melted. Oh how she loved this gentle, kind hearted man. She straightened her tiny frame and put a smile on her face.

"Okay" she said. "We will start preparing to leave tomorrow."

Ira sold his house to Alonzo for a small sum and Ozro gave him some cash for his part of the ranch. It wasn't a lot but what they gave him would get them west and give them a new start. Ira also had the money from the seven geldings that he sold when this whole "leaving town incident" started. They said tear filled goodbyes to a beloved family.

They arrived in Denver with the light wagon, the stud that Tom Ketchum had traded to him, which he now called Black Jack, and ten darling mares. Ira left Sarah and the kids in the wagon and he went to check the horses onto a cattle car and booked their passage to Rattlesnake Junction, which had recently changed to Mountain Home, Idaho Territory.

Sarah's siblings bailed out of the wagon and headed up the boardwalk to see the sights of this big city. She treated the kids to an ice cream at the parlor. Her brother was caring for little Inez. Just around the corner was that dry goods store and that blue dress that Ira kept talking about. She wanted to go sneak a peek.

When she got to the store window she could see it. Ira was right it was beautiful. It was a color like a robin's egg only darker. She began to imagine how she might look in it and she could faintly see her reflection in the big window. She began primping and holding her hair up and imagining herself in the dress. She didn't see that drunk man staggering down the street. He stopped to watch Sarah.

"How ironic does my life get," he laughed to himself. He walked up behind Sarah and forced her body hard against the store window.

"You remember me honey?" he smothered her with his hot, putrid smelling breath.

It was her uncle's friend, the gambler who Ira's horse had beaten. She tried to turn her face to look at him and tried to struggle from his arms. She wouldn't scream.

She was glad the kids were in the ice cream parlor. The last thing she wanted to do was to cause scene. The kids might hear her and come wandering out. Her brothers might try to do something to protect her and that probably would not turn out well.

She tried to start a conversation with the drunk hoping that then he might loosen his grip. But he kept going on and on saying that he had warned her half pint husband what he would do if he caught him in his territory again.

"Guess he didn't git the message I left for him at the livery," he said.

"Oh, he got it alright, takes a big man to slit a horse's throat, don't it?" she muttered coolly.

She felt like she was about to pass out from his stench and standing so uncomfortably against the wall. Just as she was thinking she couldn't take this any longer, she felt a tug and also heard a loud thud.

The gambler fell to the ground and she quickly stepped away from his grasp. Sarah then saw her rescuer. As Ira was returning from the station he saw what was happening and walked up behind them. He had pulled his pistol and hit the gambler in the back of the head.

"I guess Sam Colt really did make the great equalizer," he smiled. "I am sure glad I didn't have to shoot that snake though.

Then he commented as he put his pistol away, "I probably ought to learn more how to use this one of these days."

Ira and Sarah quickly gathered their family. He took them into the station to purchase the tickets. The train would depart in a couple of hours. He left his family and their trunks in the station and left to deliver the horse and the wagon to the livery. He had sold the whole outfit for a good price. The livery man had been good to him over the years.

Ira was busy unharnessing the horse when a couple of men came by. Clouds were forming in the sky and Ira had been hurrying in an effort to beat the coming storm. He looked up as a man with a growling voice: none other than his gambler "friend" began to poke fun at him.

"Told you not to be in my territory Shorty," he smirked, "and you've gone and disobeyed me again."

At that comment his companions began to laugh. Ira took a deep breath. He was scared. He had left his pistol in the wagon box several feet away. He wasn't that great of a shot anyway, but now it might help him.

"Why won't this guy leave me alone?" he shouted in his mind.

By this time the Gambler and his friends had come over to the side of the horse where Ira was unhitching the singletree that was a part of apparatus of hitching the horse to the wagon. He was definitely out to settle a score with Ira. The hair on the back of Ira's neck stood straight up. He knew these dogs were out for his blood.

The Gambler lunged for him, but swift on his feet, Ira leaped out of his way. The Gambler's friend however who was behind Ira shoved him hard back toward the gambler. There was no way Ira could reach the wagon box to get his pistol so he began to search the ground for some other weapon to defend himself.

The gambler's next lunge knocked Ira into the horse. The frightened little gelding skittishly pulled out of the way leaving the unattached harness and singletree on the ground at Ira's feet. He quickly grabbed the singletree and lifted it high in the air. The gambler's friend moved out of the way. And the singletree crashed hard against the gambler's head. He fell forward on to his stomach. As he lay face down on the ground, Ira's pent up rage at this man came to the surface. Ira kicked him with his boot and then took full advantage of the gambler's inability to fight. He landed another forceful blow to his legs. Bystanders heard Ira mutter as the blows came down.

"Don't ever call me Shorty again!

Again he hoisted the wooden weapon and guided it to land firmly in the gambler's back.

"Don't ever slit one of my horse's throats again!" He muttered as the administered the blow.

Ira half lifted the man half shoved him with his boot so that he lay on his back. He wanted to make sure this snake heard his next message. Then with a crushing two handed blow to the gamblers hands Ira breathed forcefully,

"And don't you ever," he landed another blow, "ever touch my wife again!

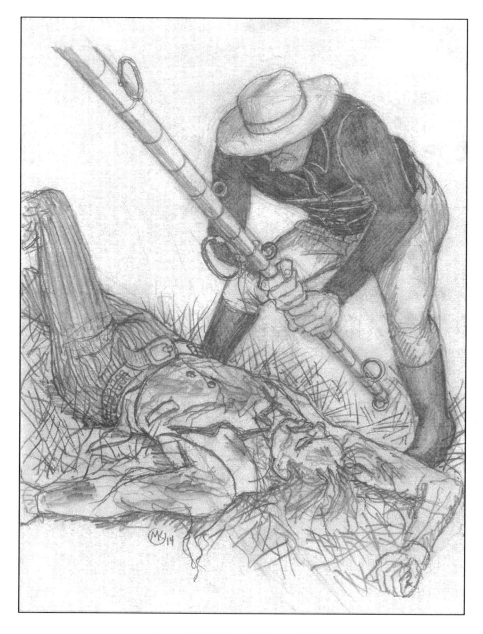

Ira gets the better of the gambler.

By this time a rather large crowd had gathered and several men pulled Ira away from the gambler. But in all reality, Ira was done. He had beaten that dog of a man for all the reasons he had built up inside.

The crowd agreed that the gambler had provoked this whole thing and they let Ira peacefully finish his business. He leaned on the wagon box and took a deep breath trying to calm his shaking hands. Then he stood up straight and tall, went into the livery to deliver the horse and the wagon as promised.

Finally, he stopped outside the train station and tried to compose himself again. He didn't want Sarah to know what had just happened but at the same time he felt an urgency to let Levi know. He stopped at the privy to see if he looked like he had been in a fight, then he went into the station to meet his family.

Chapter 22: Idaho Territory 1886

Two days after leaving Denver, the train with her weary passengers pulled into Mountain Home. The map of the Idaho Territory that Ira had gotten at the land patent office still had this place identified as Rattlesnake Station. Sarah had not been impressed when Ira told her that he had booked tickets to get off at Rattlesnake. Before they left the station Ira went to the Western Union Office. He was worried about the way they left Denver and really felt he needed to warn Levi. He sketched out a bare bones message that read:

Gambler tried me again. Watch yerself. Reached the Idaho, Ira.

Even though the telegraph was expensive Ira had to get his brother a warning. He also penned a longer letter which described more in detail the events that transpired. That letter, he sent by mail from the station.

Black Jack and the mares were unloaded at the stockyards on the outskirts of town. Ira and his family walked the short distance to gather them. Ira had packed his saddle and two others and a couple of extra bed rolls on the train with the horses. Sarah could ride now or any combination of the others. Ira had decided to quit calling the kids her siblings. Starting today a new start lay ahead of them. They were a family.

The man at the stockyards said that there was a wagon builder no more than a quarter mile from where Ira could get a much-needed wagon. The walking felt good especially after riding the train for so long. Sarah and the kids made a picnic in a shady spot near the wagon shop. Here she fed them the last of the food she had brought with them. They would get supplies after they got the wagon and harness. Ira told the wagon smith that he was looking for some good ranch land to homestead in the southern part of this territory. He asked the wagon man if he knew where the Sparks Harrell ranch might be.

"In which state?" the man retorted. As Ira inquired further the man showed him a rough map but it was similar to the one he had purchased at the Denver office. Then the wagon builder told him that honestly he would have better luck hearing about the conquers and busts at the saloon down the street. So Ira took a stroll.

Inside, the saloon was dark and it took his eyes a moment to adjust. There were only a few customers but he saw one man sitting in the corner who honestly was the oldest looking man that Ira had ever seen. Ira walked up close to the old man's stool.

"Ira Brackett is my name," he said as he held out his hand.

"You look like a man who might know this country well. Could I buy you a drink for a just a piece of your advice?"

The old man smiled at Ira. He only had one tooth in the front of his mouth.

The old man's advice.

"Of course," he said. "Eating is getting harder for me these days so beer is my main nutrient … Buy away."

Ira told him that he had come to this country looking for a good place to ranch and a new start for his family. The old man said that he had trapped beaver in every stream in this territory. When Ira asked specifically about good ranch land in the southern part of the territory the beaver trapper smiled.

He hobbled over to the doors motioned for Ira to come outside then and pointed to the south, "See them shiny mountains?"

Ira looked to the south and did see a range of mountains.

"There," the trapper said, "is where God runs his cows, I hear."

Ira liked the sound of that. He couldn't wait to tell Sarah. He was sure it would make her feel better after he had teased her about "Rattlesnake Junction."

Back inside the saloon, he drew for Ira a rough map of what he called the Three Creeks country. Ira bought the trapper a couple more drinks and thanked him for his thoughts. He took the map and left the saloon.

He found his family at the feed supply store. Sarah had purchased flour and beans and bacon. She found a really good deal on a cast iron cooker that a family leaving for Oregon had left.

They bought five hens and a rooster and an old jersey milk cow. As for the chickens, she used Ira's knife to clip one wing so that they couldn't fly.

Outside of town they made camp for the night. Sarah enjoyed having her new cooking set up and food to cook with. She might have enjoyed the whole experience more but was in a few short months expecting their third child.

The next day they pulled camp at first daylight. They were all eager to see the new country here. Still heading south they camped that night near Bruneau. A couple more days travel, always south looking for the big shining mountains. One day Sarah remarked that the mountain ahead of them looked like a big eye shining, watching over this country.

"Must be God's eye," she said.

That made Ira smile. They hadn't seen other homesteaders for most of the way. Sarah thought that the kids might like to have neighbors around. Honestly she might like that too. On the train there was much talk about the Bannocks being on the raid and their family had seen what the Indian raids were like from living in Colorado.

They spent the night near a meadow on Big Flat Creek. At least that's what they figured it was called from the Beaver Trapper's map. Nearby, someone had built a big log home with barns and horse corrals.

A short distance to the south they came to a small stream that they thought to call their own. A very tired, and pregnant Sarah said she had gone far enough.

Ira set promptly to work building a small shanty to keep their family safe from the winter cold. Come springtime however, they would find that they had too many neighbors and that all the good ground had been staked. In this Idaho Territory they would stake out several places before they found the right place to call home

Now that we have introduced Ira Brackett and got him and his kin to Idaho … we will continue with the story of Jim, Tap and his wife Ollie and their baby son arriving in Idaho after leaving West Texas in 1892 after they took care of Dick's business in Eagle Pass. Idaho had just become a state in 1890 and the west there was wild and ready for the tamers.

Chapter 23: The Idaho

It had been a long trip. They arrived in at the place Tap had chosen in the late spring. An open meadow tucked under the backdrop of a cliff, a good stream ran through and its rushing cold water promised to make the grass grow and their stock become fat. Their piece of Wild West heaven would be productive. Jim and Tap had taken patents of land next to each other in a very isolated area in the southern part of this newly formed state.

The creek, while small provided fresh clean mountain water, the coolness of it surprised them. Texas water, well it was usually muddy and warm. Another thing about the water was that, Texas streams were rivers in comparison but they soon adjusted.

Tap and Jim each took 160 acres. Three creeks seemed like a perfect little out of the way place. It wasn't really easy to access. There was a rather deep and rugged canyon that ran along the east side a fairly solid and rugged mountain range to the south and the Bruneau canyon made up the west boundary of the area. So in actuality unless someone really intended to come to Three Creeks there weren't too many passer bys. Tap and Jim really weren't hiding from anyone that they knew of but it just felt more comfortable to be somewhere you could be left alone. However, for, Ira on the other hand he would admit that he was hiding.

As the summer wore on Tap began to wonder if they would be able to grow enough food to survive thru the winter. Ollie pitched in all she could to get a home ready for the winter. They had not yet experienced it but heard tell that it did get cold here.

Tap had heard from his new neighbors of a large ranch in the area that could always use a good hand. In little more than a month they had constructed a prove up shack that would keep the weather off for the season. Ollie planted a garden and they had gotten some meat. What money they had went pretty fast.

It didn't take long for Tap to decide there had to be a better way. Tap and Jim decided that if either of them were gonna go to work it should be Tap. He was by far the best horseman of the two. And Jim, with just a little help from Ollie could do all the work required on their Home places. Tap soon acquired a job on Sparks-Harrell's Shoe Sole Ranch.

He worked hard and his talents proved valuable. It wasn't long before his talents were recognized and he became cow boss. The job did require him to be gone from home a lot that winter, but his pay served to keep his family's heart and soul together.

With the blooming of the early summer wildflowers, prosperity seemed to unfold in their way. In addition to his good new cow boss job, Tap had discovered that the Bruneau desert was plenteous with wild horses. Every time his cow crew went out with the wagon he would round up several wild horses and bring them home to Ollie and Jim. They would work at getting a fair handle on the wild ones. Then Tap would put them in his regular riding string and before too long he had some very fine mounts for sale. On his off times or on cattle deliveries he would take these finer mounts to whatever rail head and sell his horses too. With all the animals that had been lost in the harsh winter a few years earlier, horse flesh sold high. Three Creeks was a bustling community still not nearly as crowded as Texas had been.

One warm day that spring as Tap was returning from checking on his crew at Cow camp, he stopped at Faradays store just down creek from his place to get a drink. And who should be at the store? But his old friend from Colorado … Ira Brackett.

Tap had known that he was somewhere in this new state but honestly he had been so occupied with trying to feed his family and build them a home he hadn't much time for anything other than surviving. The old friends chatted for most of the afternoon. Ira told Tap that he had been going down to the Inside Desert just east of the Canyon to gather wild horses. With a gleeful look on his face he added that it had proven to be not only fun but downright profitable. He said that harvesting the horses was better than harvesting apples. He would get a few new colts each year, come back when the grass turned green again and a new crop had grown.

Tap laughed at the irony of the situation. He too had discovered that horse herd. Their kindred souls were on the same track again, he chuckled to himself.

In just a few days he said he would be headed back out and wondered if Tap might like to go. Tap said he had been at cow camp and was missing his Ollie and the little ones. But he said if he had two days at home then he would sure be game to for a roundup. That day was the start of a profitable venture for both men and a solidifying of their bond of friendship.

Chapter 24: A Few Cards in Bruneau

Tap was very happy with the cow boss job. He enjoyed the camaraderie with other proficient cowboys and they helped him hone his own horse craft.

The hours he spent a horseback on the cattle drives helped him put a real handle on the horses that he expected to later offer for sale at the next rail head or cow town. He couldn't have asked for a better life except if he had owned these cows himself instead of his boss men.

But that day will come, he vowed to himself.

With his cowboys earnings they had invested in cows as they could. They had kept the crop for the last two years. The summer had been so bounteous. The grass had come early and was tall. Tap was taking cattle for the Shoe sole to the rail head to the north that September and he decided to take also his calf crop and a few of the horses he had gathered off the desert as the year had worn on. The trip to Mountain Home and delivering the cows to the rail head had been uneventful. Even though the late summer grass was dry the grain on it was plentiful, the cattle even hadn't lost their bloom when they arrived.

Tap received a good price for them and Tap's own cattle and horses sold well. He was down to the sole mount he rode and it easily carry him all the way home to Three Creeks. Tap was feeling on top of the world. He decided that he really deserved some fun after his long summer of hard work. He stopped in the town of Bruneau and bought himself a shot of whiskey. There was a card game gathering at a corner table and several of the players invited Tap to join in. Several hands were played and the liquor flowed as freely as the cards were dealt. It was a fairly even game first one player would show well then another would get the good luck streak. Big Bad bill Hayes another Texan, was drinking heavily complaining loudly when he lost and crowing triumphantly when he won. It was getting late in the evening when the dealer dealt a once in a lifetime hand. They were playing 7 stud 2 cards down 4 up and one down.

After Tap turned his down cards up showing 4 fours the winning hand, Big Bad Bill Hays stood up said

"You Tap Duncan," he slammed his fist hard on the table,

"Yer, you're a cheating me."

"I'm taking my winnings and leaving." With that Bill reached for all of the money on the table.

Tap stood up and said. "Ahhh, not so fast Bill; we had an honest game, just because you drink too much and are a sore loser doesn't mean anything was rigged."

Bill was drunk and mad as a cut cat about losing all his money, he drew his gun and fired, hitting Tap in the stomach. Tap fell over backwards from the blow, it felt like he had been kicked by a mule. In reality it was the force of the bullet hitting his big silver belt buckle, the very buckle that many of Tap's friends had kidded him about wearing. This day however, it was that buckle that saved his life, by stopping Bill's bullet.

As Tap hit the floor he drew his gun, just as he had practiced so many times. He started shooting at Bill Hayes and he didn't stop until his gun was empty. Tap didn't make the same mistake Bill Hayes had made in shooting once and waiting to see if he had hit Tap. Tap put five bullets in that man's chest and Hayes was dead when he hit the floor.

Tap backed up against the wall and reloaded his pistol.

"Ya' all saw him fire first. It was self-defense. He would have killed me if I hadn't shot him."

Tap explained wildly. He was out of breath and very agitated.

With that Tap scooped up his winnings and stepped towards the back door. The barkeep leveled a shotgun at Tap and said,

"Hate to do this but…. not so fast Tap. Everyone saw him shoot first, but we need for the sheriff to clear this."

Later after the sheriff had made his inquest, he agreed it had been a clear case of self-defense. He took Tap aside and told him it would be better if he left town. And didn't come back.

Bill Hayes, a Texan himself had only recently come to Bruneau, but he had friends and kin in this town who might not see it as the witnesses had. With that warning, Tap gathered his horses and supplies and began the long ride back to Three Creeks.

Chapter 25: We Need to Get Out of Idaho 1898

Tap tried to stay a little closer to home after that. And that suited Ollie just fine. With four little ones at home their home now was busy and full. Charlie was now old enough to go to school and what was even better, he could pitch in on the homestead chores.

Tap was still working for the Shoe Sole Ranch and other than a couple of horse gathering ventures he spent all of his extra time at with Ollie and the kids. Their little cow herd was growing and Ollie was happy. Her only complaint was that the cold winters seemed to bother her.

Tap began to realize, much to his delight, that they were getting more cows than their 160 acres could feed. So he decided he had no other choice than to take some of them to Mountain Home to the market at the railhead He knew that he would have to drover them through Bruneau. To do that he would need to take Jim with him.

He sure would feel better if Ollie and the kids were not by their lonesome. But she assured him that she would be ok, but she made him promise to hurry home.

Charlie usually rode his horse Little Red, the couple of miles up over the hill to the school house. One lovely fall day while Tap and Jim were gone, Ollie decided to load the rest of her little ones up in her buckboard to fetch Charlie home from school. It was a beautiful fall day and she was enjoying the warmth of the afternoon. The little ones were playing happily on a quilt that she had laid out in the in the back of the wagon. She had given Byron, her five year old, the reins and was teaching him a little about handling the pulling horse. She arrived at the school pasture shortly after the big iron bell was tolled.

Charlie and some of the school kids were playing tag. The School Marm came out of the classroom and waved happily at Ollie and yelled to her that she would like to visit with her about a thing or two.

Ollie took the reins from Byron and told him to run play with his brother Charlie. She tied them to the hitching post. She lifted Tappie out of the wagon box and sent her over to the boys. As for Lora Clare, her baby, she gathered up in her arm and headed toward the schoolhouse. The teacher began friendly enough telling her that Charlie was a good boy and she delighted to have him in her school. Then her face got real serious.

"Mrs. Duncan, there have been a couple of men hanging around here the past few days, first they inquired about Duncan Children. I, I started to point Charlie out to them but then I just felt like I shouldn't do that. "

I asked them to leave and about that time some other parents started showing up to gather their children. They left quickly.

She swallows hard, "Yesterday, however, I did see them again and they followed Charlie as he headed out for home. He must have seen them too because he rode out of here faster than I have ever seen him go. Honestly it worried me so to see him go so fast."

She paused and put her hand thoughtfully to her forehead.

"I don't know what to make of all this Mrs. Duncan but those men made the hair stand up on the back of me neck!" she was sweating.

"So I truly am glad you came for him today. Mrs. Duncan."

She held her hand out to squeeze Ollie's hand.

Ollie's face turned pale. Without a word she headed out to the playground. She glanced around quickly for the boys and Tappie. She yelled for them to come at once and get in the wagon. The boys dropped the ball they were playing with and grabbed Tappie's hand. They sensed an urgency in their momma's voice.

Ollie headed the wagon back to their homestead at a very rapid clip. She was short with the kids and warned them not to be making light of things. When they arrived home they were to do their chores quickly without even one word of backtalk.

Ollie's uncertainty and fear must have evidenced in her voice. Tappie began to cry and soon baby Lora began also. Ollie had been apprehensive about Tap and Jim both being gone. But Tap had needed Jim's help getting thru to the railhead especially thru Bruneau.

Ollie took a deep breath as she drove the wagon to the barn. While Charlie unsaddled Little Red, she unhitched the wagon. Byron headed out to the pasture to fetch the milk cow.

"Mom," he yelled,

"There's riders coming down the lane, two of 'em ya think its pa and unca Jim?"

Ollie sat the girls in the corner of the barn and sternly put her finger to her lips in a "Keep Quiet" gesture. She always carried Tap's scatter gun in the wagon and she grabbed it and checked to see if it was loaded.

"Byron," she called, "You get in here now ya hear me?" Byron didn't need any other encouragement.

Charlie led Byron over by the girls. Ollie took a deep breath and walked out the barn door. She could tell at an instant the riders were not her Tap and Jim. She leveled her shot gun to her shoulder and looked down the barrel at the men who were approaching the barn. Oh how she wished she had brought the pistol with her too. This shotgun only had two fires.

"State yer business now, mister." Ollie said as gruffly as she could.

"Now here, here missy," one of the men began. "Just a looking for Duncan's."

'Who's asking?" Ollie replied. The man smiled an eerie smirk.

"Got a message for ya from Widow Hayes. Since that Tap Duncan," the man was rolling a smoke and stopped to light it. He blew out his deep draw of smoke as he spoke.

"Since that Tap took something so precious from my sister," he smiled that awful smile again.

"Well, I intend to take something precious from you ... sort of like evening the score. He drew circles in the air with his roll your own like he was balancing it all out, making it all fair.

Ollie had figured this day might come but why in the hell, she cursed in her mind, did Tap have to be gone when it did? She breathed hard. She had faced her share of tough situations, anywhere from the fighting Comanche in Texas to the rattlers that crawled this Idaho desert but this time was different, this involved her babies. She swallowed hard and straightened as tall as she could.

"You just ride on outta here mister. Now! Ollie shouted. She pulled to cock the gun in an effort to emphasize her words.

The riders looked at each other and laughed. Just about that time a single shot from near the barn reported. That shot kicked up dust in front of the horses as it hit the dirt. The dust it kicked up and the ricochet of the bullet spooked the horses.

The man who was holding his cigarette, well his horse began to buck dumping him at a pile near Ollie's feet.

Ollie seemed as shocked as the riders. She glanced over to the barn and could barely see her skinny little son just seven years old sitting on his backside. The recoil from Tap's pistol had knocked him down. She could see him mouth something she figured might be an expletive. Ollie's heart was so touched but knew that she must now make the most of the advantage her little man had just given her. She started toward the lone rider.

"And you mister, are NEXT if you don't get out of here right now."

Now!" She threatened.

Ollie's stride was forceful as she came toward him. She caught the horse that had thrown his rider. She lead that horse to the man who had just been bucked off and told him the first shot was a warning and he had to he count of three to be mounted up and off her property, or the next shot, well he wouldn't get up from... ever. The first man on horseback was up over the hill even before the man on the ground could pull himself up on his mount. Both men were gone in a very short amount of time.

Ollie didn't sleep at all that night. She sat on a chair in front of the door. Every gun that they owned was loaded and at the ready. It truly made for a long night. Tap and Jim arrived the next afternoon. As soon as he arrived she sat him down for a very serious talk.

"Tap, I love you." She said. "But, she swallowed hard to keep her nerve, "We're leaving this place now."

For the next few days as they began readying their belongings to go, Tap told Ollie you know we can't. No, I won't go back to Texas.

Ollie looked at him tenderly.

"I know that, Tap but I want to be somewhere warmer These Idaho winters they're just too cold for me."

However, truth be known, she was telling her husband that she that she was lonely for him as much as she was talking about the weather. Tap smiled and held her close.

He began to remember a letter that he had gotten from his sister Nannie. She had been such a strength in Tap's life.

Before the mess with Dick being hung she had been married to a preacher and it seemed like they were the happiest of all people. Shortly after Dick had been arrested and charged with the murders, that rascal, Man of the Cloth, as he called himself, he began to be very embarrassed of Nannie and the girls. Finally one day he came home and said she was to give him a divorce. One simply couldn't expect a Righteous Man, a man of his stature you know, to be married to a woman whose brother was a murderer.

Nannie tried to convince him that she was a good woman, that Dick was innocent. She even had Tap talk to him and tell him his story that he had been with him the whole time. They asked him all the questions that were and weren't brought up at the trial,

Such as: Why was it that if Dick was going to murder that family why go all the way to Eagle Pass to do it. There were 250 miles of wide open Texas plain between San Saba and Eagle Pass. Had he been inclined he could have shot 'em and dug a hole in the soft sand and left them and no one would have known differently.

But, Minister McKee, Sam to be exact, would not be convinced. He divorced Nannie and left her with the babies. Most of the family had left San Saba especially after the fire at the big house. The Duncan home at Richland Creek did rival some of the plantation homes that the southern states could brag about. It was a dandy. Two stories and porches all the way around on both levels. So the toll that the hanging of Dick had on the family produced yet another tragedy. The community and all of San Saba was divided between those who knew and supported the Duncan's and those who were envious of and thought the Duncan's had gotten a just comeuppance.

So Nannie. After the divorce, decided that Texas wasn't where she wanted to be. She and the girls joined a wagon train headed for California. Lot of the Indian trouble had been contained but the wagon trains still travelled with an army dispatch.

As they travelled along the captain of the Dispatch assigned to their train noticed this beautiful red headed young woman who strangely was travelling unescorted with two young daughters. He decided to take it upon himself to a keep a special eye on her.

What a treat that would be he thought to himself.

At camp as the wagons circled up for the night, Captain Greele made sure he rode by Nannies wagon, He asked her if there was anything he could do for her. She just smiled and dismissed him. But each night at the circle he would ride up and offer his assistance.

Nannie found herself looking forward to his visits. She started asking him to get off, enjoy a cup of coffee with her. By the time the wagons arrived at a place called Hackberry, Arizona, where the captain was garrisoned, they had become good friends.

Nannie decided the trail had mended her heart her and she looked forward to love again. She stayed in Hackberry as the wagons travelled on. She had a lot of life and living yet to do. She was going to make a new life for herself. Captain Greeley resigned his commission and made Hackberry his home. Sometime later, they were married.

"Hackberry, Arizona Ollie? How does that sound?

There was an excitement in his voice.

"And we've got people there. Jim won't go with us. "What with that pretty new bride of his, her people are close by, Tap winked at Ollie, "their life is here."

"You and the kiddies," he paused and twisted a lock of her soft brown hair between his fingers, "you're my family, but I sure would like to have some folks wherever we go." Ollie smiled. She loved this man so much.

"Tap. She said as she slapped his knee, "You've got folks wherever you go. You meet em and they become yours. Just for instance take that

Ira Brackett. God didn't give you all the same name but I would swear that y'all think yer kin."

Tap smiled at his beautiful wife. She would make them a happy home wherever they went.

Tap's brother James, grandmother Martha Blanchard Duncan, father Bige Duncan and sister Nannie Greele. Photo courtesy of Mackie Duncan.

Chapter 26: Bige is Looking for a New Home

Life on the Duncan Family ranch in Knickerbocker sure wasn't the same these days. After Dick's hanging and the fire they moved to this place just to get out of San Saba. Early on as the boys were growing up, the family had made big plans. They would work hard and as neighboring places came up for sale, they planned to buy them. With their hard work they would make them as productive as any central Texas ranch could be. That plan seemed to be working great until he, Jim, Tap and Richard all wandered off to New Mexico on a cattle drive. Tap took a long time to recover from a beating he took in a bar up there. That whole ordeal changed him inside he just wasn't quite the same.

Then Dick got hung for a crime he didn't commit. He was just trying to make a living and a future for his prospective new wife. That hanging seemed to take the heart right out of their old man. And now that Jim and Tap had left Texas for the Idaho, Bige missed his brothers and began to think more and more that perhaps he too should sell out and move his rather large family north for those rich and mystical grasslands too.

Bige's wife Nancy his wife had given birth nine times and seven of those little ones were still alive. Two of their babies had died at the tender age of two. Sometimes he felt that his life on this Texas prairie was tougher than the ground they tried to till.

A while ago, Bige had received a letter from his brother Jim in Idaho telling him about the great life he and his new wife had found. Jim reported that Tap and Ollie were well and their little family had grown to six. Tap had recently ended his employment as a cow boss for a large ranch in northwest Nevada and Southern Idaho and had recently moved his family to the Mohave area of Arizona, closer to his sister Nannie.

Family was important to these people. Big missed his brothers and was eager to see if this new territory where Tap had settled could be the makings of a new cow outfit for him and his family.

He kissed his wife Nancy Blake good bye and bought a train ticket to Hackberry, Mohave Arizona. He had sent word and Tap met him at the station. Their reunion was sweet. They talked for several hours just catching up on life.

Tap told Bige if he was looking for ranch country, back up north was where he ought to be looking. Tap drew for Bige several maps of the good cow country he had travelled as he managed the cattle for Sparks -Harrell Ranch in Idaho and Northern Nevada.

Bige looked thoughtfully at his brother.

"Ah Tap ... If this is such good cow country why you down here in this Arizona desert?"

Tap said that Idaho was too cold for Ollie and too hot for him[51]. He didn't even crack a smile as he said that which was unusual for Tap. So Bige gave him a look as if he expected the rest of the story.

"Back in '94," Tap began, "I got in a bar fight in a place called Bruneau. I had to shoot a man to stay alive."

He put down the pencil he was using to draw out maps. He looked thoughtfully at Bige.

"You know, Bige, back in New Mexico when they nearly beat me to death in that bar," He breathed out slowly, "I vowed I would never let anything like that happen to me again." He looked at Bige hoping for some absolution and Bige quickly gave it to him.

"A man's gotta do what a man's gotta do. What happened anyway"?

Tap smiled, "I got lucky at cards, the other guy was a real sore loser."

Tap's voice trailed off as he seemed to be remembering the sweetness of the hand. Then Tap cleared his throat,

"He accused me of cheating, he shot at me and well, I defended myself." Tap frowned as he began to relate the rest of the story.

"It was determined all was self-defense and they let me go but I tried to stay clear of that country. Too bad, too Bruneau is a great little town. I used to enjoy going there."

---

[51] Author's father, Noy Elbert Brackett I, always said and is quoted in several articles to say "Idaho was too cold for Ollie and too hot for Tap."

Tap pursed his lips, "Then one day, that dead man's kin…they threatened my family. No matter how I liked the Idaho ... It was time for us to go."

Bige asked Tap to travel with him to look for a prospective ranch that he could buy if he sold the home place in Knickerbocker. Tap liked the sound of that especially because even though he was somewhat settled in this new country, it was good enough for now but wasn't sure he would always want to be ranching here.

They took the train north to Elko and began to inquire about ranches for sale. They found a few but kept hearing a common thread about a new bank in Nevada. It seemed that this new bank held most of the businesses and most of the mortgages for ranches in the northern part of the state. The brothers decided to ride the train further west to the town where this bank was. A cow town on the railroad line called Winnemucca.

They got off the train and headed up the street to The First National Bank. Inside, the bank they said that they were in town looking for a ranch to purchase. Shortly, they were conversing with a pleasant man, the president of the bank. He said that he was a rancher himself and his place was a short distance out of town. The Duncan's spent the next several days accompanying that bank president to various ranches. They saw some that he held mortgages on and others he loaned operating capital and others that he just knew were for sale.

One ranch in particular piqued Bige's interest. It was owned by a wealthy widow who had been losing money for years. As he and Tap retired to the boarding house after their tour with the banker, Bige spent all evening and several of the wee morning hours penciling out a plan to make that ranch work. He had run this plan over and over in his mind and he finally knew what he would have to do to make it work. He would sell his place in Knickerbocker for the down payment but he would have to borrow a substantial amount of money for operating capital.

Bige slept very little for the rest of that night. He was so excited about his new plan. In the morning, he and Tap went to the bank to talk the plan over. The banker said that he felt he was a good judge of character.

"I often make loans based more on character than even collateral," he said. Then he looked the brothers up and down, slowly, he began, "You look like men of your word," He squinted as he looked at the pistols that hung at Tap's side, "Like men who would do what you say you will do." He said as he raided his eyebrows.

Bige was nervous but somewhat encouraged by his words and began to unfold his plan to his new found friend. When he came to the part about the money he would need to borrow, the banker politely laughed.

"The only way you could get that kind of money out of this bank," he paused, "Would be to rob it." He snorted.

A sort of stillness hung in the air. Tap wondered if he knew who he was talking to. Bige looked at Tap. Now was their turn to laugh.

"That could perhaps be arranged," they both said at the same time. That made it even funnier. Tap raised his eyebrows at the curiosity of this conversation. As they finished the last of their discussions, Bige left his address with that banker just in case he changed his mind about the loan. They shook hands and agreed to stay in touch.

As they left the bank, the banker studied the names and addresses: San Saba, Knickerbocker and Texas. Abijah Duncan, now that name didn't ring familiar but the name Tap Duncan did.

He kept running these names over and over in his mind. He had come to Winnemucca as an official with the railroad. He remembered hearing about a man, name of Tap Duncan that at times had been reported to have ridden with the Wild Bunch. A Duncan name or two had also come up in association with the deadly southwest Ketchum Gang in Texas and New Mexico. They had been reported to be involved in various bank and train robberies throughout New Mexico and in reality all the west. He smiled at the irony of this day.

Bige and Tap rode the train back to Wells. Not having found the new start for his family that he had hoped for, Bige headed back to Texas and Tap returned home to Hackberry.

A few short months later, Bige received a letter from Winnemucca, Nevada. It simply read:

"Wish to talk over business deal. Know more about your family now, Meet in Denver."

Bige was more than a little nervous. After he had returned home from his trip, he had given up the thought of selling the ranch at Knickerbocker and he was nestling in here looking for new workable opportunities.

But now here before him seemed to be a new breath of air, maybe this would be the opportunity he was searching for.

Arrangements were made and a short time later they did meet at the train station in Denver.

They went to dinner and finally the Banker began opening up to Bige what he was expecting to be the ranch deal. Instead, the banker began,

"You know, I told you before, that in my bank, we make more loans based on character than collateral." He paused looking intently at Bige's face.

He was getting very excited at this point.

"Does that mean you changed your mind and you're going to loan me all that money?" Bige asked trying to hide his excitement. He felt his legs shaking he put his hands on them to keep his legs still.

The banker got real quiet. He tugged at his ear thoughtfully.

"Uhhh. No," he answered. He looked at Bige very seriously, then continued, "Because you seem to me to be a man who can and will do what he says he will do," He paused. "I am here to offer **you** the deal of a life time."

He leaned in closer to Bige. In a quiet whisper nearly choking as they words came out, he said,

"My banks in trouble."

There was a long pause. Whether he was trying to compose his thoughts or his emotions, Bige wasn't sure. The banker rubbed his chin hard with palm of his hand, swallowed hard and then continued in a more authoritative voice.

"The only way I can come out of this is if my bank is robbed."

He queerly studied Bige's face for a reaction. Then continued quickly so as not to lose the effect of the moment.

"You, you can have all the money. But I have some hard and fast rules."

Now he was blabbing quickly as if these thoughts had been rolling around in his mind for a long time just waiting to spill out.

"Number 1." He held up his fore finger in exaggeration of the importance of this rule, "No one is to get hurt." Then he continued with the list forgetting to exaggerate the subsequent rules. "No one can ever know that I was involved. It would ruin me personally and politically." "I want you to get a few good men to help you. They have to be disciplined, not get drunk, throw their money and brag about their deeds. We have to do this right so that no one will ever know what happened.

Then he added, "I have heard that some of your family are braggarts and can't be trusted, don't use them."

He went on, "If you don't get caught with indisputable evidence, I promise to never identify you.

"Also," He added as almost an afterthought, "I can and will steer the authorities away from you."

Bige just sat for a long time looking at him without saying anything; He was letting this entire conversation sink into his mind. Finally he took his hat off and scratched his head.

"Well this is a shock," he said. "I can tell you honestly that I have never done anything **quite** like this before, although I do know some who have." He smiled to himself at how cleverly he had stated that.

"I will have to think it over."

"Ok," the Banker swallowed nervously and said, "I was hoping you would say that." "I ... We need only cautious men to do this deed. Do it right so we all can stay out of trouble."

The next morning, after a sleepless night, Bige met him again for breakfast. He told him that he needed some time to visit with his brother Tap, and would get back to him soon.

Photo of Noy Brackett on horseback at Tap's Diamond Bar ranch in Arizona. Photo courtesy of Kristen Scholls.

Chapter 27: A Visit with Tap

From Denver Bige sent word to Tap that he needed to talk to him about the business deal at the bank. Tap was both curious and anxious to see his brother again. Bige hadn't realized how much he missed having his brothers around. With Jim in Idaho, Tap in Arizona and Dick in the graveyard at San Saba. He was the only son left to care for his parents and the family ranch. Bige was pleased to see how well Tap was doing here and the ranch he was building was substantial. Ollie fed the brothers a good meal and they went out to the porch to talk.

"What's this about a bank deal?" Tap asked curiously. He wasn't looking for small talk he was real curious about what Bige had said in the telegram.

Bige took a deep breath and began.

"You remember when we was in Winnemucca, Tap? When I asked that banker for a loan and he smiled and commented that the only way to get that kind of money outta his bank would be to rob it, you remember that Tap?"

Tap leaned back on his chair and laughed.

"Yeah that was pretty funny."

Bige looked very seriously at his brother, "Tap," he began almost in a whisper, "He asked us to rob it."

Tap had just taken a drink and spattered out the whiskey in his mouth.

"What did you say Bige?" he asked.

This time said it more forcefully.

"That Banker, he asked us to rob his bank."

"His bank?" Tap asked incredulously.

He was shaking his head like he was trying to focus.

"Yeah, his bank," Bige replied.

Tap leaned forward. "So is this some sort of a set up you think?"

"No." Bige replied. He had his hat in his hands and was twirling it thoughtfully.

"He said he was in real trouble and he is in a real tough spot. With his political aspirations and all, well a failure at his bank would kill him. A robbery is the only way he can save his hide."

Tap leaned back on his chair. He could see by the look on his brother's face this was not a joke. Tap looked up at the night time sky.

He held his hands out, "God is smiling down on me right now." He laughed.

He looked at Bige and asked. "Well what did ya tell him?"

Bige laughed at his brother's sudden eagerness. "I told him I'd have to talk to you." Bige replied simply. They both smiled and then sat in silence for a long time.

Tap thought back through several incidents in his life. Times when it seemed that life just hadn't dealt him a fair hand. The trail drive when he was just 16. Dick's hanging at Eagle Pass. Needing to leave Texas He vowed that as he could he would try to make life fairer for those around him. He had been accused of things he never did. True, he did kill that man in Bruneau but it was in self-defense.

After the beating in New Mexico and then Dick's hanging, he vowed he would never let anything like that happen to him or his again. And when he bought that Colt pistol he fully intending to keep that vow. He didn't go looking for trouble but if you were unfair or you crossed him, you were messing with a rattlesnake.

Tap looked in the window at his beautiful wife, Ollie and his children and began thinking on his life. The ranch here in Arizona was good. Ollie and the kids were happy and yeah, he was too. But in reality he wanted more for them than he was providing for them in these days. He would like for his ranch to grow faster, but it was good. He had been to Winnemucca; he had seen the fliers that advertised how much money the bank held.

Tap smiled at that thought. Then he spoke his thoughts out loud.

"That much money could start up a couple of good size ranches."

Bige smiled, "Indeed! It would."

"Maybe, Bige, this will change our family's luck." Tap was getting more excited.

"Let me show you how we can do this." Tap began to scratch a plan out.

"We will need more than just the two of us, three men for the inside, one to get the money two to flank him and most importantly we need a horse handler for the getaway. "

As soon as Tap said "horse handler," his thoughts immediately turned to his friend back in Idaho, Ira Brackett.

Tap had always remarked that in a life or death situation there wasn't a man alive he'd rather depend on for a secure mount than Ira.

"Ira's a real straight arrow though." He was thinking out loud again.

"Okay, then who else?" Bige asked, eager to know his brother's thoughts.

"Well, now just wait a minute."

Tap's words seem to drift with his thought.

"There just might be an angle that I can use to get him."

He looked at Bige. "Give me ahh, some time, I will go to Idaho and talk to him." Curiously, Bige consented.

Then Tap continued, adding, "I will enlist Jim while I am there. Since he married that sweet, Lizzy Helsley he has settled some but he's still our blood, he'll help us out."

Bige was silently counting on his fingers, "So you, me, Jim and Ira. So we have four? Maybe, and we will need another.

They both thought on Bige's brothers in law. But Tom and Sam Ketchum although notorious already for their various episodes outside the law, Sam was in jail and Tom he was having troubles of his own.

Also with the Banker's strict rules about men that wouldn't get drunk and throw money around and keep their mouths shut…the Ketchum's weren't even candidates. Some might have said they enjoyed bragging about their robberies nearly as much as they enjoyed the money from them.

A big smile then grew across Bige's face,

"However," he said, "My other in law, Green Berry Ketchum … now he could keep his mouth shut. I think," Bige added thoughtfully, "I think that he has quietly shared in a lot of the Ketchum gang's thievery. He simply takes their money and then quietly buries it in his ranch or invests in another, and never peeps a word, Won't either even on his dying day, I'd bet."

Tap seemed to like that idea. "Ok then, we sort of have that settled. You go, Bige, to Texas and recruit Green Berry and I'll head back to Idaho to get Jim and Ira on board.

Chapter 28: Tap Goes to Idaho

Tap bought a ticket and hopped the train headed for Wells, Nevada. When he arrived he bought a horse and supplies at the livery stable and headed north for the O'Neil basin. As he rode through, mile after mile of sage brush, his mind began rolling out all the memories this place held for him. He had been lucky landing the cow boss job for Sparks-Harrell. He was surprised one day as he was returning from cow camp and stopped at old man faraday's store to get a drink. Who should be at the store but his old friend from Colorado, Ira Brackett.

The two men chatted for the most of the afternoon. Tap said he'd been meaning to look Ira up since he had gotten here but he had been busy just trying to feed his family. Ira told Tap that he had been going to the Inside desert just east of the Bruneau canyon to gather wild horses and it had turned to be quite profitable. That horse herd on the desert Ira said was better than harvesting apples. He could get a few colts every year then come back and a new crop had grown. In a few more days he was headed out for the next crop and wondered if Tap might like to come along.

True to his roots, that Ira Brackett was making a living taming and breaking wild horses, Tap smiled at that thought. Tap said that he'd been gone to check his cow camp crew for the past few weeks and needed some time to spend with his family. "But, Ira, give me a couple of days at home and then I will be game for a roundup."

That was the start of a profitable venture for both men and the deepening of an already existing bond of friendship.

It was on one of these horse runs to that the men found themselves on the 71 desert scouting for signs of the horse herd. When they camped that night, Tap brought out his flask of whiskey to share with Ira. The campfire felt good against the night chill of the late spring time air. They hadn't even cut sign on the horse trail that day and Ira wondered if they ought to head to Bruneau to see if the herd had gone closer to the Snake River.

Tap hesitated. "Uhh, not sure if I want to go there Ira," He said. "I got in a mess of trouble there a while ago." Ira searched Tap's face waiting for an explanation.

"Just ... just there was a gambler there he got his feathers ruffled when I beat his game."

Those words seemed to grab Ira's attention. Tap continued. "He tried me and I had to shoot him before he got off his second shot. It was self-defense but he's got kin who don't see it that way. Why some men aren't much more than rabid dogs, I will never understand but why the hell is it always me who has to tangle with 'em?"

Ira's blood seemed to run cold in his veins. He had tried as of late to not think of the dog of a gambler in Denver. Made life so tough for him he just got his family outta town. Then just two years later after he had left for the Idaho he got the sickening news: Levi his brother had been murdered in the streets of Arvada, Colorado, near Denver[52].

Looking back, Ira wished he would have finished beating the life out of that gambler at the train station when he had the chance. Levi would still be alive today. Tears stung his eyes every time he thought on it and here it was nearly ten years later. Sitting there by the fire Tap took a long sip of his whiskey.

"Never told anyone this Ira," he began, "but after those Rangers hung my brother Dick at Eagle Pass ... I just couldn't sleep."

He was silent for a long time. Finally he continued,

"Seems like every time I shut my eyes, all I could see was Dick heading for the rope telling those people they were hanging an innocent man."

Tap paused and took another long sip. He put his hand on the pistol that hung on his side touching it as if it were a trusted friend. Then he continued.

"I found those men who framed him. Jim and I did. And we just took care of them. That is why we came to Idaho."

His voice trailed off. Ira looked at him wondering if "Took care of them" meant what he thought it did.

---

[52] See the "About Levi Brackett" note at the end of this chapter to learn more about the murder.

Tap cleared his throat and stood up; looking at the magnificent star lit sky and shouted.

"And I have felt better every day since … I love ya Dick!"

He shot his pistol into the nighttime sky, guzzled down the last of the whiskey and threw the flask into the dark as if he was trying to make it all disappear into that black and chilly night.

There was no doubt now in Ira's mind now as to what Tap meant. He found those men who pinned the murders on Dick and he had evened the score. Ira wondered how he might feel if his own brother's killers were "dealt with". After a long time wrapped up in his own trail of thoughts, Ira said,

"Well I ain't much of a gunman myself but if I had the means, I'd send someone to clean up those filthy dogs in Denver."

Then he sighed, "Now I have mouths to feed my own as well as Levi's children. No time for what ifs."

Ira crawled into his bedroll. Ira and Tap returned from running horses this time busted, the herd they thought must have moved north to the Snake River.

This conversation was being run over and over in Tap's mind as his horse travelled the miles to Three Creeks. He smiled to himself; yes he did know a way to get Ira to handle the horses for the bank robbery.

That is, if anything could.

Out of O'Neil basin, Tap followed Canyon Creek to its source at the top of the mountain. Many a time, he had brought cattle along this trail travelling to the rail head at Deeth. Now he was making in his mind the map that would get them home from Winnemucca with the gold. By the time he dropped over the mountain and down to Three Creeks he had played over and over in his mind

The Plan.

The plan for the route,

The plan for the getaway.

But most important and now at hand was the plan to get Jim and Ira on board. He hoped it would all fall into place.

Tap's first stop was at Jim's place just down the creek from Faraday's store. He had sent a gram to Jim telling him he was coming but Jim hadn't received it. He was greatly surprised to see his favorite brother riding down his lane. Emotions burned hot inside Tap as he looked around at what just a short time before had been his home. He and Jim shared more than just blood. They shared life experiences good and not so good, He truly missed his brother, the bond and the life that they shared. And he really did love this cow country. Anger stirred inside him as he thought on the mad dogs he let chase him from this, his home.

But Arizona was good to him and his family but he did miss it here. Tap asked Jim to saddle up and ride to Faraday's with him for a drink. They got their drink and headed out into the sunshine for a more private place to talk.

"So Tappie," Jim looked at him inquisitively. "What's up?" Tap smiled.

"Do I need a reason to come to see my favorite brother?" Jim looked at him with a sideways grin.

"You and yours are a good 1000 miles from here … I look out my window and you come riding up to my door," he grinned at Tap, "what's up?"

Tap was glad to see Jim's demeanor. It was as if the miles couldn't separate their lives. Tap felt as if he had only been out at cow camp for a while and returning home.

"Jim," he began…. "I have a business proposition for you." Jim moved his chair closer to the table to catch all of Tap's words. He smiled and lifted his eyebrows in very interested gesture.

Tap continued.

"You remember awhile back when I told you I was with Bige in Winnemucca?" When he was thinking of selling the place at Knickerbocker?"

Jim was getting curious. Tap had written him about the trip and that Bige was looking for a ranch to buy so he and his family could leave Texas.

"Yeah I remember Tap," he replied.

Tap continued, "We met a banker in Winnemucca, he owns the First National. He's a young aspiring politician and seems he kept up contact with Bige. They met in Denver a while ago."

Tap stopped trying to pick the words to say next. He itched his neck with his right hand, took a deep breath and continued.

"Jim, that banker … he told Bige that his bank was in trouble."

Jim curiously raised an eyebrow. Tap studied Jim's face for a tip to his thoughts. Then he just blurted the next sentence out.

"He asked us to rob his bank." Jim hooted.

"His bank? He wants us to rob HIS bank?"

Tap nodded and was grinning from ear to ear. Jim's amazement seemed to quell Tap's nervousness.

Jim looked at his brother and asked.

"Why us?" Jim wondered out loud.

Tap looked at him and both men laughed at the question he had just posed.

"So ya gonna do it?" Jim asked curiously.

Again Tap studied Jim's face trying to choose carefully his next words. Finally he stated simply,

"We can't do it without you Jim."

Jim thought about how ranching was getting tougher and tougher on him. He was only thirty seven but he was beginning to feel all the miles he had spent in the saddle, all the bar room brawls and just plain hard knocks that life had handed him.

He thought about the pleasant things that this new life with that pretty Lizzie Helsley had brought to him in the short time they had been married. He thought about how she wanted to buy the Faraday's store and run it for their family business. If only he could get together enough money.

Jim smiled at that thought. He tugged at his ear thoughtfully,

"Well Just how much would this robbery be worth exactly?" He asked.

Tap sighed a big sigh of relief. Jim was in, and with both feet, too.

Tap was so relieved that his meeting with Jim had gone so well. He hoped it would be a sign that the next would too go well. He left Jim back at his place and headed east.

Ira too, like Jim was glad to see Tap. He invited him in to share dinner with the family to which Tap gladly obliged. After they finished eating however, Tap insisted that they go outside to talk. He hated to leave Sarah out of this man talk but she couldn't and wouldn't have any part of this. So Ira said he wanted to show him the most recent horses he had gathered off the desert. Out in the barn Ira lit a kerosene lamp and held it up near Tap's face.

"You got troubles my friend?" he asked.

Tap swallowed hard.

"No." He replied "but I do have a proposition for ya though."

Ira looked curiously at his friend.

"Yeah?" he asked.

Even though Tap had rehearsed this speech over and over in his mind nearly every mile as he rode this way he still wasn't quite sure how he was gonna spit it out.

"Ira," he began, "you remember when we was out running horses a while back and you wanted to go to Bruneau."

Tap swallowed then continued, "And I told you I couldn't go there?"

Ira was really starting to worry what kind of trouble his young friend was in now. Tap continued.

"You remember the conversation we had about, you know my brother Dick and those guys in Texas who framed him?"

Ira felt the goosebumps start to rise on his arms. He did in fact remember that the conversation well and he had thought on it many a time since. He could still see a satisfied and vindicated Tap standing there in the starlight telling him that he had evened the score for his brother Dick.

Ira looked at Tap. "I remember it well, nearly every day as I watch Ed and Levi's other young uns grow."

He was shaking his head with a very sad look on his face.

"Yes, I think about it. Tap smiled at Ira's response and felt emboldened to continue.

"Ira," he began I am here to offer you a deal my friend. But please Ira hear me out before you say anything ok? Will you promise me that?"

Ira pulled his hat off and rubbed his nearly bald head. He didn't want to promise to anything he couldn't keep but the pleading in his friend's voice made him acquiesce. "Okay Tap, I will listen."

Tap told Ira about the trip that he and Bige had taken to Winnemucca looking at ranches. He talked about the banker and Ira, true to his word didn't say a thing. When Tap finally came to the part about the banker asking Bige to rob the bank, Ira did smile.

"Why ya telling me all this Tap?" he asked shaking his head in amazement.

Tap folded his hands and simply said, "To do this Ira, we need someone to handle the getaway horses."

Ira raised his eyebrows and he settled back against the barn wall. He shook his head. There was a long pause, "I ain't never done anything like that and I am too damn old to start." He chuckled at his own response.

Then he added, "Yeah I could use always use more money but in reality I have all I need."

He smiled at Tap and leaned forward ready to end the conversation. Tap put his hand on his Ira's shoulder.

"Just a minute please, ya promised to hear me out …."

Ira leaned back against the barn wall. "Ok?" he breathed out heavily.

Tap cleared his throat. "You know Ira," Tap swallowed hard….

"This conversation we are having right here, right now, it ain't about the money."

Ira felt goose bumps again form on his forearm. Tap kicked thoughtfully at the dirt with the toe of his boot. He then looked squarely at Ira, and began,

"I am offering you, Ira, a way to feel better every day. Just like I did about Dick."

Ira looked at him very seriously. He thought for a moment on what Tap had just said.

Finally he asked, "What exactly you saying, Tap?"

Tap paused looked at Ira very seriously and then said, "I am saying exactly what you think imma saying, Ira."

Tap breathed out hard.

"Quite simply, Ira, you help me solve my problem with the horses and I will see that yours is taken care of."

Stillness hung thick in the nighttime air. Finally Ira moved forward from leaning against the wall. He cleared his throat, "Denver you mean?" he asked. Tap nodded, "Yes, I mean Denver."

A Note about Levi Brackett

Levi Brackett, Ira's oldest brother was murdered in Arvada (Denver) Colorado in October of 1888. A trial was held and the men accused of killing Levi being represented by Denver's finest were found not guilty. Interesting how a couple of working blokes in Denver could end up being represented by one of Denver's most elite Lawyers, J. Warner Mills.

Authors contention is because of the crippling that the Gambler received at Ira's hand in Denver drove him to desire to exact such retaliation as to hire a couple of henchmen to carry out a murder. He later hired an attorney who would protect them from conviction. We have and have read the transcripts from the "trial and inquest." It is hard to believe that a decent man with a wife and five children would suddenly take to getting drunk and hanging out at dances on the Black side of town. David Malone the man who was with Levi may have been the man hired by the gambler to lure Levi to a part of town that he would not otherwise frequent. The response from Levi's Father in law David Crowfoot summed it up, "There is one thing that I cannot be reconciled to, and that is that the man Malone knows more about this case than he told the jury. Why, do you think that if you and I were out on a spree that I would not know what you did and where you went? Now Malone was with Levi from 4 o'clock in the afternoon until the murder occurred and you don't think he knows what occurred? I tell you he does and it was downright cussed ness that he would not tell."

Levi's father: Well he takes it pretty hard. He arrived in town last evening about eight o'clock from his farm, where he was gathering his crop of potatoes. Then whomever is writing this paper goes on to say ..."If I had old man Brackett has I would hunt down and prosecute the murderer to full extent of the law for the crime he committed. That old man is well fixed and can afford to spend several thousand dollars in pushing the case and never miss what he has to spend on it."

Then he goes on to describe "The body was placed in a nicely furnished casket and at five o'clock the bereaved parent, father in law and brother drove off with the remains. It was indeed touching to see the gray haired father with his eyes filled with tears taking away his oldest son, who had met such an untimely death. He remarked before leaving that he had a presentiment some three weeks ago that something might happen to Levi but that he had prayed that whatever it might be would pass by.

The copy of this paper was given to a part of the trial transcripts that we found. We apologize for not having any further citation.

Levi was with Ira when he won the Gambler's horse in Denver and as Ira left Denver he sent a message to warn Levi to watch himself because he had, in an effort to save his own life beaten the gambler as he was preparing to leave on the train.

Levi's children Ed, Joseph and Cora Inez came to live with Ira and Sarah. Shortly after Levi's murder in Arvada (Denver) his wife Clara died and the children came to Idaho.

Chapter 29: Every Man Has a Job – Winnemucca Nevada, September 1900

Late afternoon everyone gathered by down by the river. They were going over the plan just one more time. Tap took charge of the group. He said that while it was because of Bige's meeting with The Banker that had set this whole game in motion, and while it was that every man present was capable, he felt that he himself had more knowledge of this sort of thing than any of the others. This group needed a man in charge and if someone really wanted the job, Tap said they could have it. All agreed however that Tap was the man for the job.

Tap began to draw out in the dirt some of the plan. They would go into the bank at noon heavily armed. Each man then checked his several pistols. There wouldn't be time for reloading if things went bad. After checking and loading their guns they placed them on their coats on the ground in front of them. Tap then started around the circle. "Ok Bige, what's your job?" Even though Bige was his elder brother, thirteen years, his senior, Bige let Tap run this show.

Bige said he was to be out in front of the First National, tell others when it was time to enter the bank and try to keep anyone from walking in on the robbery. Then after the robbery he was to help Nixon do crowd control and direct the posse. Other than that he would just sit around 'til it was over." He smiled.

"Wrong! Bige." Tap said sternly. The firmness in his voice was to let his brothers and everyone else present know how serious events of the next day would be. It seemed like he was barking out rules they all had to pay particular attention to and focus on their part because the safety of the others depended on it. Tap wouldn't admit it he knew how these jobs went down and they were not always safe.

"Yes you will be out in front and tell us when to go in but you will do whatever it takes to keep anyone from coming in! I do mean whatever. Block the door, start a fight whatever it takes. Ya hear?"

Tap looked at everybody around that circle. If someone comes in, it is a lot more likely that someone will get hurt."

Now he looked at Bige. "You will be by yourself," Tap swallowed hard. He continued. "The rest of us have back up but you will be on your own. Tomorrow you will take that fancy blooded sorrel gelding in to town, Ira says he is a true powerhouse[53].

You'll leave him just down the street at the ready if you need him." He looked at his brother and said, "Your job is probably the most dangerous and I want you to be able to get out if you must."

Then he added, "Remember to saddle him with that plain saddle Ira picked up on the way down here."

Ok, then as we leave town, Bige, what is the rest of your job?"

Bige answered eagerly, "I will help The Bankers' efforts to direct the posse. I will help him to get volunteers to the train."

"That's right." Tap replied. Then he added, "The Banker will work them to take the train thinking they can cut us off at Golconda." Tap smiled. And that should give us the head start we need to disappear."

"Ok," Tap continued. He was nervous and trying to remember to cover everything. Didn't want to write it down though.

"When we get inside ya' all let me do the talking. Do not ever call anyone by their real name.2 you all remember your aliases?" He looked at Green Berry and Jim. "You all will cover my back. I will have the money bags and I will tell the Banker and the teller what to do.

Some of the others should have left for lunch. The vault in should be open and I will clean it out then the teller's drawers. If there is too much and I can't carry it all, Jim you will help me. After the money is bagged we will take everyone out the back door and hold them until we are mounted and ready to roll out.

"Sounds good Tap." Jim said. "I will cover yer back just like I always have. I will follow your lead, just tell me what to do and I will make sure it happens."

---

[53] See the "Horses of Winnemucca and George Moore" notes at the end of this chapter for additional details.

Green Berry was holding on to his shot gun. Tap smiled at the look of him. "Green," he said, "You will be my enforcer. You'll have your scatter gun and you will look scary. Just like you do now. Make it crystal clear to everyone in that bank that if they want to be a hero….they will be a dead hero."

Green Berry looked at Tap and grinned. "You are only asking me to act natural," he sort of giggled at that thought.

Then he continued, "After dealing with Sam and then Tom, I learned how to put the fear into almost anyone." They all laughed at that.

Tom and Sam had been on the path to being hardened criminals since their parents died and Green Berry, try as he may have, he had a devil of a time trying to raise them.

"You can't leave any room for chance, if someone thinks there is room for a chance, we could get someone hurt, any of us included." Tap looked at the family and friends gathered here at the fire.

"No one wants anyone to get hurt, we clear on that?" Tap continued to look at the group and his tone got just a bit softer.

"You all are my family and I promise that each and every one of you is going home to your wife and family."

"Ira," Tap exhaled deeply. "Your job started weeks ago. Compliments to you my friend. I don't know how you picked these horses no two really look alike. You tell me they can run and I trust you completely. My dad told me years ago that some people just know horse flesh like it is a gift from God.

Tap smiled and paused, "The story goes that an average settler can ride a horse hard and fast for twenty five miles before he drops dead. The Cavalry men, with their travel routine can go forty miles on that same beast. A good horseman which I know we all are can take him seventy five." Tap looked around the circle at his kin and his friends,

"Then you got your Comanche buck with his knowledge of how to pace and motivate can make 100 miles before that mount drops dead."

Tap looked at Ira as he continued. "Then he will jump off, eat a chunk of that raw horse flesh and run another fifty. I can tell you now boys I don't want to run that last fifty miles." They all chuckled.

"But with you pacing us Ira," Tap continued, "we will be able to ride those 100 miles." Everyone was smiling and nodding.

Ira now cleared his throat. As he stood he straightened as tall as he could somewhat conscious of how short he appeared as he stood near Tap. Tap folded his legs and sat on the ground near the fire.

"My job," he said as if reminding himself more than the rest, "I will be out behind the bank in the alley holding the horses. I will also make damn sure no one comes in the bank from that direction."

As if he were making them a promise he added, "There won't be any delay…As soon as you come out of that door we will get you mounted up and we will take off. You all will need to trust me and switch your horses or vary your speed according to my say."

Ira looked at the hobbled horses.

"They may look like a motley bunch but I promise you, they have the heart and they will travel. They will take us farther and faster than any set of horses around. You must however take the horses I tell you to take. And at the time I tell you to take it. Ira shook his head and continued.

"No questions, no back talk. If you do as I say, we will outrun any posse. No one will be able to catch up with us or get ahead. I have cut the fence along the railroad in at least a dozen places, so we will be able to cut north when we need to."

Ira smiled at his friends, "The last they see of us will be our dust disappearing into the sagebrush north and east of here," he said.

The 'over the hill' gang.

Horses of Winnemucca and George Moore

Like many of the other settlers in Three Creeks, George Moore came from New Mexico, West Texas. Tap and Jim Duncan's homesteads in Idaho were located just to the west of him. From time to time old friends from the south would stop by his ranch. His ranch was on Deer Creek a short distance south of where it runs into Three Creek. He had enough cattle to be respectable, enough horses to be profitable. His ranch while near the main road & community of Three Creek, was far enough off and isolated you had to want to see him to go to his ranch. He always had a good supply of horses of a variety of horses. Something for everyone. From old gentle horses anyone could ride, to good cow horses, any ranch would be proud to own

Probably his specialty was stout seasoned horses that could carry a man a long distance in a short time. He was always ready to trade horses, no questions about origin, or where the rider was coming from or going to. He would trade either a fresh stout horse for two tired worn horses or one for one with a bit of cash to boot. Any Law coming through would usually have a description of the rider, general description of the horse he was riding, usually a brand or other description of the horse. George had a short memory and couldn't remember the description of the riders that passed by his ranch. Horses were usually a sorrel, bay, or buckskin, never could remember head or foot markings, he had seen too many horses to try and remember any distinct marking of a particular horse.

BRANDS, well, brands were a specialty of George's. He had a shelf full of Bill of sales for all the horses he had bought over the years. Any horse of any description, with any brand. George had a bill of sale that would match. Another specialty of Georges was his running iron. He was an artist. He could take any brand and turn it into another. The Diamond, became the Diamond Bar. The 71 became 7Z, or the 76.

The Faraday Store and later the Jim Duncan Rock Store were nearby so George always had a few supplies on hand for anyone needing food or supplies and not wanting to ride the mile or so over to the store and risk being remembered. Again George would never lie to the law. It was just that he had a poor memory and couldn't remember the description of who had been by or what their horse looked like.

Not liking too many people at the ranch, George had a few cabins scattered around for his ranch hands to live at. It was better if not too many people lived at the ranch, that way no one could remember who had stopped by. He had to have food and supplies in these cabins so his hands could stay there. If someone stayed in one of these cabins when his hands were not there, it wasn't his fault, he couldn't check every cabin every day could he?

One of Moore's more famous dealing was when he allegedly supplied some of the horses for the Winnemucca Bank Robbery of 1900. The robbers wanted horses that could not be traced to them. Shortly before the robbery some of Moore's horses were stolen. Four fine big grey horses. After the robbery one showed up lame, in Mary's River south of Jarbidge Mountain. Three more turned up on the ridge south of Moore's Ranch. No one claimed them or had any idea where they had been or who might have had them. So George was just glad to have his horses back and didn't ask any questions.

There is a story told about a young man who was given one of the horses that the bank robbers had used. Our version of the story is that As Bige sat at the front of the bank watching to make sure that no one entered the bank during the robbery, he had a powerful little horse at the ready and tied to the hitching post just down the street if he had any trouble. When Bige left town. He left on the train leaving the horse on the street after they left the bank and switched horses they told the guy at the ranch that there was a fancy horse on Bridge Street tied to the rack

A Note About Ira's Alias

A few weeks ago I ran across an Owyhee Co. Directory at the museum in Murphy. There I found a section that shows what Jim and Lizzy Duncan's store looks like in winter. Along with that picture there is a directory of the residents of Three Creek in 1898. There is an A.H. Bracket listed as the owner of sheep but there is no Ira Brackett listed. Very odd indeed. We know for fact that Ira was in Three Creek having settled here in 1886. Yes he did have sheep as well as cattle. As Chet and I talked this over we remembered the story of Ira leaving Denver and the murder of his brother Levi. We decided that Ira was still trying to live under the radar so to speak and at time used an alias. His brother's name Alonzo Haines (A.H.) Bracket may have made a convenient pseudo name. Side note, G. T. Duncan was still listed in Three Creek in 1898).

Alonzo Haines Brackett was Ira's step brother, the oldest of the children born to Ozro and Lucy Stone. Ira mentions earlier taking Alonzo to Denver with him in Chapter 21. We had read that in an effort to not leave a trail that could be easily followed, Ira purchased train tickets to another destination so that the gambler that Ira had just beaten with the singletree could not trace them.

Another interesting point on this is that Ira's death certificate was filled out by his son N.E. or Bert Brackett as he was called. Perhaps he fulfilling his duty as oldest son in doing this for his heartbroken mother, as he did so he got his dad's birthdate off just a bit and neither did he know anything about Harriet Blackstone (Ira's Mother and his grandmother.) but most interestingly he filled out the name of Ira's father as Alonzo. We think that Alonzo was a name they had commonly heard at their home as Ira used it as a pseudo name. But then (this gets even better) I read in a book: the Sundance kid: The life of Harry Longabaugh. By Donna Ernst. Page 115.

"Nixon claimed that the outlaw identified as Jones was the outlaw who was called

ALONZO, by his partner." The point of this discussion being is that one of the bank robbers had called his partner ALONZO. Jones was in fact let go but still someone had heard the name Alonzo. Donna Ernst attempts to connect the name of Butch Cassidy (Harry Longabaugh whose middle name was Alonzo). It seems to have been proven that Butch Cassidy and his gang were in Wyoming at the time of the Winnemucca robbery and could not have committed the robbery.

Chapter 30: Leaving Winnemucca September 19, 1900

Out in the alley behind the First National, Ira waited with four of the Banker's finest blooded colts. The one he rode and three others for his fellows in the bank. The Banker's foreman had been training these sweet little power machines for the California race tracks. They were fidgety. Ira didn't try to settle them.

He was there to hold the horses and to make sure that no one walked in through the back door on a robbery in session. Bige was in the settled on the window seat outside the front door. His job, like Ira's was to prevent anyone from just wandering in the front door. Last night they as they had gathered at their campfire going over their plans for what seemed like the 47th time, Green Berry, who would soon turn fifty years of age had looked at them all and remarked that they should call themselves "The Over the Hill Gang." So, Bige had carved himself a cane from a branch that he cut from a willow down by the creek.

Ira smiled at that thought.

Then muttered out loud," I **am** a little old to be doing this." He quickly forced his focus back on the task at hand. Nervousness was twisting his stomach up. He now circled his prancy little colts a few times just to keep their blood up. And maybe to give him something to do.He wanted them ready when the boys came out into the alley. Everything depended on it.

Everything.

He hadn't waited long when the back door flew open and none other than the Banker himself burst into the alley. The colts startled at the noise and lunged forward but Ira had a good grip on them. Directly behind the Banker was Tap with his 45 pistol snugly against his back. Next to him was a man who was obviously a teller. Jim was covering him with his pistol. Green Berry had the shotgun sighted on them. He had concealed that gun in his long duster when he entered the bank.

Tap gave the banker a shove to the ground. The teller took cue from the Banker and laid on the ground too. Ira circled the colts as they again skiddishly lunged away from the confusion. They were ready to get going.

Tap grabbed his colt's reins from Ira and swiftly stepped in to his saddle and swung his leg over that colt in a liquid motion. The colt didn't even seem to notice that he had gotten on. Green Berry was pointing his gun at the prostrate men.

"Guys," he said clearly trying to cover his soft Texas drawl, "I'm just a bit nervous here and I can promise you that if ya move, it'll make my finger twitch and I am afraid that this scatter gun'd blow a hole clean through ya. So ya all just lay there real quiet and be still, ya hear?"

Jim had mounted his colt and he and Tap were covering the men now so that Green Berry could saddle up. The speed with which they mounted up was incredible. Those little colts were fresh and they were tired of standing around in that alley. As the robbers hit the steel of their spurs to their sides, they hit the open streets of Winnemucca on a dead run.

The Banker watched them head out and disappear around the corner. At that point he jumped up and ran back inside the bank and grabbed his own six shooter. Exiting the bank through the front door he began to shoot his gun in the air in an attempt to draw attention to the bank. After a few men had gathered he ran towards the train station and was calling for a posse. He gathered several men and suggested they all hop on the train. The robbers, he pointed out were headed east and if he and his men could take the train they could beat the robbers up the Humboldt River to the next station. From there they could grab horses and ride back to catch those thieves. Bige who had been at the First National's front doors joined the volunteers in following him. His own eagerness to follow the banker's lead helped influence the crowd.

By now the Banker and his few volunteers loaded up in the engineer's car. Excitedly they instructed him to head east as fast as the train could go. The train at one point did pass the bandits and soon after it did, the riders headed north, no longer following the tracks, they simply found a hole in the fence and headed north. Everyone, especially the Banker looked shocked. The volunteer's hopes began to sink. They began to realize that the slight advantage that the train could have given them was disappearing into the sagebrush sea.

At the station in Golconda, the Banker and his horseless posse hopped a train and headed back to Winnemucca. Bige, too got off at this point as if to switch trains, but instead of hitting the cars headed back to Winnemucca, he slipped quietly through the crowd into the station and purchased himself a ticket to Elko. As he boarded that train he smiled. The four riders by now would be changing their exhausted colts. With no one really following them out of town, their lead would be substantial and if they kept moving at Ira's pace, there would make it safely home and there would never be a trace.

The robbers were riding faster than any of them had ever gone. Ira took the lead. True to the plan they headed east out of town so as to draw the train. When the train drew near, they headed north. About the time the colts were starting to play out, they were only a short distance from the first of their exchange corrals, north and east of Golconda on Evans Creek. Those little colts had played well their part: they had run fast and hard. At the corrals, acting on his experience from his pony express days, Ira told the men they had only two minutes to change horses and hit the trail hard again.

The four men had much incentive to make sure this getaway was successful. But even as they were hurrying they were steady in their preparation. These new horses were fresh and somewhat green too. Ira had chosen them carefully for their will and stamina. The men carefully tightened cinches after they set their saddles straight. A stop to retighten or reset could cost them precious getaway time. At this exchange they would leave those spent little colts and now would each have two horses apiece: one to ride and spare to travel. They also had two packhorses that would carry the stash and their gear. Back at the bank, more of the money was gold than they had anticipated. So here they roughly split the take just for travelling purposes. Tap ran his fingers through the gold coins in one of the bags just to hear that sweet tinkling sound of the pieces hitting together.

Tap was the first to get his new mount ready. He turned the Bankers colt loose in the sage and spent a few seconds scouting the southwest horizon for signs of a posse. He didn't see one but he was not willing to gamble that one wasn't coming. As soon as the others turned the colts loose and got mounted they hit the trail again fast and furiously. They headed north and east toward the town of Tuscarora. This leg of the journey would be fast but not as fast as the first.

They followed a wagon road to Evans Creek and later to Willow Creek. Later that night when they stopped near Tuscarora, Winnemucca would be nearly 100 miles behind them. As the day wore on they began to feel more confident that the Banker had been true to his word and steered the posse from them.

Now the sun was sinking fast in the western sky. September nights in this high desert chilled off fast. The horsemen were travelling more at a trot than a gallop allowing the horses to pick the best route. A stumble that might hurt or break an animal's leg would be a cost they could not afford. About the time they figured that they would have to stop for the darkening of the nighttime sky, much to their delight, a full yellow moon began to light the southeastern sky. It was as bright as a reading light. Tap and Jim remembered many years ago leaving New Mexico in a hurry just like tonight. A giant moon appeared in the night sky to aid their flight. The two men shared a laugh as the riders travelled on.

Sometime in the early morning hours, cold, beat and weary, they stopped for a very few winks of sleep. There were a few scrub trees near the creek. Here they used their lariats to make a rope corral for the horses. While the bedrolls felt good against the September's night chill, not a man even though weary slept well. As Ira closed his eyes his mind kept playing over and over in vivid colors the happenings of the day.

He had just participated in a bank robbery. Green Berry had told them about Sam Ketchum being shot, he had heard of others too killed as they robbed and plundered. But most of all, what would happen if Sarah found out? He examined some "what if" scenarios none of which had a pleasant ending.

"Well," he said out loud ..."She'll never find out!"

We won't get caught and neither she nor anyone else would ever find out,

"I will carry this secret to my grave," he looked up at the stars andvowed.

That thought spurred him out of his bedroll. The dawning early sun was starting to color the early morning sky. Ira was now fully awake and eager to get moving. He washed his face in the cold, cold creek water. It made him feel alive and focused. He filled every man's canteen and woke his fellow robbers. He winced at the thought of calling them that. He decided not to ever refer to them that way no matter how true it was.

"Let's get moving boys, we are burning daylight." He said. He handed each of them some of Sarah's jerked meat. "This ain't much," he said, "But tonight we can fill our belly at Dinner Station." Let's head out."

The horses were packed and saddled and ready to go in less than ten minutes. True to their word there was no grumbling or back talk to Ira's command. When he told them to get their horses and go...they did. Even though they were far from the bank and even though they hadn't, as of last night seen even a sign of the posse, not a man in the group wanted to be responsible for lagging behind. They all had wives, families, and yes, a certain standing in society. Not a one of them wanted to be caught.

They rode mostly at a rapid clip throughout the day. They traded the horse they rode for the spare every so often when Ira told them to. Even though the horses were in fact travelling, not carrying a man made a difference in that horses endurance.

Near evening the dusty crew wandered into Dinner Station.

Here they bought a place to sleep for the night in the barn and a warm meal. They chose to stay in the barn near their horses just in case they might need a fast getaway. They all thoroughly enjoyed the feeling of food in their stomachs. At this point in their journey they felt increasing assured that they were not being followed. So, this night bedded down in the Dinner Station barn with full bellies, they slept well. After two days of little sleep, fast riding and adrenaline pumping through their veins, yes they slept well.

But at the rising of the sun the men took the money from the saddle bags and divided Greenberry's split. He also added Bige's split to his saddlebags. The men took breakfast at the diner. Green Berry caught the early stage for Elko. His part of the plan now was to meet Bige at the train station and take the train back home to Knickerbocker, Texas.

Horseback, they were now three men travelling and anyone who might be looking for the bank robbers would be looking for four. That made them feel somewhat more at ease. It would be good for Bige and Green Berry too.

Tap, Ira and Jim headed north toward the town of Charleston. A few miles south of town however they headed over the big mountain and they dropped down into Mary's River. As the horses moved, sometimes the gold would make the sweetest tinkling sound as it rattled around in the bags. Jim smiled every time he heard it. This meant a whole new life, a whole new start for him and his darlin' wife Lizzie.

They camped that night on the banks of the Mary's river and early the next morning at the first light of dawn they headed up the steep mountain. The climb up to Hummingbird springs was steep and at times treacherous. The horses were sweating freely. Ira instructed them to climb for always then slow and turn the horse sideways to the path to let him catch his wind. That pace made for a slow ascent to the top but the horses made the tough steep trail that way. Everyone was extra glad for this morning's brisk September air. When they reached the top of the mountain they stopped at the spring to water the horses and let them rest.

Ira watered his horses and he also drank from the cool, crisp water in the springs. As he stood up he looked down the mountain. Oh, what a beautiful sight lay before him. Home. They still had a good twenty miles to go before they made it to Three Creeks. Fortunately it would all be downhill and much, much easier than the grueling and grinding ride of this morning.

He turned his view more toward the east and where his home lay. His thoughts drifted to his beautiful wife Sarah. He sure hoped that she and the kids were getting on well. He had been gone for a really long time both physically and mentally. As far as Sarah knew he was down on the desert running horses. What would she say when he returned again, busted, no horses, he wasn't sure. But he had to do this little deed for his brother Levi. She wouldn't understand but now it was almost over.

The ride north was easier than anyone had thought, it was if the mountain was welcoming them home and rolling them safely to the clutches of their families. Before they arrived at Jim's place they decided to stop at Faraday's place for a celebration drink. There were more people than usual at the store and all the place was buzzing about a ROBBERY. Ira's face paled white. Just this morning he had begun to feel they had safely conducted their doings, gotten away with it.

"How in the HELL do these people know?" he wondered. The men ordered their whiskey and sat down. As they drank, Tap asked the man near him what the noise was all about.

"You ain't heared?" He snorted. "Ole man Faraday was robbed in the middle of the night a while back." This man got more animated as he told the story. "A couple of men held him and his wife up at gunpoint scared the dirt right outta them. I hear now he wants to sell out. The men didn't get much money but took some hats and coats grub and course some whiskey."

Tap smiled and a visible relief washed over his face and that of Jim and Ira also. All three men enjoyed their whiskey more after that. Pretty soon they decided the time had come to be getting on home. Tap would be staying on a few more days with Jim and the sinking sun dictated that Ira too would stay one more night with Jim and Tap.

Early the next morning before he left, Ira looked seriously at Tap. "When you pass through Denver," he paused thinking how to put forth his meaning, "There was a beautiful blue dress at the Dry Goods store, years ago…"

He paused waiting to see if Tap knew what he was saying, "I meant to buy it for Sarah when we left but never did. Could you send one like it to me?" Tap studied his face to be sure he understood.

"From Denver ya mean?" He queried, then added,

"You have my word, my friend." He winked at Ira. Ira giggled his horse and headed east into the rising sun towards Sarah and his home.

Jim and Tap rested up the most of that day. They had been running on nerves and adrenaline for the last few days. Now that they were home they needed to make up for the stress and strain. Lizzie always a great host fed them a good dinner. When they finished and went out to look at the place that just a few years before, he and Ollie had called home, Tap told Jim he had the most ingenious idea ever.

"Jim I know how we can make this robbery cover our tracks from Winnemucca forever."

Jim was listening anxiously. Tap continued.

"Cassidy and his Wild Bunch have used my name to cover some of their deeds in the past. This time I am gonna use theirs to cover us. They owe it to me." He smiled that joking smile of his.

"Tonight," Jim, was getting more excited every word he spoke, "Tonight we are gonna take two of these $100 gold pieces and the money sack from the bank, we will leave it on the door to Faraday's store with a note. "

Around midnight, Jim and Tap snuck up to the store and nailed the sack and a note to the door.

The note read: Sorry for the scare old timer. We needed the grub and coats to get to Winnemucca. Hope this'll cover yer trouble. Til we meet again. Butch.

Tap nailed the note and the sack to the door. They headed back down the creek to Jim's place. Tap chuckled to himself all the way back and every time he thought of it for many days to come. He was tickled by his ingenious idea.

Jim and Tap snuck up to Faraday's store in the middle of the night. They left the money sack, $200 .00 and a note they hoped would cover their tracks forever from the bank robbery. The note read:

Sorry for the scare old man. We neeeded the grub,
coats and the money to get to Winnemucca.
Hope this will cover yer trouble. Til we meet again.

Butch

Covering their tracks.

Family Lore and Other Stories

As we have visited with cousins and others relatives of the Duncans we have begun to uncover some treasured stories. Talking with our friend and relative Tim Whitaker he related to us that he had always heard insinuations of a bank robbery at home but wasn't sure what it was all about until one day when he was sitting watching a show on tv at his grandmother's home. It seems that a group of kids from UNReno had proven that Butch Cassidy didn't rob the Winnemucca Bank, that they were Tipton Wyoming. Tim made the comment to his grandmother who was the wife of Byron Tellis Duncan. Taps daughter in law in other words. Tim innocently remarked to asking if she really thought that the Cassidy gang had robbed the bank. Tim said much to his chagrin, his grandmother came out of the kitchen hopped over the couch and got right in his face. She shook her finger close to his nose. "No matter what anyone ever says your great grandfather did not rob that bank." Quite bewildered Tim wondered what she meant but was too scared to ask. So he began listening and just being aware. He concluded that his great grandfather Tap Duncan did indeed, rob that bank.

In The Humboldt Historian by Lee Berk fall 1982 edition: Berk reports that George Nixon described in detail the three men who came in to the bank. "One of the robbers he said was about 5 feet 10 inches tall, had a dark complexion, a rather plump face and regular features and was clean shaven. (Green Berry Ketchum), the second was smaller man, perhaps 5'7 inches tall and weighed about 145 to 150 pounds. His hair was heavy and he wore a little reddish moustache which curled around his mouth, (Jim Duncan) His beard had a two week growth and he had a sandy complexion…other was perhaps 5'9 or 10" in height. He further described him as having a light complexion and a very scraggly and light faded beard which stood out all around from his ears down. Nixon at first thought it was false. The man had very small hands and they were freckled. His nose was fairly long but not roman. While emptying the gold from the counter till into the ore sack, he told Nixon he was lame in the hip. Was this man Butch Cassidy? Nixon said, "No!" For months, he referred to the leader of the bandits simply as "Whiskers."

Authors note: The Duncans were a family of light skinned and fair-haired people. He was for the most part of his life clean shaven. Although at times he did grow a mustache. Nixon did not describe the other two bank robbers because Bige spent the duration of the robbery outside the front door of the bank and Ira was in the bank holding the horses.

Authors note: In the Humboldt Historian by Lee Berk fall 1982 edition: Also states that "Word of the robbery was sent by telegraph to all the neighboring towns including Tuscarora, on the route the robbers were believed to have taken. Officers there were asked to organize a posse. A reply came back that the men would not start until their expenses were guaranteed. They were but by the time the posse formed, they were far behind in the chase."

The 'bank robbers'.

Chapter 31: Ira Returns Home

Ira left Jim and Tap early the next morning. He was anxious but apprehensive to return home. He missed his sweet wife and his children but wondered how he could convincingly explain to her that running horses with Tap was again a bust. Earlier this summer while they were planning the route to Winnemucca, they had used the excuse that they had gone running horses. Ira had told her that he had a new horse market possibility and he needed new horses to break.

Sarah in her dutiful and loving way had cooked him up some biscuits and jerked some beef to send with him. She also sent him some salt pork and beans and a bag of coffee. She was doing her part to make it easier for him.

When they rode the route down Tap told them that he had been many times to the rail head at Deeth to sell the Shoe Sole cattle. He thought they should take the O'Neil basin route. Ira had another route in mind and took him south of Jim's place. From there over the top to Hummingbird Springs, where they dropped down to the banks of the Mary's River and just kept following the creeks south and east to that little cow town called Winnemucca.

When Ira mentioned that he might be a little old for an undertaking such as this Tap told him that wisdom and wit of old age would trump the agility and enthusiasm of youth any day. If they planned this deed well they would be successful, Ira agreed careful planning would make it go a lot easier.

Sarah wasn't happy when they returned without horses. It was more out of concern for their family's wellbeing than Ira had realized at the time. Tap had spent several days with their family as they were planning their new business venture.

Now trotting along on the road back toward Butte, he realized that again was several short months later in the same spot. Returning home, empty handed after telling Sarah he had gone to gather horses.

As he rode along the road he was trying to construct in his mind what he was going to say to her. Just before he reached his yard, he saw his sons, Bert and Chet and his nephew (Levi's son) Ed coming down the road to greet him. As he watched Ed he thought about his brother Levi and the problems in Denver. Thinking on that gave him even more resolve that what he had just done was the right thing. Justice would be served maybe not by a judge but justice all the same.

"After Tap finishes in Denver, I won't have to worry so much about my family. Maybe I can even use my own name." He said out loud.

Most anything that was available the general population Ira was known as either A.H. Brackett or Alonzo. He had used this alias hoping that someday when that gambler sent folks after him, like they had done for Levi, unless they could recognize him, he would simply be known as Alonzo. His beard served to cover up a lot of the recognition and that boded well for him because he just hated to shave.

The boys were anxious to see the horses that Ira had gathered. He hated to lie to them but he reported to them that unfortunately, the horse herd, had either been all gathered or had moved on north to the Snake River.

Bert stood as tall and straight as he could before his father and told him that he would make a good hand on the next gather. After all he was fourteen and nearly grown. Ira ruffled the young man's hair and said he would have to think that one over.

Sarah and Inez were out in the garden picking the last of the vegetables. These September nights were getting nippy and a frost was sure to be here soon. Ira walked up behind his pretty wife and gathered her up in his arms. He pulled her close to him. She sent the kids off to milk the cow and finish the other chores.

She looked at him matter of factly. "I am glad to see you home Ira," I did miss you and the children missed you too. "She swallowed hard and continued, "What…no horses again?" There was an odd sounding tone to her voice. "Not even a sign," Ira said trying to sound convincing. Think they've all moved to the Snake for permanent.

"Ira," she said softly but in a queer tone. "Is it really horses you been a chasing?"

He looked at her for a long time not quite certain what she was asking. Finally he took her hand in his. "You Sarah, are my world" His eyes got very misty. Besides that Sarah, look at me, I am tired and filthy and I smell worse than a rattlesnake den."

"No other woman has ever even turned my head since I met you."

With the look he gave her, she knew that in this pledge of devotion to her, he was telling the truth.

So, satisfied that her marriage was okay, she pulled away from him then she added,

"I really don't want that Tap Duncan hanging around here anymore. I was glad when he left this country and I just wished he would stay gone, He is just bad news and he'll get you…us in trouble Ira."

With that comment Ira smiled at her.

"Sarah," he said, "I don't look to see Tap in this country much anymore. The wild horse trade in these parts seems played out. Those Wilkin's with the diamond brand seem to have captured anything that runs for their own herd. They are running from Bruneau across the desert up to the Wilkin's Island. As they move across from range to range they take it all…feed animals, everything."

She thought about what Ira said about the horses for a moment then switched her thoughts back to Tap.

"Well, I hope he doesn't come back ever!" She said.

Ira was actually relieved that Sarah might have thought he was chasing women he glad that was what she might have suspected of him instead of bank robbery.

Ira settled in at home and got to work taking care of all the things that he had let pile up all summer while he was working on the Winnemucca deal. He thought about how ironic it seemed that when most people thought about a life of crime they often referred to bank robbers as being too lazy to work. Truth be told Ira had never worked so hard on anything in his life, this deal had consumed his time resources and his abilities. But now he felt an odd sense of accomplishment but the worst part was he couldn't talk to anyone about it.

A few weeks after he had returned home. Sarah received a package at the Butte post office. She was curious as to who might send her a something. This package was wrapped in a brown paper and tied with a thin leather strap, knotted at the front.

The return address read, Tap Duncan, Denver.

She looked curiously at Ira and put the package down. Somehow seeing that the package was from Tap irritated her. Ira picked it up and told her if she wouldn't open it then he would. He too, was curious what might be inside. Sarah relented and took the package, she carefully cut the leather tie with Ira's knife. Pulling the paper back she couldn't believe her eyes, There folded neatly lay a beautiful blue dress, similar to the one she had seen in Denver many years ago at that dry goods store. Sarah's eyes filled with tears. A note lay on top of the dress.

She handed that to Ira. It read: The promise is kept. Tap.

Now Ira's eyes filled with tears. His worries would be over. No more worries about the Gambler from the Denver years coming to find him. It wouldn't bring his brother Levi back but it would make his world safer and more peaceful.

Sarah was so delighted with the dress that she seemed to change her heart about that Tap Duncan. She put her dress on and was spinning around watching the flow of the skirts.

"That Tap sure knows the way to a woman's heart," she remarked.

"Now, now just you wait a moment here!" Ira scoffed.

"It was my idea that he should send you the dress!" He smiled at her as she teasingly swirled in closer to him allowing the dress to brush against his legs.

She smiled and hugged herself closely as she admired her reflection. "Oh, Ira I just love it!"

In the spring of 1901, as the snow melted and it was time to move the sheep south to the mountain, Jim came to visit. Ira was glad for his company and Jim helped him take the stock to the to the spring range. It gave them a chance to visit as they rode.

Faraday's selling the store and Lizzy and I are buying it." Jim said.

"He's old and worn out and that robbery last fall just took the more than store goods it took the heart right outta him."

Jim mentioned Tap's note and that Faraday had gotten a lot of attention and fame over being robbed by "Butch."

Everyone had assumed that it was Butch Cassidy and the Sundance Kid that had done the robbing. News had travelled fast to Winnemucca and even to the Wild Bunch. Seems that they had even sent a picture of themselves to Nixon thanking him for the cash. Jim was impressed by Tap's genius in writing the note and their good fortune. Ira smiled at that thought. It felt good to have someone to talk to about the deeds they had done even if they didn't say that much.

Ira's thoughts drifted back to another note that Tap had written and what it meant to him for his brother Levi's sake and what the dress had meant to Sarah. This past winter it seemed that they had shared the best relationship since they had married. If Ira had known how much happiness that new dress would bring her he would have bought her several throughout the years.

Jim and Lizzie had gotten the mail contract and they were going to be in the merchant business.

"This really does give you and Lizzie a new lease on life," Ira said as he remembered how Jim he kept sharing his plans on the way home from Winnemucca.

"I am happy for you Jim!"

"Thanks" Jim said.

"But Ira, there's one thing I really need your help with, didn't you and your father build a stone jailhouse in Colorado?"

"Now that was a life time ago Jim," Ira replied.

Jim continued. "I want to move the store down the creek to my place Ira, That old log store's gonna burn one of these days, I want a sturdy stone store," Jim paused.

As Ira looked at him he seemed somehow younger than he had remembered maybe it was his fresh ideas, hope for the future.

"Would you help me build my stone store, Ira?"

Jim offered to pay well. Both men laughed at that. The Brackett boys, Bert and Chet now 12 and 14 were old enough to care for the home fires while Ira helped in the construction of the store.

Photo from shorpy.com. Jim and Lizzy Duncan's store and Post office in Three Creek. Lizzy was awarded the postal contract in May of 1901.

Jim and Lizzie Duncan's store in 2015. Photo compliments of Michelle Drumheller.

Chapter 32: The Texas Filly Comes to Town 1911

Ira helped Jim build a good and sturdy store. And life in Three Creeks resumed. Since Tap's ingenious note to Faraday it was widely accepted by the strong arm of the law and everyone else that the Wild Bunch had committed the robbery in Winnemucca. The Pinkerton detective agency added that robbery to the list of debauchery attributed to that gang.

And Green Berry, Bige, Jim, Tap and Ira, true to their pact never spoke a word of it. All the men returned to life as usual. Their ranches and businesses were prospering and their families were growing.

Last Christmas, Jim had sent a letter to his brother Bige in San Saba. He was so enthused with this new merchant business. In the last few years gold had been discovered just to the south and west and a new boom town called Jarbidge, Nevada had sprung up overnight. He mentioned that the gold strike had grown his business and enterprises substantially and he was looking for some help. Seems that he and Lizzie were overworked and it was taking a toll on their marriage.

Ora Lee Duncan Brackett.

When Bige read that Jim needed help it was like this letter was sent from on high. His younger daughter Ora Lee, now 19 years old was a spitfire. She was gorgeous and she loved to have fun.

She had been as of late, associating with some young men that Bige considered less than desirable, especially as candidates to be his son-in-law. She had heard about the escapades of her uncles (The Duncans and the Ketchums both), and she seemed to feel they had much glamour to their lives.

When Bige figured enough thaw had come to Three Creek that spring, he decided to take his little girl to Idaho to get her out of Texas. Jim had eagerly decided she would be great help at the store. There was a rail that ran now to Rogerson so they could take the train most of the way there. Bige and Ora were so impressed by the fancy buckboard that Jim drove to pick them up. Ora began warming to the idea of leaving Texas and her friends.

As they were crossing the Salmon, Jim pointed to the south and talked about the dam that was being constructed where the canyon narrowed.

"A reservoir for homesteading farmers' downstream," he said.

Bige remarked that soon this Wild West would be as populated as Texas. As they continued Jim suggested that they stop at Whiskey Slough to see their old friend Ira. Bige eagerly agreed.

Ira was so tickled to see his old friends. Especially so as Bige introduced his daughter. Immediately Ira thought to his son Bert and what a striking match these two might make. Ira asked if they planned to stay and Bige said he would be there until after the 4th of July but that Ora would be staying on with Jim and Lizzie.

The boys, Bert and Chet and Ed were all gone on a horse gathering trip with Tap. Seems that he had just purchased a substantial ranch in Arizona, Grass Springs[54] and was looking to stock it. While there were perhaps closer herds of wild horses, Tap knew this country like the back of his hand and if there were horses available, he knew how to get them. Especially so around Clover Creek where there were some small, dead end box type canyons where a guy could cut a set of horses from the larger herd and slow them long enough to convince them they didn't have to travel with the rest of the herd. In the open desert, young colts could run a man and a horse to death before you could get them settled to head a new direction. Before the turn of the century, catching and breaking these wild horses had been a major part of Tap and Ira's income. It didn't seem quite fair that when the Wilkins moved in they had taken all the horses. When

---

[54] In 1904 Tap purchased the Hookedy H ranch in Hackberry, Arizona. Then in 1901. He sold those holdings and purchased the Grass Springs ranch from the widow of Wellington Starkey. He changed the name of the ranch from Grass Springs to the Diamond Bar as the Diamond was the brand that the ranch held.

Tap and Ira had harvested the wild bunch they took a few but always left some too.

Several people spoke of the horses that still ran free farther north and east all the way along the Snake River from Glenns Ferry to Hagerman. From Arizona, Tap brought up a crew including some of his nephews and he had every intention of taking some of these wild Idaho horses back to his Ranch. They had stopped by Ira's place for a visit and Tap had invited him along. Ira however had a new enterprise going. He was supplying meat and fruit to the dam builders and he had negotiations to complete. He did however, agree to let his boys go along.

It took two days heading mostly north and west to arrive at the banks of the Snake River. They camped there that night. Chet was amazed at the size of that river. He hadn't known there was that much water in all the state of Idaho. They didn't break camp until the sun was well up that next morning. Tap said this was the waiting part. They did pack their gear and have their horses ready for a later time that morning.

When the sun seemed high, probably near noon, true to the legends that he had heard they watched as massive droves of horses began pouring off the hillside and down to the river to water. It was a magnificent sight.

As a group of horses watered and began making their way up the hillside to graze, Tap and his boys tried to haze a group of them to the west. Tap hoped that the sheer number of cowboys would be enough to convince the horses to head where they wanted them to go. Without a natural corral Tap had realized this was a gamble but he was willing to try. They would just start to get a group headed to run fast and hard. And just as they would think they had them, the colts would bust away with the mares following close behind. They would head in all directions. As one cowboy would break out to bring a horse back, another would bust back. The riders tried all day to get some horses headed out. It seemed as if the horses had a plan: If those humans come near scatter then see if they can catch you.

After a few days of this failure Tap finally called the boys off and they set camp for the night. That evening a few men rode up to their camp. They too had been running horses and were headed back to Bruneau. One man recognized Tap.

Tap originally hadn't planned to spend much time in this country and now a man from these parts had seen him. He didn't want anyone to know he was in these parts especially not the kin of the man he had shot.

He made the hard decision that he needed to get on south away from this country. They traveled that day back toward Clover Creek. Tap was not happy. He needed horses for his ranch but needed to stay alive more. That night they camped in one of those box type canyons.

Early the next morning, Tap woke to the sound of horses' hooves in the camp. Panicked, he rose quickly, thinking that their horses had escaped the lariat corral his men had set. Tap pulled his boots on and ran over to the man who was night watch for the mounts. Their horses were all ok. Seems that sometime during the night, they had drawn in a herd of horses traveling the desert.

The dawning of the sun colored the sky just pink enough for him to make out the shadows of about 200 head of horses. Tap began to chuckle.

"If I was a praying man, I would just have to say thank you." Tap woke his men. He told them quietly but quickly saddle up. His plan was to make a circle north of the horses. Because they would take the whole of this herd they could avoid the horse races and busts of the previous days. They would need a couple of their fastest and most agile cowboys in the lead to keep the leaders headed south and the rest would form a corral to follow up behind.

Tap's men were mounted and ready to go in mere minutes. The excitement of finding these horses fueled their hopes especially since just yesterday, the thought returning to Arizona busted was a real possibility. The cowboys surrounded the herd and headed them south and east.

As the sun began to light the desert, Tap began to realize that these horses carried a brand. A diamond in fact. How easily they would fit in at the diamond bar ranch, he smiled. Tap didn't say anything to his crew. They just kept moving. Tap began to think about how he and Ira had gathered horses here on this very desert. Those horses that they gathered broke and sold were sometimes the difference in lean and prosperous years. They never took more of the horse herd than they needed or could put to good use, leaving some for others and seed for the next year. When Wilkins began sweeping the desert clean as they moved their herd Tap and Ira both had find ways to make up for the lost income in those years.

Tap kept the herd moving as quickly as he could. By the time the herd reached the big corrals at Smith's Crossing on Big Flat Creek, night was settling in. There the crew and the horses spent the night. Early the next morning they headed the horses east until they hit the big springs at the head of Antelope Creek. The herd was traveling fast and every so often, one of the younger cowboys would rope a new mount and break him to ride simply and buck him out and get him ready to carry another cowboy. It would be a long trip back to Arizona and they would need a lot of fresh fast horses to keep up with this herd.

Near Whiskey Slough, Bert, Chet and Ed headed for home. Tap promised to send them their pay from his Diamond Bar Ranch in Arizona when he returned. Bert said he guessed the money would be great but honestly for him this trip was the most fun he had ever had. With a chuckle, Tap and his men headed south, across the Salmon, past the San Jacinto and the Boar's Nest. Always south, these horses were headed to Arizona.

Chet, however, was more than a little confused. He could read a brand too. He knew those horses weren't wild. He had just participated in horse thievery. "I think they hang guys for that!" he thought. They had just stolen thousands of dollars in horse flesh and now Tap wants to send us a week's worth of cowboy's wages. Chet was disgusted thoroughly. Through family legends he had heard of Tap and he knew his mom didn't like him. Now he knew for himself what a rascal he was.

At home, Ira was glad to see his boys. He had in fact missed their help. A few weeks later he announced to them that there would be a family vacation this year. Things were looking good. The contract had been signed and he was selling beef and fruit to the dam builders and at a good price too. Years ago, when Sarah sent to Colorado to get those trees, Ira thought that she had gotten too many. She spent so many hours laboring over them, pruning, watering and harvesting and canning. This year he would have to apologize to her. Their fruit was worth twice as much as his beef. The men building the dam would buy all the fruit he could produce. They had given Ira 16 cents a pound for the plums and they would receive only 8 cents a pound for his beef. The spring had been wet and without frost. Things looked good for a bumper crop.

There was to be in the new boom town of Jarbidge a huge Fourth of July celebration. Back in Denver there had always been a celebration for the nation's birth. Ira was glad to be able to take his family to attend a celebration. It would be their first ever. Jim and Lizzie and their pretty niece from Texas would be there too.

Chapter 33: The Fourth of July

Ora Lee had settled in at her Uncle Jim and Aunt Lizzie's place. She was surprised at how well she liked life at the store. With the mining activity at Jarbidge there was a constant stream of customers at their establishment.

Actually there was more interaction with people than she had ever had in Texas. And at this time in her life that was something she enjoyed. The weather here was cooler than in Texas and that too suited her just fine. She kept busy helping Lizzie sort mail and they had even begun serving some meals. Bige, her dad, and Uncle Jim were really enjoying their time together. They were working on building a new horse corral behind the store.

In late June, Jim announced that the store was to be closed for a couple days the first part of July. There was to be a huge celebration in the boom town of Jarbidge and they would travel there and be a part of it. Ora was so excited. She had watched the young men who stopped at the store on their way through to Jarbidge. There were definitely a few she wouldn't mind seeing again.

She spent the next few days sorting through her clothes trying to decide on just the right dress to wear. The morning came to head south to Jarbidge. Jim loaded up in the buckboard. They took bed rolls. They would be camping out. Most of the residents of Jarbidge lived in tents.

Buildings had been built but land was scarce and there would not be rooms to rent. The drive over the island was like nothing Ora had ever experienced ever. This country sure wasn't Texas. In Jarbidge, they pulled up to a spot just north of town and decided to make camp. Late afternoon was now upon them and the barbeque would start soon.

Lizzie helped Ora lace her corset and get her dress on. Just up the canyon from their camp, another young lady Ora had befriended at Three Creek was camped. Ora asked if it was ok if she went to find Vada, her friend. She promised to meet up with her kin at the barbeque later. She was glad when the sun began to set low against the canyon walls and the air began to cool. Sporting a dress wasn't entirely to her liking but for such an occasion as this it was entirely appropriate. She soon found her friend and the short walk to the bustling town was a lot more fun in the company of another young lady. They watched handsome young cowboys as they traveled the streets and young children as they played. The food at the barbeque was great.

As the sunlight completely faded, several bonfires burned in the streets and lanterns were lit outside the buildings and the tents lining the main street. A band struck up and Ora made the comment that she would like to hear a type of music from her home. Vada told her to just wait. As soon as one band tired another would strike up. A street dance was in full swing. Suddenly Vada stopped what she was saying.

"Oh my gosh, Ora," she turned to face her.

"There he is." she whispered excitedly. She grabbed Ora's arm. "I look okay, right?" She asked.

Vada had seen this young man on various occasions in Three Creek and thought he was the most handsome guy she had ever seen. Ora looked at him curiously. He was indeed handsome but standing next to him was the cowboy who caught her eye.

"Vada" she said. "You can have him," her voice trailed off, "but that one's mine," as she said that she pointed at Bert[55].

About that time the cowboys saw her gesture their way. The girls were a little embarrassed but they smiled sweetly.

"They are coming over here." Ora said.

Vada's young man did ask her to dance and that left Ora and Bert alone. Bert seemed to fumble over his words. He wasn't sure if he should take his hat off when he spoke to her. Finally he just took a deep breath and asked her to dance. They danced and they danced some more.

When Ora told him that she was from Texas he asked if she knew Jim and Lizzie Duncan. Their conversation began to roll from there. They spoke of common interests and common people, and pretty soon they were talking as if they had grown up together. He told her about running horses with her Uncle Tap only weeks before and that he had met her brother

---

[55] This story must have made an impression on many of Ora's family. This story was written in Uncle Chet's writings but also was related to us by Ann (Brackett) Gilbert and also Ronda (Patrick) McCaw, grandchildren of Ora and Bert

Loys Boy on the gather. He left out the stealing the horses part, hoping she would know. After the fireworks show, Bert walked Ora back to her campsite. She shivered in the cool mountain air and Bert quickly took his own coat off and placed it around her shoulders.

"You are quite the gentleman, aren't you Bert Brackett." He liked the way she said his name and the teasing in her voice.

They could have kept on talking 'til the sun rose again but that just wouldn't have been appropriate. Agreeing to meet for breakfast the next morning, Bert left for his own campsite. Jim, Lizzie and Bige could see the huge smile on her face even in the campfire glow.

The next morning their camps were pulled early. Ora had met Bert at the breakfast and he had asked her to accompany him in his buckboard back to Three Creek. Last night when he returned to camp he told his dad that he had met a beautiful young lady and she was staying with Jim and Lizzie Duncan. She was helping at the store and oh was she beautiful. Bert wondered if he could take the wagon and the fancy black team and escort her to her home. Ira smiled when he remembered meeting this Ora. She was beautiful and he had immediately matched her with his son. Without mentioning that thought they seemed to be on the same path.

So Bert drove up to Ora's camp with the fanciest set of black horses she had ever seen. Ira's one indulgence was that he drove fancy wagons with even fancier high stepping horses. The two young folk headed up and over the top of Wilkin's Island and on over to Three Creek. Ora was impressed with the gentle but strong way he handled the reins and the horses. The horses seemed to understand his commands and respond quickly. The trip to the store seemed to end all too quickly. Bert helped her carry her things to the house and then just seemed to linger a little longer. He liked the sweet way she smelled. Soon Ira and the rest of the family pulled up. He told Bert they had best get a move on to make it home by nightfall. He asked Ora when he could see her again.

She just smiled and said, "Soon I hope."

Jim and his crew arrived shortly afterward. Bige needed to catch the train tomorrow to return to Texas so after dinner that night he asked Ora to go walking with him. He asked her if she would like to stay on in this country.

"I would like that very much, Pa," she said.

She smiled warmly. Bige had seen that look on his own Nancy Blake's face before they married and on the faces of the other girls as their time for love had come.

There was an uneasy silence then she swallowed hard and said, "I, uh I think he's the one Pa."

Bige stopped short. She had only met this fellow days before. True, he himself liked the idea of having them together but marriage, and so quickly?

"I'm gonna have to talk to that young man then." he said.

Ora grabbed her father's arm "Uhh. You can't do that. Pa. He, he doesn't know we are getting married yet, not yet anyway."

Bige laughed. "My dear beautiful Ora you have always been strong willed and what you have wanted you have gotten. Maybe, I should warn him before I leave!" He laughed and so did she.

He pulled her tight and hugged her.

"I am happy for you baby but I am sure gonna miss you." The cracking of his voice made tears come to her eyes. He continued. "I worry about leaving you here but with your Uncle Jim well you are blood and he always cares for his own, and from what you are telling me now, you'll be alright. However." he stopped and pulled something out of his coat pocket. "I want you to have this," he said. He handed her a small carry pistol nestled in a leather sheath.

"What with coyotes and rattlesnakes both the human and the animal kind, a pretty girl like you needs an equalizer." He swallowed hard like he was trying to fight back the tears. "Hope you never have to use it."

Ora hugged him. "I will be okay Pa, but I am sure gonna miss you."

Picture of Uncle Chet and Loys Boy Duncan also our uncle.

Chapter 34: Courting the Texas Filly

It had been nearly a week since the 4th of July and Bert had been busy helping his father at the ranch. Some of the fruit had already begun to ripen and had to be picked and delivered to the dam site. When the last of the first crop was delivered he asked his father if he could take the fancy buck board and go to Three Creek on Sunday. Ira knew he shouldn't ask why but couldn't resist seeing his son blush.

Truthfully, Ira had wondered if the romance was off but he could quickly see by Bert's reaction that it was still hot. When Saturday night bath time came around Chet thought that Bert spent longer than usual getting clean When Chet teased him about getting all clean for a girl he just told him he wished he was so lucky. Chet very truthfully thought "Yeah, you are right."

Ira got up early the next morning to help Bert hitch up the black team. When Bert arrived at the store, Ora was surprised, pleasantly, to see him.

"Beginning to think you'd forgotten me Bert Brackett." she smiled.

He took his hat off his head trying to remember his manners. Holding it to his chest he asked her to go riding with him. She glanced at the chores she needed to finish and then to her Aunt Lizzie. Fond of young love herself, Lizzie told her to go but to pack a picnic from the kitchen. They rode in the wagon looking for a good spot to share that picnic. It didn't take Bert a week before the next time he came to call on his pretty Texas filly.

Later that fall, they attended several dances at Rogerson. After one dance, as Bert was driving her home, they were quietly riding along listening to the clop of the horses' hooves as they pulled along. Bert pulled the horses up.

He looked at her and said, "You know Ora, you'd do a lot better coming home with me and raising kids and horses than sorting mail and selling groceries."

She looked at him for a long time. Then she began, "Well not until after you ask me to marry you Bert."

Bert was fumbling so terribly with his words. He was holding his hat to his chest, he looked so humble. He swallowed hard and said, "I thought that was what I was asking you, Ora."

She smiled. "Oh," she said.

He waited for more of a response and didn't get one, so he gigged up the team and drove on. He felt so bad, he wanted this to be just right and he was sure he had messed it up. Why didn't she want to marry him? He was sure she liked him. The horses traveled on about a mile or so. Ora then knew she had waited long enough. She thought she saw his striking blue eyes begin to tear up. I better respond she thought, before he changes his mind. Ora then reached up and put her soft hand on his as he held the reins.

She looked at him, "Okay," she smiled. "Okay."

When Bert returned home that day he met his father at the Cedar Creek. From the smile on the young man's face his dad knew this hadn't been just an ordinary dance. Bert told him what he had been feeling for Ora and how he felt bad that courting her had taken so much of his time.

"It's like this unseen force is just drawing me to her, Dad, I think about her all the time."

Ira smiled at Bert's words. He thought back to his courtship days with that lovely Miss Sarah when his colts seemed of their own accord to travel by the Mauldin place. And Ira shared that with him.

"Dad," he said. "I asked her to marry me." This time those blue, blue eyes of Bert's did fill with tears. But so did those of Ira.

"Well son, this is a good start."

Through the next months as the wedding plans were made, Ira told Bert that since he and Sarah were spending more time at Cedar Creek, Whiskey Slough should make a good home for the newlyweds. A few days later when Bert was at the Three Creek store to pick up Ora for a date, he was waiting outside for her. He began looking at the outside of the store and he marveled at how well the stones were fitted together. It occurred to him that Ira had built this stone store using the stone mason skills that he learned from Grandpa Ozro. Bert remarked to himself that the store seemed put together more solidly than any building he had ever seen. Then a thought came to him, sort of like a whisper from on high, from his grandpa.

"Build a house for her." He felt those words more than heard them.

Bert was filled with emotion. He had to quickly compose himself when she came out the door.

"Let's go riding," she smiled and hopped in the wagon seat.

Wherever you go I will go, wherever you lodge I will lodge.

Your people will be my people And your God will be my God.

Ruth 1:16

Bert and Ora take a ride.

When Bert returned home he stopped off to see his dad first. He found him out feeding.

"Dad," Bert began, "I uh I want to build a good solid house for a good solid marriage." He blurted it out quickly so he wouldn't change his mind.

"You were always the most sentimental of the kids, you know." His father said.

Bert explained what had happened earlier that day at the store and what he had felt. As he heard the story, Ira knew that he had no choice but to help Bert build a house.

"Your grandpa wants us to do this," he said.

A few days later they all met at Whiskey Slough and picked a place close to the fruit trees that Sarah had planted years before. Father and son worked together on constructing a solid rock home. Ira decided that if they put a lot of time and effort on this project, it could be a honeymoon home for his son and new daughter-in-law come the third of February.

Picture of rock house, the honeymoon house that Bert built for his bride, with the help of his father, Ira. Courtesy Ronda McCaw

Photo of Ora Lee and Bert Brackett

Chapter 35: Tick Fever

With Bert and Ora starting a family and living at Whiskey Slough, Ira and Sarah settled into their lives at Cedar Creek. He continued running sheep and cattle up on the mountain to the south of them. Even though he was getting on in age, he still enjoyed working with wild horses. He would do much of the ground work but depended on Chet and Bert to do much of the riding. It was still a matter of pride with him that he have the best looking team in the country.

Ira gets tick fever.

About 1919 word came to Ira that a reputable sheep breeder from Montana was coming to town. Because he was constantly on the lookout for ways to improve his herds and flocks Ira hitched up his team and drove to Rogerson. The train the sheep man was riding in on was late so Ira busied himself buying the supplies he needed for the ranch. Ira determined he wanted to meet with this sheep man. The train did arrive later and Ira got a good look at the information on this new bloodline that he was considering for his flock. Ira was eager and he agreed to buy a couple rams and a few ewes. They shook on the deal and the sheep man departed.

Upon leaving the hotel, Ira was a bit concerned at the lateness of the afternoon. His concern increased as he reached the springs they call Antelope and a heavy rain began to fall. He had his usual high stepping black geldings that ate up the miles so he was sure he'd make it home before too much storm settled in. But as the wind carried the black clouds straight overhead and the thunder began to roll around him he knew he was not gonna beat this storm it was just moving too fast.

Now the occasional flash of lightning seemed to strike ever closer to him. It was almost completely dark when he pulled up to the gate about a half mile from home. As he pulled the team up, he carefully tied the reins to the wagon brake handle and got off the wagon to open it up. As he opened the gate and turned to head back toward the wagon, a huge flash of lightning struck the fence not 20 yards away.

Ira watched the icy blue flash travel down the length of the wire until it hit the nearest wooden post to which the wire was tied. The thunder clapped at almost the same instant that he saw the flash. His team already skittish from the now nighttime blackness, spooked and bolted forward knocking him to the ground. As they did they pulled the heavily loaded wagon over his leg. The wagon headed down the road and toward the house, without him.

He lay there in the mud and rain for a few moments, then he began to shiver.

"I guess I am still alive," he said out loud.

As he tried to get up his one leg gave way underneath him. He now realized that he was in a bad, bad way. At first he thought to wait and hope that Chet would come to look for him or wait until morning, when someone would see his renegade team and come looking for him.

But as he lay there in the cold wet rain and that even colder mud, he realized that if he stayed there, he probably wouldn't live that long.

He decided there was nothing other to do than to crawl back to his house. Crawling on the ground soaked him to the bone. But between the shock of breaking his leg and the tremendous exertion it required to pull his body closer to his home, he thought he was warm.

At long last he made it. Their old cow dog Jack, growled and barked warningly at the approaching sight, until he recognized it was Ira out there in the dark. With his last bit of strength, he crawled up on the porch and began banging on the door. Sarah and Chet both came out. They immediately drug him in the house and cleaned him up. They put dry clothes on his except for his pants, which they cut off of him. Chet headed to Rogerson to fetch the doctor. Even though he did reset that leg, it never healed properly and he never really recovered.

The sheep did arrive and in the spring, Ira and Chet were working them. Ira was excited to see how the new lamb crop would bring. A few days later, while they were out choring, Ira excused himself from the corrals. He said he really needed to go lay down and rest for just a little while. Chet noticed that his dad's hands and arm were red and spotted but he thought it was just from working in the cold of the spring day.

That evening however, Sarah realized that there was more wrong with her husband than just being tired. He had a terrible rash on his hands and feet and it was growing up his extremities. For all that night she sat up with him. She put a wet cloth on his forehead to try to break his fever. At the crack of dawn, Chet took a fast horse and again headed to Rogerson to fetch the doctor.

When the doctor arrived, he took one look at Ira and knew the prognosis…and it wasn't good. Ira had Rocky Mountain spotted fever. Recently the doctor had attended a conference talking about this disease, this Tick Fever. It was most common in the sheep country of Montana and he wondered if Ira had maybe been there.

"No," Sarah replied, but he has bought some sheep from there.

The doctor said that unfortunately there wasn't a cure yet for this sort of thing. Ira could perhaps recover, but most likely it would be just a matter of days before he died. Sarah felt so sick inside.

What would she do without her Ira? They had lived so much life together and what an adventure it had been. Yes, the boys now grown men would be able to manage the ranch but for her personally, she wondered how could she live without him, he was her anchor in life. The doctor gave him some medicine mostly a pain killer to try to make him comfortable. He said that whiskey might be better. But he would give them all the help he could.

The next few days, Ira slept some but mostly just want Chet to sit with him. Sarah tried to keep herself busy with her house work and chores. She left it to Chet to try to keep his father comfortable. He would give him the whiskey when he would ball up in pain. As they sat Chet told his dad that he had something that he wanted to get off his chest.

Ira said, "Well son, we're a talkin', let's have it."

Chet asked him to recall when they sold the fruit to the dam builders then he continued,

"You were busy but you let us boys go with Tap to round up horses you remember?" Chet swallowed hard. Ira smiled by looked curiously at his son. No telling what he had to say if it involved his friend Tap.

Chet continued. "I, uhh…we helped him steal a bunch of branded horses, Wilkin's horses,"

Chet blurted it out quickly before he got scared and changed his mind. He hated keeping that secret. In the first place it was something that he wasn't willingly in on. Chet was scared of what his dad might say but he felt surprisingly good, after saying it, like a huge burden was lifting off his shoulders.

Ira, seeing Chet's angst, patted his son's leg with his feeble spotted hand. He seemed lost in his own thoughts for a long time, actually long enough that Chet was afraid his father hadn't heard him or that the shock of Chet stealing horses finished him off.

Finally, Ira cleared his throat, he took a very long sip from the whiskey bottle and sighed.

"Son," he smiled, "Let me tell you a thing or two about that Tap Duncan!"

Ira spoke of leaving Denver and the fear he felt for his family. He talked of hiding out and worrying that the Denver crew might find them. And do to him or his family just like they had done to Levi. When he came to the part, later about the bank robbery in Winnemucca, he made Chet promise to carry that secret to his grave.

"Your mother doesn't know and she can't EVER! You hear me? I want her to still love me even after I die." He got real sad and added, "Keeping these things from her has been hard on me, hard on our marriage."

"Son," he said, "I have tried to do things straight." He paused. "I wouldn't take the money from that robbery, but Tap made me an offer worth more to me than gold."

Chet tried not to show the shock on his face as his father told him that Tap had cleaned up the streets of Arvada. (Denver) That was his price for handling the getaway horses. Chet thought on his own brother and all the siblings that the family had called their own. His mom's siblings, his Uncle Levi's kids and Inez's kids and Bert's too however they didn't live with them.

The tales of Ira's contact with that Tap Duncan made simple horse theft seem like child's play. He wondered if it was the whiskey or maybe the fever that loosened his dad's tongue, but either way, it truly was no wonder that his mom didn't want that Tap hanging around. Chet knew how much better he felt after telling his dad his secret about stealing those horses, he hoped his dad felt better after telling him about his.

Chet sat at his father's side for the next few days. When visitors came to call he would leave his father's side long enough to let them visit but would then return. He never tired of hearing his father's tales of life, a grand life lived.

Somewhere in the night on the 28th of March, dad just silently slipped away. At another time in his life a simple tick bite might have caused him to feel sick, but because his system was weakened by trying to heal from his broken leg, the chill and stress he suffered from the crawl, the bite this time was deadly. He was the first known to succumb to this disease in this part of the country.

The lifelong friendship of Tap and Ira did finally result in them becoming "Kin" as taps niece Ora Lee was espoused to Ira's son Bert in 1912.

Chapter 36: Cleaning the Streets of Denver

It was back in 1900 that Tap had gone to Denver to pay his debt to Ira. Only one person knew Tap had gone there, and that person did not, did not want to know the details of the visit.

An old man shuffled quietly down the hall from the saloon/ gambling hall to the luxury hotel that was his home. Though he was indoors, he was impeccably dressed. His fawn colored hat nearly new, was perfectly creased, not a speck of dust, nor was there any other imperfection to marr it. His black pin striped suit was perfectly tailored to fit his misshapen figure. No amount of tailoring however, could cover the damage that had been done to his broken body. He walked with a limp, to his room and looked around. Out of habit, he checked to be sure that no one was watching. He pulled the key to his room out of his pocket, started to put the key in the lock, and then realized that the door was unlocked. With a concerned but somewhat irritated look on his face, he pushed the door open. He went in and looked warily around.

Not seeing anyone, he called for Darcy.

Darcy was a pretty 19 year old girl, his latest romantic conquest. She had never been inside of a saloon, when the gambler had first seen her. He had been out collecting on his debts.

Much money was owed to him by various merchants, (a toll he called it) for the pleasure of doing business in his fair city. Her father was behind on his toll and the gambler said it was time to collect. As he eyed Darcy's trim little figure and her pretty face he decided that the toll could be up for trade.

Her father had said no! Not his daughter! But by the time the Gambler's business managers had explained what would happen to the merchant and the rest his family if Darcy did not come to work for the Gambler, as his personal secretary, Well, Miss Darcy was practically begging to come down to the gambling hall.

Now in his room and not seeing or hearing anything out of the ordinary. The Gambler hurried over to his wall safe. He opened it and looked inside to make sure nothing was missing. As he was finishing the count of a large stack of bills, he sighed out loud. He sat down heavily on the bed. He leaned back against the pillows. And he began to relax, he looked over and saw a pair of boots behind a window curtain. Quickly as he could, he opened his desk drawer and pulled out a small pistol.

Somewhat startled he said, "I have got you covered with a gun. So whoever you are, come on out. Come out now, or I'll shoot you through the curtain."

A tall, muscular cowboy, Tap Duncan, stepped into the room. He looked at the crippled old man and nearly had compassion for him. Then Tap shook his head as if to scare those thoughts from entering the recesses of his mind.

He looked squarely into the eyes of the Gambler and asked, "Do you remember me"?

The Gambler replied with more than a little irritation in his voice, said, "No, I don't remember every two bit cowboy that comes through here, get out before I shoot you."

Tap smiled and spat tobacco on the floor. Then he asked, "Well, then do you remember a little horse wrangler from Cherry Creek? Ira Brackett?"

Anger seemed to cut the air in the room like lightening.

"Do I remember him?" The Gambler's voice seemed to squeak a little.

"Yes, I remember him … with every step I take, with every breath I take, and every damn time I try to pick up a deck of cards. He held up his broken and crooked hands.

"Yes I remember him! If you are here to collect the reward for killing him, you will have to give me proof that he is dead, and I want proof that you are the one who killed him. Something like his head on a platter."

He tried to catch his breath.

"After you give me the proof and I will check it out." He said.

The gambler wiped the sweat that was forming on his brow with the covers from the bed. Then he continued.

"If he is dead and if you have proof that you did it, and it checks out, THEN you will get your reward. Now give me the proof and get out of here and let me have some peace and quiet."

Tap smiled at the wretched man in front of him. The compassion that he had fleetingly felt was erased by the Gambler's despicable arrogance. Tap smiled slightly at the old man.

"Ira, that little horse wrangler, is my friend." Tap began. "And I need you not to bother him or his again."

"Or you're going to what?" The Gambler sneered.

Then he continued, trying to cover his fear with strong words. "Get out of here or I will shoot you and get you thrown in jail for breaking in here and threatening me."

"Now get out."

He might have sounded quite commanding at another time but the sweat on his face and the squeak in his voice really betrayed his confidence.

Tap started walking towards the Gambler. The Gambler pointed his pistol at Tap's chest. His crooked hands fumbled but he managed to pull the trigger. Tap continued walking towards the Gambler with a pillow in his hand. Again and again the Gambler pulled the trigger. Realizing his gun was useless the Gambler started to yell for help. His cry for help was cut short by the heavy pillow pressed against his face.

After a brief struggle, the Gambler lay quietly. For several minutes more Tap kept the pillow in place over the Gambler's head. As he looked at the lifeless body on the bed, Tap began to think about Ira.

"This won't be bringing Levi back, but Ira," Tap whispered, "He won't be bothering any of yours ever again!"

Tap swallowed hard.

As he turned to leave Tap smiled. That open wall safe contained a rather large stack of bills.

"You know there is a bunch of orphans from down at Cherry Creek that could use this money." He said out loud.

Tap walked to the safe and feathered the stack of money. With a quiet nod he pockets the money and slipped into the night.

He spent several more days in Denver just listening and looking.

Several days later in The Bucket of Blood saloon on the wrong side of town a couple of "wannabe" toughs sit drinking. They are lamenting that fact that it's hard to make a living. "Putting muscle on people and roughing them up doesn't pay as well as it used to." One complains to the other. "These days it seems that the new sheriff is always on our asses."

One of the toughs slams his glass down hard on the bar displaying his irritation about the deputies who always seem to be hounding them.

A well-dressed Tap pushes open the swinging doors to the dark and dirty bar. He looks out of place in this dingy hole. He paused for a moment allowing his eyes to adjust to the dim light. He finds a quiet table in the back and orders himself a drink and a meal.

After looking him over for a few minutes one of the toughs goes over to his table and sits down.

The tough looks him over, "You're a stranger to these parts ain't ya?"

Tap wiped the man's splashing saliva off his cheek and continues to eat his meal as the wannabe slid his chair nearer to his own.

"Buy me a drink and I'll give you some advice." Tap smiled.

He thought about how this man reminded him of the scrawny, mangy dogs that guarded the alley near this hole.

He could hear his thoughts say, "Advice from you?"

He swallowed hard to stifle the laugh and coolly, Tap said, "Advice I can use but what about your friend over there?"

Taking that as an invitation the man signals for his friend to join him at Tap's table.

The two Toughs alternate between threatening Tap and bragging about how they run this part of town, how they enforce their law on the people of the area. As their talk flowed Tap kept the whiskey coming. The Toughs continued to drink the free drinks, eat a good meal, and brag to the stranger of some of the deeds they have done. Tap smiles and pretended to be intrigued by the tales they tell.

Finally when they begin to tell the story about nearly being caught for knocking off a dumb dirt farmer a few years back. Tap began to smile. He knew that he had found the vermin who actually killed Ira's brother Levi.

They told how they had been arrested and had to scramble to call in a bunch of favors to get off. Tap was now getting bored with their bragging and disgusted with their arrogance. But every time he started to get up and leave, they told him to sit down, and buy them another drink.

The Tough with the biggest mouth pulled at Tap's jacket to make him sit back down. Tap swallowed hard, and fingered the colt pistol that hung at his side. Then took a deep breath and sat back down. Stick to the plan he muttered to himself.

As he sat down the Tough said, "It would be unhealthy to leave just yet. This, my friend is a bad part of town. A feller might get hurt if he went out on the street."

The hair on the back of Tap's neck bristled at this man calling him "Friend."

At long last Tap decided that it was very late he must be going.

Bidding them good night, he reached under the table and pulled out a bottle of very fine whiskey as a parting gift for them. Being assured of plenty to drink for the rest of the evening they wish him good night. They tell Tap that they plan to see him the next day. He smiles and laughs audibly.

"You betcha. My friends," Tap says.

At the door Tap looks back, and with a smile, he tips his hat to them. They wave him off, they don't need him anymore, and they have plenty to drink. They continue to drink, play cards and talk of what they would do next. Suddenly, one of them feels a twist in his gut, it feels like someone has reached inside him is trying to tear him apart. He has spasms and falls out of his chair to the floor. There, he twists and turns, kicking wildly.

His companion at first at first laughed at him, tells him to quit acting stupid and get up. Then concern reaches his befuddled drunken mind.

He calls for help, "Someone, get a doctor for my friend. " He yelled again and again.

About this time the second man grabs his stomach. He too, falls down and thrashes around much like his companion had. By the time a doctor is gotten out of bed and brought to the saloon both men are dead.

The doctor looks them over, says he will have to look at them the next day to be sure, but, "It sure looks to me that they got into some bad whiskey." The doctor said.

The barkeep looks at the bottle, "This is not one of mine." He says as he tosses it on the one man's back." The he added,

"These two were all the time coming in and buying a few drinks and then drinking their private stash the rest of the night."

He was so concerned that he not be blamed for the bad whisky that he forgot all about the stranger that had been with them earlier. Later that evening the sheriff came. He looked at the men, the strange whiskey bottle, and listened to the barkeep and the doctor.

"Let's just say good riddance to bad rubbish. The town would be a better place with them gone." He patted the barkeep on the back and said, "Close her up, for the night. I'll be back to collect "em in the morning,"

CASE CLOSED

It was the spring of 1901 that Ira got a letter from his half-brother Alonzo back in Cherry Creek. He said he had heard some news that surely Ira would want to know. That Gambler up in Denver had been declared dead. Died quietly in this sleep, from complications of a beating he had received years ago. Maybe (no justice in this world) but he would have to answer to a higher power now!

Chapter 37: Chet's Writings

The following was taken from writing of my great uncle Chet. These stories he wrote in the late 50's and early 60's. Some of the stories were from his dad Ira who died of tick fever in 1920, some were from his mother Sarah some from his old friend Jim Duncan (Tap's brother) and some from his personal observation of various family and non-family members.

Chet was the stay at home son. He was there when his people needed him be it family or friends.

It was in responding to one of these calls that the information in this chapter has been written. Chet received a letter from Arizona. Jim was asking if he could come to stay with Chet for a few days, he said he had some unfinished business in Three Creeks and he would need a place to stay and some help in getting around.

Over the course of the visit, as was his want, Jim drank more whiskey than he should have, waxed eloquent on old times and by gone days. And in the comfort and safety of a trusted friend, he ran his mouth a bit more than he should have. He commiserated with Chet about losing the love of his life as he knew that Chet had also lost his. Jim told tales of long ago, many perhaps best forgotten. At first Chet was dismayed then later fascinated by these stories. Many of them confirmed what Ira or Sarah had told him, some filled in gaps that he had often wondered on while others were completely new stories that Chet had never heard of. They all made for fantastic and very interesting stories but Chet did not want to hurt any of the players or their families. So he wrote the stories down hoping that someday maybe someone would find the stories.

And if enough time had passed, then they could tell these stories to their family members.

Chapter 38: Jim's Musing on Marriage or Ollie Lays Down the Law

Taken from Chet's notes on marriage and what it takes to be a man.

I had taken Jim over to visit with Lizzie. He had visited at length and had a few drinks with her by time I got back to pick him up and take him back to my place. They had an affectionate leave taking and promised to meet again before Jim went back to Arizona. Jim seemed pretty mellow and in the mood for conversation. It was a long drive with nothing to do but drive slow and visit. I ask him how he still felt about Lizzie. He told me that she was the love of his life. He would give anything to go back and undo the troubles that had destroyed their marriage. I ask him if that was how they felt, why they didn't try to work it out and enjoy the rest of their lives together. He said no! It was too late, too much water under the bridge, both had commitments to others that could not be broken. He began a rant:

"If only he hadn't been so pig headed. Just had to be the man, couldn't listen to my wife, and had to be the man in charge even if he was wrong. I would show them that Jim Duncan wasn't no panty waist with a ring in his nose that a pretty face could lead around. He wasn't like his brother Tap."

He looked at me, "You know Chet, after Tap brought those Diamond horses, you know from Three Creeks here… down to Arizona, him and Ollie, oh let me tell you, they had a real big fight.

"I had told him to stand up for himself, put that woman in her place. Show her who was boss." Jim lit his pipe and puffed a bit. After a deep draw he continued.

"But he wouldn't listen to me. That, Tap he caved and just gave in.But me," He patted his chest like he ought to be proud of himself,

"I stood my ground. The Mint, my bar up in Jarbidge, was making just too much money, but the store & livery at Three Creek it was minting money."

Jim looked at Chet with tears in his eyes, "I wish, oh how I wish, I would have had realized how hard it was for Lizzie to keep the Three

Creeks store going without me. How much she missed me when I was up in Jarbidge! She sent me a letter on Eddie's[56] stage and told me she couldn't do this any longer. I hopped in with him on the return, when I got to the store she gave me the ultimatum: We needed to give up the bar in Jarbidge or the store in Three Creek and live together as man and wife... He scoffed at her and told her to just man up and be his partner and keep things running. They were doing so well building a very comfortable future.

"Lizzie got her hackles up when I told her to straighten up."

He held up his bottle of whiskey looking at it, then he began again.

"She told me that if they weren't going to live as man and wife she was done. She wanted out!"

I told her if she wanted out, she could just go, they would ahead and split up, she could have the store and he would keep the bar in Jarbidge. That was it! That was the end. There was no going back. He was a man, wouldn't have no woman bossing him around.

"So when Tap got back to Arizona with the Diamond horses and changed the ranch name to the Diamond Bar." He smiled in the middle of this sentence like he was chuckling to himself.

"How perfect! Just using a running iron to add that little bar to the Wilkens Diamond brand, ya know." He chuckled at the thought of it.

"Those horses stocked the ranch and set them up good." Ollie said she was worried for him, worried that something might happen to him.

She said "Tap you do live a charmed life, but something could happen to you. We have everything we could ask for. Let's just enjoy what we have. The kids and I need you. Sooner or later something will happen to you if you don't change your ways."

---

[56] Ed Brackett son of Levi Brackett came to live with Ira and Sarah shortly after Levi was murdered in Colorado. Ed herded sheep and helped at the Brackett's ranch. He later he ran a stagecoach route from Buhl, Idaho to Jarbidge, Nevada.

He just grinned and hugged her, told her he was ok, he was careful and nothing would ever happen to him. Ollie then said, well maybe he was right. He did always come through where other men failed and died.

Then she started to cry. "But, Tap now we have four kids, kids that worship the ground you walk on."

She wiped her tears and got real solemn, "They want to grow up and be just like you.

"You might get away with it but yer kids might not be so lucky. And in that case, I would never forgive you or myself, if one of the kids got bad hurt trying to be just like TAP DUNCAN."

Tap and Ollie kissing outside the Diamond Bar Ranch house. Photo courtesy of Myrtle Stowe Duncan Estate

She told him she loved him and he meant the world to her, but either he changed his ways, stay home, cut out this skirting the law or she was leaving. She didn't know where she would go, just that she and the kids would be gone. So he had to make a choice, either her and the kids or his wayward good time buddies. She just couldn't, just wouldn't live like this any longer.

Well,Chet, Ya know he didn't even have to take time to think on it, Tap caved and he and Ollie have continued to live the love of their lives. To this day every day, I swear is like a honeymoon for them.

Jim got real quiet. Then he choked out the words, "I look at them and think of what Lizzie and I could have had."

Jim took a deep breath and a long draw off his whiskey bottle. He looked over at me and says "Chet what about you? You never got married, why not?"

I felt like the dark recesses of my soul would be safe with him so I began:

It was the fall of 1919. I thought that things were going well on the ranch and I had some time. I started attending some socials and dances around the country. Down at Buhl, I started seeing this one good-looking girl at most of the socials. I got myself introduced to her so as not to seem too forward. When she spoke her name it was like the sound of angel bells tinkling in my ears. Conversation with her seemed to come so easily. I don't really remember what we talked about, but at each social it seemed like we just spent the whole time visiting.

I told her about the ranch and how Bert had built Ora a honeymoon home and now they had a couple of the cutest kids. She said that sounded like a good life. She had always dreamed of living on a ranch and especially out in the country. We talked about marriage and what life together would be like. While we did not have solid wedding plans, we talked a lot about the future, our future.

That spring, Dad got sick of the Tick fever and died. Bert and Ora were off running their ranch. Frank and Inez were off running and growing an operation of their own. This left the responsibility of running our ranch to me. Mom did a lot but she was pretty broke up. Seems that some days, all she could do was get up and stare out the window like she was waiting for dad to come home.

Truman and Edna were spending a lot of their time with us. In some ways it was good, but they still needed lots of time and attention too. They needed us and it certainly wasn't the first time that mom had taken in family members who needed the safety or love of her home[57].

I found out that just because you are a Brackett, it don't mean you have money. Dad had invested in a ranch that I hadn't known about. It had taken quite a bit of money. He had also invested in one of the mines in Jarbidge before it went bust. All of these things added up. The ranch, though it had lots of livestock and land, it had a lot of debt too. It seemed there weren't enough hours in the day nor days in the week to get everything done that needed done.

One day I woke up and realized that since the spring, I had only seen Miss Emily three times this year and the last was about six weeks ago. There was a social coming up and I determined to go and make up for having neglected her. When I walked into the dance hall, my heart jumped. There she was and did she look beautiful. My heart sunk however when I saw standing next to her the dirt farmer that had always tried to cut in on us. Shyly, I went over near her to say hello. She seemed a bit miffed but she told her dirt farmer to go get her something to drink, she needed to talk to me. When I tried to tell her how I missed her, she said she had missed me too. But while I had been so long gone, she had found someone else. She was gonna get married. My heart hurt.

"What about us?" I asked. "Our life and the new home we were gonna build at the ranch?"

She said she loved me and probably always would but a girl has to have more than dreams, she's gotta have reality, something solid. She

---

[57] When Sarah and Ira married several of her siblings came to live with them. Sarah's mother had passed away and her father had been shot shortly before the marriage by his sister in law Mrs. Gibson. Siblings Joel, Mary and William lived with Ira and Sarah (Lizzie) according to the 1880 Colorado census. All three of those siblings accompanied them to Idaho. When Ira married Sarah it was with the understanding that he was taking on her siblings as family. Later, when Ira's brother Levi was murdered in Colorado son Edward and daughter Cora Inez came to live with the Brackett's. There may have been others but we are certain of those two.

needed something to actually build her life on. She told me that it was the hardest choice she had ever had to make but she had made it.

Then she cradled my face in her soft hands, "Please, don't make this harder on me than it already is." She waited as if she expected an answer from me but, dumb ol me, I just stuttered.

With that she turned and walked away.

She walked over to her dirt farmer, kissed him lightly and said, "Let's go." I was too shocked to do or say anything. My world was walking away. In a daze I stumbled out into the blackness of the night. I returned to the ranch and dug back into the needed work.

As time went on, I tried to find another fiancée. Every time I met someone and said this might be the one, I went home and looked at Miss Emily's picture on the wall. No, this new girl, I would decide didn't come close to comparing. I would then decide to keep looking. I'd rather not have anyone than have a marriage like some of those around me.

As the years went by, I found myself looking at the girls less and less and talking to Miss Emily's picture more and more. Oh….

The could have dones.

The should have dones.

And more regrettably…

The what ifs.

I had finally just given up trying.

Jim looked over at me and said "Chet you pig headed fool. She was asking you to stand up like a man and ask her to marry her. She wanted to marry you. Was just tired of waiting for you to make up your mind. Poor Girl, You broke that poor girl's heart."

Oh the things we might do different, if only we knew then, what we know now.

Chapter 39: Is Your Life Worth a Few of Old Tap Duncan's Cows?

Jim and Chet both sensed that this conversation was set to make for a very depressing evening. Neither wanted to be sad. Chet searched for another topic to change the course of the conversation so he asked Jim if Tap really was as tough as it was said! And if he still had it? Jim laughed

"Yes he was tough as all that…. and still as tough as ever." He smiled as he reached in to the deep recesses of his thoughts. Let me give ya an example…

This story told to Chet by Jim Duncan:

It was late in the fall, they had spent several days gathering, sorting and getting the herd ready for winter. One herd of cows and young stock was headed off to winter range. Another herd of old fat cows and steers headed for a holding area ready to be taken to market. There weren't much for fences, just use areas with limited water that pretty well held stock in one place.

One of the hands rode in and told Tap of what looked like tracks, maybe a small herd headed south.

"But Boss.they'se headed off of the Diamond Bar range. I couldn't really tell if they were just drifting, or if someone was herding them."

It would take all hands to get these herd where they belonged before that storm that was building broke. Tap decided he would check out that stray herd. Probably nothing, but could never tell unless ya took a look-see.

Several hours later Tap did cut the tracks of a small herd headed south. Definitely someone was driving them, and with the way this storm was building those tracks would be gone tomorrow.

Tap thought he ought to go get some help, he would surely be out numbered. But if he went for help, by time he got back the tracks and cattle would be gone. He would just have to check this out by himself, be careful. No one, by god, could steal Diamond Bar stock and get away with it if he had any knowledge of it.

After carefully checking the loads in his pistols and seating them right in his holsters, Tap headed his horse down the trail left by the small herd.

Keeping an open eye for the range ahead, he followed the tracks and tried to figure where they might be heading. He had followed them down a small ravine. Didn't look good, couldn't see very far, maybe needed to get to high ground and take a look around. Suddenly there were the cattle, definitely Diamond Bar stock.

As suddenly as Tap had found the cattle, three mounted riders came out of the brush behind him. The leader a big scar faced man, his hand just over his pistol rode up and asked what tap was doing. Tap told him that he was just looking for stray Diamond Bar stock, and it looked like he had found some. He would just gather them up and be on his way before the storm blew them away.

Scar just laughed and said he reckoned that these were his cattle now.

Tap calmly said "no," then he feigned an innocence as he pointed out to Scar that they were carrying a diamond brand and, Tap looked Scar squarely in the eye, "that brand mister means that means they belong to the Diamond Bar."

At this all three riders edged closer, their hands hovering over their pistols.

Then Scar pulled his pistol, looked at Tap and said, "look old timer, if you just throw your pistols on the ground, turn around and ride off, you might live another day."

He smirked at Tap "Think of it, are a few of Old Tap Duncan's cows worth dying for?"

Tap knew that if he threw his pistols on the ground and turned away he would never make it. He would be shot in the back, left to die in this hidden ravine. Suddenly the rain started to fall and in cold and drilling drops. It was just enough of a distraction that Tap drew his gun shooting Scar and at the same time spurred his horse into the nearest rider. The horse he had spurred into spooked and began to buck.

With Scar down, Tap shot again knocking the third rider from his horse. The bucking horse finally got the best of his rider. He landed in a heap on old tree stump, breaking his shoulder.

The rider that Tap had shot held up his hands and said, "Please mister, I give up, don't shoot me again."

Scar was dead, the bullet Tap had put in his chest had made a clean kill. Tap herded the two survivors out into the middle of a small clearing, had them throw their guns out into the brush. He then gathered up the horses and brought them over.

He made the crippled men to drag Scar over the muddy ground to a nearby cliff that had a small cave in it.

Told them put Scar in there and cover him up with dirt. They complained that they were wounded and couldn't do it. Tap told them they could and had better get on with it before he shot them and buried them too.

After Scar was buried, Tap got them on their horses. He pointed his .45 at them for emphasis as he said. Boys, this here is Diamond Bar Range and these well these are Diamond Bar Cattle. You best get going and when this rain erases your tracks, you never make em this way again. And ya tell all your friends to stay away from this range."

Tap paused and started to ride away but then he turned back to the two men and said, "Think of it, in the words of Scar… Are a few of Old Tap Duncan's cows worth dying for?"

"But you know Chet." Jim began, "That ain't my favorite……….."

Chapter 40: Too Many Thieves in Hackberry

"When Tap first settled in Hackberry it seemed like he had come home. It was everything his sister had told him would be. It was good to have family, his cousins the Ketchums, and other friends nearby. Tap made friends with the local ranchers, the Bacons, the Neals and others. He was a good hand, he helped them and yes, they helped him."

Hackberry was a major shipping point, cattle always moving through. Often the trail herds would lose a few head. After the drovers were gone, there were always strays left there for the taking.

Tap's old friends came through, often they were trailing a few head, some needed to be branded and you know...maybe held for a spell before they could be marketed."

Jim was drawing circles in the air to indicate there was more to the story that Chet would understand.

"Now Tap worked with them, and truthfully it helped him build his herd. He fixed springs for water, to water and hold his cattle on his range. Without water all the feed in the world was of no use ya know."

Chet nodded at that saw that on his own ranch.

After a drag on his smoke, Jim continued, "Old friends would show up with half a beef. They would have a barbeque, rope some horses or steers, and in general just have a good time. Tap was really enjoying this, the visits, the roping, and the comradeship of old friends. Life was good, Tap was becoming a respected rancher in the community.

Jim smiled, "Then one day as he was riding, back tracking some of his friends trails, he came upon one of his own beeves butchered. The hide and part of the carcass just left there for the varmints.

After that, that free beef that his friends were sharing. It just didn't taste as good as it used to." Chet thought about how mad it would make him to know someone was rustling and a cooking up his cow, especially if they were feeding it to him in a gesture of friendship.

Jim continued.

"Then one day one of his riders came into the ranch his horse all lathered up. Tap started out to chew him out for working his horse up that way.

The hand said, "Tap, Tap you got to come now. They are loading our cattle on the train at Hackberry." Tap got his horse and headed for Hackberry, His rider rode alongside and told him that Bob from the Rocking B was shipping cattle. Mixed in with the Rocking B cattle were a number of Tap's Hookity H cows. When Tap got to the stockyards they were still loading cattle. Tap saw one of his in the pen they were getting ready to load.

Bob came over with a big smile on his face, good to see you Tap. "What brings you to town?

Tap says "Bob ya got one of my cows in that pen!"

Tap looked him squarely in the eye and proceeded, "I hear that you have already loaded some others. I want them unloaded. Now."

"Bob says, "Well we might have loaded a few, don't really matter none Tap, we got a real good price and we will finish sorting and pay you for yours at delivery. Ain't no big thing."

Tap was getting kind of riled," Jim shot Chet a look that they both understood, knowing Tap.

Well Tap says it is a big thing, we are going to unload them all and get mine out before you ship. And being Tap, he just walked over to that railcar door and begins to unlatch it.

Bob yells "Oh, no you don't Tap, we are shipping today!"

So Bob that he pulls his gun and shoots the panel by Tap's hand.

Tap luckily, jerked his hand back from the splintered gate. Just in time

He pulls his own gun, turns and shoots Bob in the shoulder.

Tap says "If you weren't a friend and neighbor, Bob, you would be dead right now. We are unloading and the Hookity H cattle and they are staying here till I get ready to ship for me."

After this Tap began looking for a more isolated place, maybe a little more like Three Creeks, where he could run his ranch by himself without neighbors interfering and messing with his cattle.

He heard that Starkey's place up on Grape Vine Creek was for sale. Ever since Wellington had died, the place had headed downhill. It was bigger than the Hookity H, but more important, it butted up against the Grand Canyon, had the Hualapai Indians for neighbors. Not many white men to share with, to run with and against.

He would still be close enough for company, but far enough out to avoid conflict. It would be a big step up if he could sell the Hookity H and buy Starkey's ranch. He would need the help of his friends like Henry Bacon if he was to raise the money to do this.

John Neal, Henry Bacon and Tap Duncan sitting on the corrals at Hackberry. Photo courtesy of John Steele

Tap and Boys at the Shipping Corrals in Hackberry, Arizona.

Hackberry was the third largest shipping point in all of Arizona.Photo compliments of
Myrtle Stowe Duncan Estate

Chapter 41: Tap Was Scared

Chet began:

After Jim told me about Tap taking on those cattle thieves alone. By himself a few years back, I got to thinking "These Duncans are just something else. They have no fear… they can do anything and never blink an eye!"

So I asked Jim if there was ever any time that he or Tap had ever been scared. Jim thoughtfully rubbed his chin, "You know Chet, there's lots of times I've been scared but as long as I was with Tap I just figured we'd come out ok."

He smiled more to himself than to me. Holding up his forefinger, however…he added, "Now Tap, on the other hand, aside from when he was a kid in New Mexico and truthfully after the bar fight in Bruneau, he admits to only being really scared one time in his life."

Jim seemed pleased with Chet's renewed interest in this conversation. So he continued:

"This time it wasn't for himself but for his girls. It was one cold fall back when the girls was just teenagers."

He took a short swig of his whiskey cleared his throat and continued.

"They were moving cattle to the winter pasture. The girls were home. More hands to move those cattle ya know?"

Chet smiled at that.

"There was a cold wind blowing. It was truly cold and miserable day but Tap figgered there was more to come so just best to gut it out this day and get the critters moved. When the snow began to lightly fall it surely made a man want to just hole up by a warm fire and look out his window and count himself blessed to be inside, not out there with the cattle and horses. But not Tap and not his Diamond Bar crew. They had started at day break. The now weak sun was barely glowing on the horizon. Barely enough light to make out the outlines of Music Mountain. The crew split up and headed for their gather.

By noon, cold and wet, everyone was back together everyone that is except for the girls. They had had just a short ride those and those two, they should have been the first ones in."

Jim stopped here and cleared his throat. Then he continued.

"Tap kept the crew working, a sale bunch was cut out and Tap sent them with some boys on back to the ranch. An hour or so more and strays were cut out and headed back to their home range. Still no girls to be seen. Tap was now fit to be tied. He alternated between being mad that they were goofing off somewhere to being worried that something had happened to them. Finally he sent his crew and the restless cattle on to the winter range."

Chet didn't really know what it felt like to worry about his own but sure worried at times for Edna and Truman. Even though they belonged to his sister Inez, he loved those kiddies as if they were his own. Chet listened nodding in appreciation of they fear Tap must have felt. Jim continued.

"Tap headed over to the blind canyon tracking what should have been the girls' ride, he hadn't figured there were many cattle up that canyon, but still, someone needed to check. As he drew closer to the canyon he could smell wood smoke. He remembered that old prospector cabin down under the cliff. Thinking that the girls must have gotten cold and stopped to build a fire, Tap himself started heating up. His mind was racing and he was reciting over and over in his mind his thoughts."

"It was damn poor of them not to consider the rest of the crew, that someone, not the least being. He might worry about them.

He would sure tell them about how inconsiderate it was of them when he found them.

It would have been one thing to build a fire to warm ya up but it was quite another to lay back, keep the fire warm and enjoy it especially while everyone else was out working!"

Jim looked at Chet, "Can't you just imagine how Tap was going on." Jim asked.

Chet smiled thinking of how red Tap's face got when he got riled. He didn't get the red Duncan hair but his complexion was light and sure showed his sentiments.

Jim drank some more whiskey then continued his story.

"As Tap rode closer to the cabin, he saw five horses tied out to the hitching post. Now he was really hot. It just wasn't right for the girls to be so irresponsible and stay with friends while everyone else was out working and worrying about them. One of their horses could have fallen or one of the girls gotten hurt. It wasn't right for them to worry him that ways and they were gonna hear about it when he saw them!

Tap quietly tied his horse up to and headed for the door. When he stepped on the porch he heard the sound of a slap and an angry voice, the voice of his sweet Lora Clare saying:

"You Keep yer hands off me!"

Tap's insides boiled, and then he heard an even deeper voice say

"Ah come on girly, we're just having a little fun here."

Tap already full of fire kicked open that cabin door. What he saw inside chilled him to the bone. Two men were sitting at the table with his daughter Tappie. She was tied to the chair at the end of the table over by the window.

Another man held Lora by the arm on the bed in the other corner, "Daaaad!" Lora screamed as he entered the cabin.

"Help me." Her tear filled blue eyes looking at him made him want to rip the arms and legs off each one of these bastards with his bare hands.

Tap tried to act calm so as to not scare his girls any more.

"Let me you get outta here girls." He calmly replied.

An older dark haired man sitting behind the table got up and said, "I don't think so mister, you just drop yer pistol!" He sneered at Tap. Then he added,

"If you turn and walk outta here you might live to see another day."

With that he shook his gun in Tap's direction.

Tap looked at the younger man sitting at the table. Recognizing one of his own crew he smiled.

"I can bet you it was not a good smile either," Jim added.

"Tommy?" he began, "You can't be involved in this are ya? Come over here and help me get my girls outta here." Tommy gave Tap a sheepish grin.

"Sorry Boss man, ye see we ain't a fixin to really hurt these girls…just take 'em down a notch or two."

He put his hand over to the side of his mouth as if to whisper as if to whisper some friendly advice to Tap. "You best do as the big guy said and drop your gun and leave the cabin. I'll make sure they ain't hurt. After we take 'em down a notch or two we'll let 'em go."

Tommy grinned at Tap. His decayed teeth left a stench in the air.

Tap paused as if he were actually listening to what this dimwit young man had to say. Using his poker strategy, he carefully looked around the room as if he were realizing the odds were not in his favor. He pulled his gun out of its holster with his left hand, stepped forward as if to lay it on the table. But instead with the speed of a rattler strike, he lifted the table with one hand and shoved it into Tommy and the dark haired man shoving their chairs over backwards.

Tap shifted and shot the man holding on to Lora. Quickly, he turned back and shot the dark haired man who had been gang the leader as he was scrambling to get up from where the table had fallen on him.

Tommy, who was lying flat on his back in his chair, was frantically fumbling for his own pistol.

"That's really the wrong choice Tommy."

 Tap said as he pumped a lead into his chest. Lora raced over to untie her sister. The other two men were not going down easy; they were trying to line their sites on Tap. By now Tap had drawn both of his guns and he gave each of them two more ounces of lead. One in the chest then in the forehead. The room grew silent and the smoke from Tap's pistols seemed to dance happily in the air. The game was now over.

Tommy was still breathing and he looked at Tap. "Boss Man, we was just funning never meanin' no harm. We'd have turned 'em loose in just a bit."

Tommy then gave a big sigh; blood started dripping down over his chin. His eyes closed head dropped and he quit breathing.

Tap quickly gathered his daughters in his arms. He asked them if they were ok.

"We are now Pa!" they both answered at the same time. That expression filled Tap's heart with emotion. He just held them close for a moment. "Oh how he loved these baby girls."

He took them outside and got them mounted on their horses. He told them to ride to the mouth of the canyon and wait for him there.

"If anyone comes along just send them on their way. Ya hear? Do not let them come up the canyon. "

He glanced around at the cabin as if he was trying to figure what to do next.

"I will be there shortly. "You girls, you wait for me." They mounted their horses and Tap slapped Lora's horse on the rear end to get them moving. A few tiny flakes of snow began to fall.

When the girls were out of sight, Tap quickly pulled the bridles and saddles off the three horses. He stacked them in the middle of the cabin with the three dead men. Back outside he began to pulling the corral down. As he would get a pole loose he would throw it into the cabin adding to the pile inside, when the cabin was full he finished by stacking the rest of the corral on the front porch. Taking the lamp oil he found in a rusty can, Tap poured all that it contained on the logs stacked on the front porch.

By now Tap had burned off all of his adrenalin and was ready to take a break. He leaned on the porch railing and he rolled himself a cigarette. Along with the makings was a brick of Lucifer's in his left pocket. He peeled one off and struck it to light his Bull Durham. As he inhaled deeply savoring the rich flavor, then he flicked the burning match on to the oil soaked timber. The fire slowly sputtered slowly then began to grow as the hungry flames licked out searching for more fuel for their consuming appetite. At first lapping up the oil then dancing on to the dry timbers themselves that had once been a corral to hold cattle. Soon the entire cabin was a hot burning funeral Pryor.

The dryness of the timbers burned hot making little smoke. But now even if someone came, the fire was so hot that no one could do anything other than watch it burn, Wait for it to burn out. After the ashes had cooled they could then sift thru those ashes. As hot as this fire was burning the guns and any other metal would be unrecognizable blackened globs. Tap finally felt his heart beat normal and steady again.

Tap slowly mounted his horse. One of the dead men's horses stood nearby even after Tap had unsaddled and unbridled them so he chased it on further up the canyon. As he drew nearer the mouth of the canyon where the girls were waiting for him, he took a deep breath so as to compose himself. He couldn't let them know how scared he had been. He put a smile on his weary face and got off near where they were standing. He walked over put his arm around both of them. We got some talking to do he told them.

He sat them down and told them that neither of them could ever speak a word of this. Even though the girls had not been physically hurt there would always be suspicion, little whispers, and maybe ugly rumors. And if their mother, his Ollie, ever found out, oh how she would worry and have suspicions that perhaps more had happened. She always watch them with a cautious eye.

"And more than that!" Tap added with a nervous laugh, "She would give me holy hell for not being a better dad. For not. .. Not taking enough care for you girls." His voice started to break. He hugged them both as he said that. Tap suspected and Ollie would tell him that this might be some sort of payback for some of the things he had done when he was younger. If Ollie knew, Tap feared that she would never trust him again to take care of his family.

As Jim spoke he realized that he had just broken a trust with Tap. Even though this had happened years ago, and no one could ever find that cabin or identify its contents Tap had trusted his brother to not ever tell his secrets.

Tap was now safe from the law but not from his family. Tap's family loved him, looked up to him and relied on him. This was the very sort of thing Ollie had warned Tap of many times and years before.

Jim swallowed hard. "Chet." He began in a half choked please, I shouldn't have told you that. Ya gotta keep that a secret for me ok."

Chet just smiled, "Jim I swear I'll keep it silent." Just another of those family secrets that we can't ever talk about.

Chapter 42: Tap Takes a Beating or Tap has a Heart

Chet and Jim sat in the silence of the evening staring at the fire in the stove for a while letting the story Jim had just told settle into the night air.

"What a man that Tap is," Chet thought.

After a while the Chet rolled himself a cigarette. "Ok,"

He began, "maybe a silly question but besides the beating in the bar did Tap ever get beat up again?"

Jim looked sideways at Chet and laughed. He thought a moment then with a huge smile on his face he began there was this one time:

"It was along about early winter and a light snow had started to settle on the ground. Tap had been riding the winter range checking the cows. Lots of days he likes to just get out and check on the cows. Ya know, fond of saying the master's eye fattens the beast."

Chet and Jim both smiled at that knowing that a man who owns stock sure likes the chance to check up on 'em and see how they are doing.

Jim continued. "Tap had ridden for several days and kept seeing some tracks heading up a canyon. Looked like just horse tracks at first then he cut a cow track alongside the horse. Tap could not figure who he had sent up there and why so he decided to follow the marks. The trees got heavier and thicker toward the top and he lost the tracks but could smell the smoke of a fire. He dismounted his horse and walked on up to find a squatters camp. Tap was a more than a bit miffed especially when he arrived at the fire and they was cutting the hide off of one his Diamond steers."

Chet nodded in agreement at that, He wouldn't be real fond of anyone taking freely of his beef either.

As Tap neared the camp he intentionally pulled his coat tail to one side and put his right hand in the pocket of his trousers, deliberately showing his pistol. He man cutting the beef was very thin and wiry. Tap almost felt sorry for him but he felt more that he had to stop this thief.

"Ya know that ya can't just be taking a man's beef because ya feel like it. Tap began.

"The wiry man kept his back to him and just continued his work almost as if he hadn't heard Tap. That riled Tap's feathers ya know."

Chet smiled. He leaned in a little closer to focus on this interesting story. "I can imagine," he replied.

Jim continued.

"Tap began to speak a little louder and a bit more forcefully. I can't let you take my cow, you know that. Don't you?" Tap just kept getting hotter and hotter and that hider just kept focusing on his work. All of the sudden from behind Tap felt a sharp blow to his back, he whirled full force gun pulled out ready to shoot. As he turned he couldn't see anyone. Whap! Another blow to his knee. Angrily he looked down. Luckily he hadn't fired.

"Course ya know Tap don't shoot till he knows what he's shooting at." Jim added.

" Anyway Tap looked down and there in front of him stood a five year old boy about two and a half feet tall. He had a huge tree branch in his hand,

"Don't you shoot my daddy," he yelled at Tap. "We's just hungry."

Chet got a real laugh out of the picture he painted in his mind. Tap did have a kind and soft heart.

"So what did Tap do?" Chet asked Jim.

Smiling Jim replied "Exactly what you would imagine he would do. That squatter's wife was sick with a little one and Tap took em down to the ranch house,"

He paused and held his hands open, "Well you can guess what that good woman Tap is married to does…. Ollie nurses them back to health and Tap even gave that squatter honest employment for the rest of the winter. But come spring...Like drifters do… they left for the greener pastures.

Ranch house at the Diamond Bar. Photo. Courtesy of Myrtle Stowe Duncan Estate

Jim paused like he was reliving these old days. He looked at Chet. "Ya know, my brother was an opportunist but in all those opportunities, he always found a way to help somebody out. Sort of like he was paying back.

"That reminds me of a time,"….Jim began….

Chapter 43: Moonshine and Hogs

Always one to take advantage of a good situation and… always one to help those in need, Tap found just the opportunity he needed in the roaring twenties and Prohibition. Prohibition or passing a law, didn't dry up the desire for liquor in Kingman or Hackberry. Sugar, grain, water, a holding vat and a still were all that was needed to make moonshine. That and an isolated place, a few good men. Tap certainly had an isolated place in the Diamond Bar. And truth be told, good men with certain tolerance for skirting the law just seemed to be attracted to Tap. He had already boxed up the spring, running its water down the draw into a trough for his cattle.

So he got some sugar, mixed it with the grain and started brewing. The still worked great, soon he had a good batch of white lightning. But the grain mash left over begin to stink and draw bugs and birds. Tap decided it needed to be hauled off it because it could be a defining sign to revenuers combing the outer parts of town for these kind of stills.

Always one to use what was at hand. He set up a hog pen near the springs not far from the ranch. It was the greatest, now the hogs ate the mash and the ranch had plenty of bacon and ham. Having more hog meat than he needed he began hauling the hogs to Kingman & Hackberry. Always a generous man he gave much of it to those in need. This was in addition to the old cows he had always dropped off at the butcher shop, stockyards or homes of those in need.

Everywhere there was a desire for liquor, there was someone to supply it. Anywhere someone might be making illegal liquor, there were federal agents. Soon there were federal agents watching Tap's operation and getting ready to raid and shut him down. But, to do this they had to find his still, catch him transporting and selling the liquor. But with the Joshua Trees as a very formidable barrier on one side, the Grand Canyon to the north of him Tap had an isolated location with only a few ways in. He hired some of the Hoolapie1 Indians to live on the hills overlooking the roads in. When they saw strangers coming they would warn Tap and his crew. Tap had tried having them brew his brew, but it seemed they could not resist having a few drinks and sharing with their kin, then after they had their fill of the hootch, they didn't care for the still. This shut down operations till they had ran out of liquor and then they would start up again. The other men Tap hired to run the stills could take a few drinks but still keep the stills running.

So finally with trusted men running the stills, the Hoolapie[58], watching out for federal agents, Tap had the brewing working like a well-oiled machine. Once the federal agents headed up to the still, the Hoolapie sounded the warning system, the still operators dumped the mash into the hog feeder, and the pigs ate it. They were some very happy hogs I might add....grunting and laying in the sun.... Then they dumped the moon shine in the stock water trough, and the cattle were happy.

There was no sign of liquor there by time the feds got up to the spring where the hog pen was. The still had become a water holding tank for the cattle water trough. Though the agents knew that Tap was brewing, there was nothing illegal there by the time they had arrived at the spring.

The roads into Kingman were rough, no one could drive very fast, there were narrow places, and it was easy for federal agents to block the road. You couldn't out run them, so you had to outsmart them. To do this Tap had special truck built to haul his hogs and cattle to town for slaughter, for a few friends and those in need, ya know. Well this truck, it had a false floor. After the liquor was loaded in, the planks that formed the floor were put in and the hogs were loaded.

To get to the liquor you needed to unload the hogs, pull up the floor, unload the liquor, then put the floor back in. No agents wanted to mess with a hog delivery truck. When Tap's boys got to town they would park the truck at the butcher shop overnight. The hogs would be unloaded, the liquor unloaded, the truck washed out. The boys would then take it down to the feed store for another load of grain for the still and hogs.

Just another example of Tap helping those in need of a little help. And maybe, just maybe, helping himself a bit in the process.

---

[58] Uncle Chet spelled the Indian tribe Hoolapie. In learning further about the people of the area we think it must be Hualapai. But that is our assumption.

The Diamond Bar ranch is situated in the midst of the densest Joshua tree forest in Arizona and all of Northern America. You can see that the corrals created for holding cattle was made of cut Joshua tree trunks. Photo courtesy of Myrtle Stowe Duncan Estate.

Old boiler from stamp mill used for making moonshine. It still serves a purpose as a cattle watering trough. The still photo courtesy of Michelle Drumheller

The following story is not from Jim's tales. Jim passed away in November of 1943. Tap lived for another year and died in 1944 at the age of 80. This is a story from Uncle Chet's writings. We are not positive where he got it but we think that Chet perhaps accompanied his sister in law Ora Lee to the funeral in Kingman and heard this story. At this stage of their lives, Tap and Ollie spent the bigger portion of their days at their home in Kingman.

Chapter 44: A Day Like Any Other

Tap got up before daylight as he was always did. Washed his face, performed his morning rituals. By this time Ollie had breakfast ready, and as they ate breakfast Ollie ask what he was going to do today. Would he be home for lunch or when should she fix dinner. He said he was going to meet with some financiers and men from the government. There was speculation that there might be some of what they called rare earth minerals in the King Tut. If these mineral were there it would help the war effort, it would take a lot of money to develop them, but it could make them lot of money. Ollie told Tap, you do what you need to, but remember, I'm not going to sign on the Diamond Bar for money for this money pit. These money men can risk their money if it's such a good deal. As Tap prepared to go, he put his pistol in his shoulder holster. It was increasingly difficult to keep his gun belt up on his thinning hips. It seemed like it just sagged down, and he had to keep pulling it up all the time[59].

He walked the few blocks down to the Beale Hotel, up to his usual room on the second floor. Had a cup of coffee, prepared himself mentally for the upcoming meeting. His friend his long time banker came in first. He told Tap, he had talked with the engineers and other bankers. If the government agents in fact wanted these minerals, that they should pay for the mining of them. The gold and silver that would be produced would be a byproduct. The government agents said yes, if these minerals were there, they needed these minerals, mixed with ore, it made a stronger steel that would make a better more bullet proof armor.

They appealed to Tap's Patriotism, said he should do it for the war effort, you know. For the boys fighting overseas. The financiers said yes they could provide the financing needed to develop the King Tut, just needed to sign a few papers pledging the Diamond Bar as security. At the end of the meeting everyone except Tap and his banker friend agreed that Tap should finance further development and research on the King Tut. It

---

[59] Ollie and Tap had a home on 5th street in Kingman, Arizona. Located a few blocks from the Beale Hotel. Tap conducted his business at the hotel and had a room there for persons who came to town to do business to stay. In his elder years he would go there to conduct business, gamble, drink and socialize. The Beale was located across the street from the train depot in Kingman.

was for a good cause and would make Tap a lot of money and help the war effort.

After the meeting Tap walked his friend out to his car parked near the rail tracks across from the Beal. After a few minutes conversation, Tap said goodbye and began walking behind his friend's car to go home.

Another friend called, "Hey, Tap, got a minute? I need to talk with you."

While Tap was standing behind the car responding to his second friends hail. His first friend thinking Tap had gone home began backing up, knocking Tap to the ground.

What should have been a minor bump, turned into a life threatening situation. Tap fell backwards striking his head on the iron rail track. At first it appeared to be a minor injury. Tap was taken to the local hospital to be checked out.

Then an aneurism developed and Tap fell deathly ill. He died later that evening in bed surrounded by his loving family. So died one of the most feared and respected gunmen of the old west.

Tap Duncan on his gray. Photo compliments of Margaret Pehl

Ollie on horseback. Margaret Pehl reported to us that Ollie rode her horse up until the 80th year of her life. She told us that Tap and Ollie had such good relations with their friends and neighbors the Walapai Indians that she would often ride her horse up to visit the tribal elders even after Tap had passed away. Photo compliments of Carol Hardin/Dennie Anderson.

John Neal, Tap Duncan and Harrie Avery. Photo courtesy of Margaret Pehl.

Tap on his horse.

Kevin Stockbridge told us a story that Tap would use up a box of cartridges a day shooting.

He often would have cans set up on the fence posts on his way home so he could ride along and shoot them.

Afterward

As we have been exploring life that our great uncle Tap Duncan lived, we have come to know some very wonderful and fascinating people. Two of these folks are our cousins Margaret and Lewis Pehl. They live in Arizona and Margaret is the great granddaughter of Nannie Duncan Taps sister.

Margaret grew up in Hackberry, Arizona, hearing and loving the stories about her extended family.

We were sitting at Margaret's kitchen table one day discussing Stories that we had heard about Uncle Tap as we all referred to him. Someone mentioned that it was quite humorous how some historians tend to try to make what is written in some publication as "gospel" fact.

It was brought up that it was reported in a newspaper that Tap had died after the bar fight in Bruneau in 1894. Then someone else brought up the fact that it was written somewhere that Tap Duncan had been killed in a robbery in Parachute, Colorado.

Margaret got quiet then she told us a story: She said that Ollie was a great homemaker and an incredible seamstress. She made all of Tap's clothing including his jeans that he wore. She would lovingly sew them for him then as a token of her love for him, she would sew his name into every article that she produced.

Then Margaret went on to tell us about how Hackberry, Arizona, was at one point the largest rail head for shipping cattle in the state of Arizona. So lots of people wandered through there especially down and out cowboys maybe looking to hide out for a bit. Often they would show up running fast from the law and had often left with not much more than the shirt on their back. Some of these folks Tap might give a job, some of them a meal and some of them she said he would even give a coat or shirt if they needed. Some of them stayed awhile but some other just drifted through. She said that one time they had received news that a man had been shot in a robbery in Utah and as they pulled the shirt off the dead man they saw the name sewn inside Tap Duncan. So she said there is a grave in Utah marked with Tap Duncan's name.

Appendix: An American Icon

Buster Keaton

Bruce Kiskaddon

Will James

Louis L'Amour

Growing up with a fascination for the old west there were certain icons that one would turn to for learning what a cowboys life might be like. Will James and his stories and artistry. I could look at those pictures that he drew and be sure that the horse was going to jump straight out at me. Louis L'Amour could fascinate and draw me into a world that held you captive for weeks. Those characters came ALIVE and the reader of his books was transported to another place and another time.

As we have been riding the trail to find out all we could about the fantastic life that our Great Uncle Tap lived, we have stumbled on to some very interesting tidbits. We were at was his Diamond Bar ranch in Arizona about two years ago now. We ran into a fascinating fellow who was, as he called it, "On the Will James Trail." As we talked with Claude he began to draw for us what he saw as the connection between Will James and Tap Duncan. Will spent much time with Tap Duncan learning about cowboy ways, many of his drawings and some of his works, especially The Three Mustangeers," was inspired and influenced by Tap Duncan. We have a copy of a book that Will's wife Alice started to write. (UNReno Library). She describes living at the Diamond Bar and Will working on his art and his writing. Other stories are told of Tap providing notebooks and supplies for Will to draw. What an honor it seems to be related to a man who shaped such an icon of the American West as we know it,

Then we learned that Buster Keaton of Hollywood fame filmed at least one movie (Go West) 1926 silent film at the ranch with Diamond Bar hands as the supporting cast. If you haven't seen this movie you are missing out on some good old fashioned entertainment. So Buster who was another icon of the American west that was influenced by Tap Duncan.

We enjoy cowboy poetry. It speaks our language. We learned that Bruce Kiskaddon, who is acclaimed to be the Father of Cowboy Poetry, worked for Tap Duncan at the Diamond Bar. Think about this scenario, Tap this rough and tough cattleman taking time to read the poetry written by one of his cowhands, not only does he read it, he sends it to Hollywood hoping they would publish it.

Finally we discover that Louis L'Amour worked for Tap Duncan at the Diamond Bar. He wanted to cowboy and live in the west. It has been told that he has credited "everything he learned about being a cowboy to Tap Duncan." How interesting to me that these icons that shaped the romance and image and love of the American west were all influence by the strength and goodness and character of one man…Tap Duncan and his amazing life. We take our hats off to you dear Uncle Tap and thank you for the stories and the goodness and the way you have influenced our family and the world we live in.

34234477R00152

Made in the USA
San Bernardino, CA
23 May 2016